"Why are you so defensive with me?"
Sean asked softly.

"Because you're like an ad man selling a product," Stacey told him candidly. "Your line is too slick. I want a man to be honest with me."

"How much more honest can I be than to say I'd like to make love to you?"

"You can admit that's all it is without pretending to feel the same passion that Romeo felt for Juliet."

Sean sat back, his eyes narrowing slightly. "That's very illuminating. You're looking for true love?"

"I'm not *looking* for anything, but you make it sound as though it doesn't exist," Stacey replied.

"Do you know of any cases?" he asked dryly.

Stacey gazed at his handsome, jaded face. Sean Garrison had everything—looks, wealth, position. Yet he was like the Tin Man in *The Wizard of Oz*. He didn't have a heart....

Dear Reader,

Sophisticated but sensitive, savvy yet unabashedly sentimental—that's today's woman, today's romance reader—you! And Silhouette Special Editions are written expressly to reward your quest for substantial, emotionally involving love stories.

So take a leisurely stroll under the cover's lavender arch into a garden of romantic delights. Pick and choose among titles if you must—we hope you'll soon equate all six Special Editions each month with consistently gratifying romantic reading.

Watch for sparkling new stories from your Silhouette favorites—Nora Roberts, Tracy Sinclair, Ginna Gray, Lindsay McKenna, Curtiss Ann Matlock, among others—along with some exciting newcomers to Silhouette, such as Karen Keast and Patricia Coughlin. Be on the lookout, too, for the new Silhouette Classics, a distinctive collection of bestselling Special Editions and Silhouette Intimate Moments now brought back to the stands—two each month—by popular demand.

On behalf of all the authors and editors of Special Editions,
Warmest wishes,

Leslie Kazanjian
Senior Editor

TRACY SINCLAIR
No Room for Doubt

Silhouette Special Edition

Published by Silhouette Books New York

America's Publisher of Contemporary Romance

SILHOUETTE BOOKS
300 East 42nd St., New York, N.Y. 10017

Copyright © 1987 by Tracy Sinclair

ISBN: 0-373-09421-3

First Silhouette Books printing December 1987
Second printing November 1987

America's Publisher of Contemporary Romance

Printed in the U.S.A.

Books by Tracy Sinclair

Silhouette Romance

Paradise Island #39
Holiday in Jamaica #123
Flight to Romance #174
Stars in Her Eyes #244
Catch a Rising Star #345
Love Is Forever #459

Silhouette Special Edition

Never Give Your Heart #12
Mixed Blessing #34
Designed for Love #52
Castles in the Air #68
Fair Exchange #105
Winter of Love #140
The Tangled Web #153
The Harvest is Love #183
Pride's Folly #208
Intrigue in Venice #232
A Love So Tender #249
Dream Girl #287
Preview of Paradise #309
Forgive and Forget #355
Mandrego #386
No Room for Doubt #421

TRACY SINCLAIR

has worked extensively as a photojournalist. She's traveled throughout North America, as well as parts of the Caribbean, South America and Europe. Her name is very familiar in both Sihouette Romances and Silhouette Special Editions.

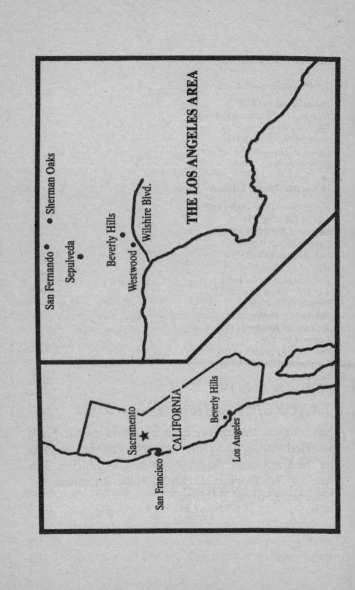

THE LOS ANGELES AREA

San Fernando
Sherman Oaks
Sepulveda
Beverly Hills
Westwood
Wilshire Blvd.

San Francisco
Sacramento
CALIFORNIA
Beverly Hills
Los Angeles

Chapter One

I don't see why you can't look for a real job instead of wasting your time on these get-rich-quick schemes." Eileen Marlowe looked at her daughter disapprovingly.

"I don't expect to get rich." Stacey Marlowe's patient tone indicated this was an ongoing argument. "All I'm trying to do is make enough money to live on and still have time to write."

The older woman pushed aside her coffee cup and picked up a section of the newspaper lying on the breakfast table between them. The paper was opened to the classified section. A circled ad read:

CALL YOUR MOTHER! Remember who was always ready to help in a crisis? Mother Marlowe wants to do the same thing. Need someone to water your garden while you're out of town? Pick up your cleaning? Write those thank-you notes that are so long overdue? No job too small or too difficult. Call Mother Marlowe, 555-1269. She wants to take care of you.

"What kind of nonsense is this?" Eileen demanded. "You aren't anybody's mother. You aren't even married!"

"It's just a gimmick," Stacey explained. "If I'd said, 'Would-be author needs odd jobs to support herself while she writes the great American novel,' no one would give my ad a second glance."

"They still won't. Who's going to pay to have those things done?"

"People with more money than time."

"Is that what we sent you to college for? To be a . . . a handyman?"

Stacey's green eyes sparkled with laughter. "No, I suspect you sent me to find a rich husband."

"A lot of good it did!" This was obviously a sore point with her mother. "That nice Walter Caldwell was crazy about you. Not to mention all the other eligible young men. But no, you had to find fault with every one of them. I honestly don't know what you're looking for!"

Stacey's mouth curved in a smile. "Someone very special."

"You're going to wind up an old maid, mark my words. Do you realize you're twenty-six years old?"

"My birthday isn't for three months yet."

"Time flies," Eileen warned darkly. "Pretty soon you'll be thirty, with nothing to show for it."

"Maybe I'll be famous by then."

"It's all right to dream, but you have to be practical, too."

"I don't know what you're worried about," Stacey protested. "I've saved enough money to live on for a while. I'm not exactly destitute."

"That's another thing! How you could quit a good job with a top advertising agency is something I'll never understand."

"You would if you had to write copy for Bow Wow Bones and Kitty Nips all day."

"You're exaggerating."

"Well, maybe a little, but it isn't deathless prose. A trained chimp with a short attention span could do it. Merkle and Walston will get along fine without me." She shrugged her slender shoulders in dismissal.

"*You're* the one I'm concerned about."

"Don't worry, Mother, I'm starting a whole new life." Stacey grinned mischievously. "Who knows? I might even meet that someone special and be swept off my feet."

"I just hope you don't meet him in the unemployment line," her mother muttered. She stood up. "Well, I must run. I'm meeting your Aunt Sophie for lunch, and you know how she carries on when anyone is late. Are you sure you won't join us?"

Stacey laughed. "No thanks. One lecture a day on my spinster status is enough. Besides, I have to stay home to answer Mother Marlowe's calls."

Stacey's phone calls were all from friends that day, but she refused to be discouraged. After all, the ad had just appeared.

She spent about an hour straightening up the house before sitting down at her typewriter. The small house was another bone of contention with her mother. It was in an unfashionable part of the San Fernando Valley, peopled by young couples with little children.

Mrs. Marlowe would have preferred her daughter to live in a chic apartment in one of the glitzy buildings with a swimming pool. But for the price of a tiny cubbyhole there,

Stacey had a two-bedroom house with a backyard. She preferred it to the swinging singles life-style.

When the phone rang at dinnertime, Stacey was no longer expecting an answer to her ad. Her expectations rose when a strange man's voice greeted her. It was deep and authoritative.

"I'd like to speak to Mother Marlowe."

Stacey felt a thrill of excitement. Her first client! "This is Mother Marlowe."

There was a slight pause. "How old are you?" he asked unexpectedly.

She was thrown off balance. "I...uh...does that make a difference?"

"No, of course not. You just sound younger than I expected."

"I assure you I'm quite competent," Stacey replied with dignity. "Did you have something you wanted done?"

"I need somebody to walk my dog. Do you do that sort of thing?"

"Yes, definitely. No job too big or too small," she said brightly.

The man hesitated. "This one might be somewhat unusual. Do you like dogs?"

"I love them. They're so cuddly. I had a darling little cocker spaniel when I was growing up," she said, getting slightly carried away in her excitement. A curious silence greeted her enthusiasm. "Will this be one time only, or did you have something like once a week in mind?" she asked hopefully.

Dollar signs danced in front of her eyes as he said, "I'd like you here every day if you can manage it. I'm out at night, and I sleep until noon. It's hard on Lobo. I try to take him out when I get up, but very often I have appointments in the afternoon."

"I understand." Stacey wondered what kind of business he was in to keep such odd hours, but she couldn't very well ask. "What time would you like me to come by?"

"Around ten in the morning would be fine. Can you start tomorrow?"

"I haven't told you the price yet."

"Whatever you charge is fine," he answered carelessly.

"No, I think we'd better discuss it. I know *I* don't like surprises."

His voice was filled with rich laughter. "I guess I was wrong. You're older than you sound."

"I just don't want any misunderstandings," she insisted. She quoted him a price, which he agreed to immediately.

"My name is Sean Garrison. I'll give you my address if you have a pencil."

The address placed him in one of the large, expensive apartment buildings on Wilshire Boulevard in West Los Angeles. Whatever Mr. Garrison did for a living, it netted him a handsome income, Stacey reflected.

"Tell the doorman who you are, and he'll bring Lobo down to you," he instructed.

"I'll be there promptly," she promised.

Stacey was amused by the dog's name. He was probably a Mexican hairless, or one of those fluffy little mops that scarcely looked like a dog. Sean Garrison didn't sound like a man who would have a toy animal for a pet, but voices were deceiving. He could be short, stout and bald—with bloodshot eyes, if he ran around every night.

Was Mr. Garrison one of those wealthy playboys who lived on inherited income and never did a lick of work? Much as she disapproved of the breed, Stacey decided it was none of her business. He was a promising source of income, and she'd never meet him anyway.

* * *

Promptly at ten o'clock the next morning, Stacey pulled up in front of Sean Garrison's apartment building. As she'd suspected, it was an elegant white tower with a circular driveway and a canopy over the entry. Her modest compact car looked out of place next to the Rolls Royce and Lincoln Continental parked in front.

A uniformed doorman came out of the building at a leisurely pace. After Stacey had stated her business, his condescending manner became friendly.

"Hi, I'm Mitch." He opened the car door for her. "Mr. Garrison told me to expect you."

As they walked into the lobby Stacey said, "This is a beautiful building, but I always feel sorry for city dogs, cooped up in an apartment."

"It could be worse. Lobo has the run of the place. Mr. Garrison really dotes on that dog." Mitch grinned. "It wouldn't surprise me if he lets him sleep on the bed."

"A lot of people become very attached to their pets. Especially when they don't have children."

"Isn't it the truth? Mrs. McAllister in 14-B treats her poodle better than she treats her husband."

Stacey wasn't interested in Mrs. McAllister. She was angling for information on Sean. His voice on the phone, plus his unusual life-style, had piqued her curiosity. Was he married? *Did* he have children? How old was he? But Stacey wasn't destined to get any answers.

They'd reached the elevator, and Mitch said, "I'll be right down."

Stacey watched the indicator go all the way to the top. The one bit of knowledge she'd gained was that her client had the penthouse apartment.

When the elevator returned a short time later, Mitch was leading the largest dog Stacey had ever seen. His head was massive, and his long tail added at least three feet to his impressive length. The creature had four legs and a shaggy coat—but so did a lion!

"What's that?" she gasped.

"Meet Lobo. Isn't he a beauty?" Mitch asked fondly.

The dog yawned, showing impressive canine teeth. Stacey inched back. "What kind of dog is he? Assuming he *is* a dog."

"An Irish wolfhound. They're the largest breed in the world. You don't see too many of them around."

"They've been hunted to extinction?" she asked dryly.

Mitch chuckled. "I gather Mr. Garrison didn't prepare you for Lobo, but you'll get used to him. He's very well trained."

"For what, fighting gladiators in the coliseum?"

"I'll show you. Sit, Lobo." The huge dog sat obediently. "Speak," Mitch ordered. The lobby was filled with a sound not unlike a thunderclap.

Stacey wasn't impressed. "What does he do for an encore, go for the jugular?"

"Come on, he's a real softy. Lobo thinks he's a lap dog."

"The only lap big enough to hold that animal would be Godzilla's," she said crisply.

"If you're afraid of dogs, why did you take the job?"

"I'm not! I love animals," Stacey declared. "I was . . . he just came as a surprise, that's all."

"You'll get along fine together," Mitch assured her. "Lobo's a real sweetheart. The only thing that drives him wild is cats."

"The fur gets stuck in his teeth?"

Mitch laughed. "He wouldn't actually hurt one, but he does like to chase them. If you see a cat, be sure to hang on tight to the leash." He handed over the leather strap as a car drove up to the entry. "Have fun together. I have to go to work."

Stacey looked apprehensively at the dog. Lobo looked back mildly. After a long moment she tugged gently on the leash. He followed her out to the car docilely.

She pulled back the bucket seat on the right seat, and Lobo climbed into the back seat, which he filled completely. Stacey slid behind the wheel and drove onto Wilshire Boulevard, trying to ignore her passenger. It wasn't easy. As she entered the flow of traffic, Lobo rested his huge head on her shoulder.

Stacey kept her voice very even. "I know this isn't the kind of car you're used to, but you aren't exactly what I was expecting, either. We'll both have to make allowances."

Lobo turned his head and licked her ear with a long pink tongue.

Stacey began to laugh. "You really are a lap dog at heart, aren't you?"

It was the start of a love affair. Lobo was everything Mitch had promised. He was well trained, affectionate and intelligent. Stacey found herself talking to him as though he were a person. And Lobo acted as if he understood.

Stacey had planned to walk him around the city streets when she was expecting a small dog. After discovering his size, she didn't feel that was adequate. In a rapid change of plans, she drove up into the Westwood hills above U.C.L.A., where Lobo could stretch his legs.

Stacey was afraid to let him off the leash, so she ran with him over the hills covered with yarrow and wild mustard. It was exhilarating but strenuous. The only respite she got was when Lobo stopped to inspect rabbit holes hidden under the tall weeds.

Finally, Stacey sank to the ground, panting. "How do you feel about entering the Kentucky Derby?" she gasped. "You could win enough to buy your own penthouse."

He flopped down beside her and rested his shaggy head in her lap.

"Poor baby." She stroked his wiry coat. "I don't care how fancy your home is. You don't belong in an apartment. I can't change that, but maybe I can make things a little better for you."

That evening Stacey called Sean.

"Is there some problem?" he asked after she'd identified herself.

"None at all. He's a wonderful dog. I'd like to keep him permanently."

Sean's slightly forbidding tone relaxed. "That would be like parting with one of my family."

"The doorman told me how fond you are of Lobo."

"There's nothing like a dog to come home to at night. Where else can you get such a greeting?"

"Some people think that's the function of a wife," Stacey observed.

"I gather you aren't married," Sean answered dryly.

"No, but I've never considered it a fate worse than death."

"You sound very young, Miss Marlowe."

"And you sound very cynical, Mr. Garrison."

"Now that we've aired our opinions of each other, what can I do for you?" he asked mockingly.

Stacey decided he was a most disagreeable man, in spite of that sexy voice. "I called to ask if I could take Lobo to the beach," she said stiffly. "A dog that size needs more exercise than a walk around the block."

Sean's derisive tone disappeared. "It's extremely nice of you to care," he said softly.

"Lobo is a very nice dog," she answered, her annoyance dissipating. The man could be irritating, but he had undeniable charm. His voice was like dark velvet, creating an intimate mood—and then he spoiled it.

"Of course I'll pay extra for the service."

The illusion that they were on equal terms vanished. Stacey was reminded that she was merely a paid employee.

"I wasn't trying to pad the bill," she said crisply. "I quoted you a fair price, and I'll stick to it."

"You aren't a very good businesswoman." The mocking tone was back.

"Perhaps not, but money isn't everything," she replied distantly.

He chuckled deeply. "You're even younger than I thought."

Stacey's green eyes continued to sparkle angrily after she hung up. How could she ever have considered Sean Garrison attractive? The man was impossible! He was one of those people who thought everything in life had a price tag. No wonder he had such a low opinion of marriage. He'd probably added up the pluses and minuses and decided a wife cost too much!

The following week was a busy one for Stacey. To her surprise and delight, she got several answers to her ad. Stacey never would have admitted it to her mother, but she hadn't been sure her idea would pay off. Now the future looked rosy. With the steady income from Sean, and the extra jobs that kept coming in, she could support herself on a modest scale.

The time she spent with Lobo was a delight. She almost felt guilty about charging for what was essentially a vacation. Sometimes they went to the beach and ran along the wet sand just above the curling surf. When Stacey's legs gave out, she built sand castles while Lobo raced in and out of the water, barking at the breaking waves.

On other days she took him to Griffith Park, where they strolled through acres of wilderness area. Lobo would disappear into the underbrush as soon as Stacey stopped to admire the abundant wildflowers. The only indication of his whereabouts might be a distant crackling, but he always returned the minute she whistled for him.

Without realizing it, Stacey began to feel as though Lobo belonged to her. She started keeping him out for much longer than the agreed upon time.

One morning the phone rang as she was getting ready to leave for Sean's. It was a new client who wanted Stacey to board a couple of dozen African violets while the woman went on vacation. It sounded simple enough except that the woman, a Mrs. Henderson, wanted to bring them over right then.

"That won't be necessary. I'll pick them up this afternoon," Stacey offered.

"Oh no, I must see where you're going to put them. They need to be kept away from drafts and out of direct sunlight."

"I'll be very careful with them," Stacey assured her.

"These are prize-winning plants. I have to leave detailed instructions," Mrs. Henderson insisted.

Stacey was beginning to have second thoughts. She wasn't a very expert gardener. Her mother had once declared that a century plant would only live fifty years if Stacey took care of it. But a job was a job, and she *had* advertised that nothing was too difficult.

"All right. You can bring them over anytime after one o'clock."

"That won't be possible. I have a million things to do this afternoon. If I came over right now, we could get everything settled," the woman coaxed. "It won't take long."

Stacey knew that was wishful thinking. Instructions for two dozen plants could stretch on endlessly. She needed the money, but she couldn't afford to jeopardize her major source of income. Lobo was a firm commitment.

It posed a problem. There was no way she could reach Mitch to tell him she'd be late. And since she was always prompt, he'd have the dog waiting in the lobby. The only solution was to get Lobo and bring him back to the house.

"I was just leaving for another job, but I can meet you here in an hour. That's the best I can do for you, Mrs. Henderson," Stacey said firmly.

Lobo didn't seem to mind the change in routine. When Stacey brought him home he inspected the whole house thoroughly before stretching out happily in the middle of the living-room floor, his big head resting on his paws.

Stacey was in the kitchen filling a bowl with water for him when the doorbell rang. "It's open," she called. "Come on in."

The sound of the door opening was accompanied by a loud bark and a louder scream. Stacey raced into the living room to find Mrs. Henderson frozen with fear as Lobo sniffed with interest at the tray of violets clutched in her hands.

"It's all right, he won't hurt you," Stacey said hurriedly. "Sit, Lobo."

Although the dog complied immediately, the woman continued to tremble. She seemed incapable of speech or movement. The color didn't come back into her face until Stacey put Lobo in the backyard. Even then it took several cups of tea until she was calm enough to discuss her plants.

When Mrs. Henderson got on her favorite subject, however, she went on endlessly. Stacey learned more than she really wanted to know about African violets. She was look-

ing for a tactful way to cut the woman short when Lobo did
it for her. He set up a frenzied barking.

Mrs. Henderson sprang to her feet. "I have to go! You
will take good care of my plants?"

"Don't worry about a thing." Stacey frowned as the
barking became strangely muted.

It reassured Mrs. Henderson. "Now don't forget, every
pot needs a half turn daily. Otherwise they get lopsided."

"I'll remember." Stacey was anxious to see what had
disturbed Lobo, although he was quiet now.

"And be sure to fill out the chart I left. It's very important to keep a record of when each plant was fertilized."

"You told me all that," Stacey said firmly. "Have a nice
vacation, Mrs. Henderson."

Whether it was rude or not, she had to get rid of the
woman. Stacey's intuition told her something was wrong.
She discovered just *how* wrong when she went outside to an
empty backyard. Lobo was nowhere in sight.

The little boy next door had climbed up on the fence.
"Are you looking for your dog, Stacey?" he asked when she
called and whistled frantically.

"Yes. Have you seen him, Billy?"

The child nodded. "He jumped over the fence after Mary
Ellen's cat."

"Oh, no! Which way did he go?"

Hardly waiting for the boy's vague gesture, Stacey ran
back into the house and grabbed her car keys. If anything
happened to Lobo, she'd never forgive herself!

She drove around the block looking for him, but he was
nowhere around. Then she drove up and down the cross
streets with the same lack of success. It didn't seem possible for an animal that size just to vanish, but that's what
he'd done.

The worst of it was that he might not be able to find his way back on his own, since he'd never been to her house before. Stacey's heart started to pound when she realized that Lobo was really lost. She forced herself to calm down and think clearly. A dog that huge was bound to be noticed. The best thing was to start ringing doorbells.

After hours of inquiring and searching, she came up empty-handed. No one had seen him. Since she couldn't think of anything more to do, Stacey went home. She had been too frantic until then to even think about Sean's reaction when he found out. He was not a reasonable man. Would he remember that murder was against the law in every state?

Her green eyes darkened to jade as she anticipated the biting recriminations awaiting her. It didn't help to realize she deserved them. How did you tell a man you'd lost his best friend?

After long moments of agonizing over the prospect, Stacey drew a deep breath. Sean had to be told.

She got a reprieve when his answering machine greeted her reluctant phone call. Her initial feeling of relief faded as Stacey realized it only prolonged her misery. She couldn't very well leave a message on the tape. That would be cowardly. Actually, news like hers should be delivered face-to-face.

Stacey panicked at the thought. She'd never met Sean, had no idea what he was really like. Even a mild-mannered man would be upset—and Sean Garrison was far from the patient type. But even as she tried to talk herself out of it, she knew this was a duty that had to be performed in person.

Part of her punishment was getting through the long hours until he got home. She couldn't count on it being much before midnight. Maybe a miracle would occur, and Lobo would return on his own!

Since she couldn't rely on divine intervention, Stacey decided to help matters along. She made up dozens of Lost Dog posters, using a broad felt-tipped pen. Under Lobo's description she put her own name and phone number.

She tacked some of the notices on supermarket bulletin boards and distributed others to various stores and gas stations. In an attempt to cover all bases, she even taped them to lampposts over a wide area.

By ten that evening she had run out of things to do, and she couldn't sit still any longer. Why couldn't Sean keep regular hours like everyone else? A sudden thought struck her. What if he picked this one night to come home early? That was the deciding factor. As long as she had to mark time, it might as well be at his place.

She debated changing out of her light blue jogging suit, then decided against it. Sean was only going to see red!

It hadn't occurred to her that Mitch wouldn't be at his customary post. When she saw the unfamiliar doorman, Stacey's heart sank. He'd never let her into Sean's apartment.

But when she told him who she was, he smiled broadly. "Sure, I know who you are. You're the one who walks the big fella. Mitch told me about you."

"I thought he'd be here tonight," Stacey said tentatively.

"Mitch is on the day shift. Is there anything I can do for you?"

"Well, I...I have a message for Mr. Garrison. Is he home yet?"

"No, this is a little early for him. Would you like to wait?" As Stacey was resigning herself to hours in her cramped car, the doorman said, "I can let you into Mr. Garrison's penthouse."

She couldn't believe it was that easy. "I'd really appreciate it."

"No problem. If he trusts you with Lobo, that means you're a-okay."

Sean's apartment was the most beautiful one Stacey had ever seen. The spacious entry had a black marble floor that contrasted dramatically with the white carpeted living room. The black and white theme was carried out in large couches and chairs covered in a striking print.

Color was furnished by the excellent paintings on the walls, and by fascinating objects on the highly polished tables. At a quick glance Stacey saw a lacquered Russian box with a detailed miniature painted on the lid in glowing oils. A jade tree nearby was decorated with pearls, and an antique Chinese bowl had a red and gold cloisonné pattern.

There was much more, but her dazzled eyes were drawn to the floor-to-ceiling windows. Beyond the broad terrace outside, the city lights glittered like a million Christmas tree ornaments. She walked to the windows and looked out at the moving panorama. The freeways were loops of diamonds that tied the city together like a gift package, and the sparkling ruby, emerald and sapphire signs were the contents.

In spite of its elegance, the apartment had a lived in feeling. There were bowls of candy and nuts on the tables and evidence of a recent fire in the black marble fireplace. A huge rawhide bone of Lobo's had been abandoned in front of one of the chairs, reminding Stacey of her errand. Poor Lobo. Wherever he was, it certainly wasn't anyplace this luxurious.

She sank down on a couch facing the entry, wishing she'd thought to bring a book. It promised to be a long night.

Stacey was asleep when Sean arrived home. The long, emotional day had taken its toll. Tension couldn't be sustained for that many hours. As her body relaxed, her eyelids had drooped.

"What a delightful surprise."

Sean's remembered voice woke Stacey instantly. Her eyes flew open, and she stared into a face that was darkly handsome. Her first reaction was that this couldn't be Sean Garrison. Where was the dissipated little runt she'd pictured? This man looked fit for anything. His square jaw was lean, like the rest of him, and his wide mouth, although smiling now, was firm. She also had an uneasy feeling that his deep blue eyes could turn icy.

"I presume we've met, but I must admit to a shocking lapse of memory." Sean's face was filled with amusement. "I can't seem to remember your name."

Stacey sat up hurriedly, running her fingers through her tousled hair. She was acutely conscious of her rumpled state, since he was so elegantly groomed. His dark hair was faultlessly cut, and his expertly tailored suit looked as though it came from London's Saville Row.

She moistened her lips nervously. "We...uh...we've never actually met. Didn't the doorman tell you I was here?"

"Didn't see him. I came up through the garage. But wait—don't tell me! I know that voice. You're Mother Marlowe!"

"I...yes."

"You're certainly not what I pictured." Sean echoed her reaction.

He inspected her with keen interest, from her shining auburn hair and thickly lashed green eyes to her baggy jogging suit. From the look of male appreciation on his face, Stacey got the impression that he was quite familiar with what it concealed. This was a man who had known a lot of women. It was the only thing about him that she'd pegged correctly.

"You aren't what I was expecting, either," she said.

His white teeth flashed in a grin. "From your grim expression, I gather I'm a disappointment."

"Not exactly."

"You can tell me. I don't have a fragile ego."

"Mr. Garrison, I have to talk to you," she began desperately.

"Sean, please. And I'd like to call you something other than Mother Marlowe, if I may." He chuckled. "I find it difficult to summon up the proper filial feeling."

"Mr. Garrison . . . Sean . . . I really—"

"Aren't you going to tell me your first name?"

"It's Stacey."

"That suits you much better than Mother." His warm voice curled around her like a caress. "Why don't we have a drink and get acquainted?"

"That's not why I'm here." Stacey hesitated before taking the plunge.

His expression changed as her tension registered. "Is something wrong?"

"Yes, it's about Lobo."

His manner cooled perceptibly. "You're quitting?" He looked around. "Where is Lobo, anyway?"

"He's gone," she answered in a voice that was almost a whisper.

Sean frowned. "What do you mean?"

Stacey explained, almost wringing her hands in distress.

Sean's reaction was everything she'd feared, and more. The charming, sophisticated man vanished instantly. He was replaced by someone with cold, ruthless eyes. Fury permeated every inch of Sean's muscular body as he told her what he thought of her incompetence.

"I'm sorry," Stacey murmured when he paused for breath. "I loved him as much as you did."

"Don't talk as though he were dead!" Sean ordered. "I'm going to get him back."

"I'll do anything I can to help," she said eagerly. "I've already left notices all over the neighborhood."

"Did you put an ad in the paper?"

"No, I . . . I didn't think of it."

Sean gave her a disgusted look. "What's the name of your local newspaper? First thing in the morning we'll phone them and offer a thousand-dollar reward. I'll put it in the city newspapers, too."

Stacey swallowed hard. A thousand dollars! She had to offer to pay it, since she was responsible, but it would bankrupt her.

"I'll take care of the reward," she said in a muted voice.

"That's the least of my worries, right now," he answered curtly. "How long have you been here? What if someone called while you were out?"

"I have an answering machine."

"Well, what are we sitting around here for? Let's go see if there's any news of Lobo."

"It's the middle of the night," Stacey pointed out.

"So what? Give me your address, and I'll meet you there."

A red light showed there had been phone calls while she was out.

Tension filled the air as Sean waited, grim faced, through messages from her mother and two friends. Stacey was sure it was hopeless, when suddenly a strange voice sounded on the tape. It had the slightly stilted form that people use when talking to a machine.

"This is John Cuzak. I have your dog. I found him in my garage. You can call me at this number."

Sean grabbed a pad and pencil from the table and wrote down the number. "I told you we'd get him back!" he exclaimed gleefully.

As he reached for the phone, Stacey stopped him. "You can't call now. It's three o'clock in the morning."

Sean relinquished the receiver reluctantly. "I suppose you're right."

"I know how you feel, but Lobo's safe. That's the main thing. He'll be all right for a few more hours," she reassured him.

"What time do people get up around here?"

"I wouldn't call before eight o'clock."

Sean jammed his hands into his pockets and glanced around the living room for the first time. "I won't get any sleep if I go home. Would you mind if I stayed here until morning?"

"Well, I . . . I guess it will be all right." Stacey figured she owed him that much, although she was exhausted as reaction set in. "Would you like some coffee?"

"That would be nice." He examined her pale face. "On second thought, don't bother. You look done in."

"I'm fine," she lied, "and it's no trouble."

"I'll bet you don't usually have those dark circles under your eyes," he said gently.

"This hasn't been the most restful day of my life," she admitted.

"Poor little Stacey. I'm sorry I was so hard on you."

Sean's abrupt change to concern made her wary. He seemed like a very physical man, and he, too, might consider that she owed him something. Was his request to spend the night really because of Lobo? If she rejected his sudden friendliness, he should get the message.

"You had every right to be upset. I took on a job, and I made a mess of it." Stacey made the statement matter-of-factly.

"I think Lobo was more than a job to you," he said softly. "I should have realized you were as upset as I."

"Fortunately everything turned out all right. I'll make coffee."

Sean followed her to the kitchen. "It seems very quiet around here. Is there a Father Marlowe?" he asked casually.

"Yes," she answered without turning around. Stacey did have a father, although she knew that wasn't what Sean meant.

"Maybe he'd like to join us for coffee."

"If you were sound asleep, would you want to get up and make conversation?" she demanded, reaching into the cupboard for cups.

Sean captured her left hand. There were no rings on it. "You aren't married, are you, Stacey?"

"No," she answered reluctantly. It was all right to be evasive, but she didn't like to risk being trapped in an outright lie.

He held on to her hand when she would have withdrawn it. "Why all the elaborate pretense in your ad?"

"It was just a gimmick," she mumbled. Sean seemed overpowering in her small kitchen. "Mother Marlowe sounded like someone dependable." She laughed self-consciously. "I guess I blew that image, didn't I?"

"It was an unfortunate occurrence that could have happened to anyone. Don't dwell on it."

"I'm glad you—" Stacey let out a yelp as Sean leaned against the wall and absentmindedly plucked a leaf from one of the African violet plants clustered on the kitchen table. "Don't do that! Mrs. Henderson probably counted every one of those leaves."

Sean raised a dark brow. "Is that some kind of hobby?"

Stacey sighed. "I think it's more of an obsession. If she notices that leaf gone, she'll never use my services again. I can't afford to lose another client."

"Who else did you lose?"

She stared at him, afraid she was misinterpreting. "You don't mean you'd want me to continue after today?"

He returned her gaze blandly. "Lobo would miss you."

"I'd miss him, too. He's been a great deal of company."

"I shouldn't imagine that would be a problem for you."

"Lobo is in a special category," she said lightly. The deepening note in Sean's voice told Stacey it was time to change the subject. "The coffee's ready. Shall we take it into the living room?"

He looked at the mass of plants covering the kitchen table. "I guess we'll have to. There's no place to put anything down in here. Where do you eat?"

"Standing up mostly, although I was too upset to bother tonight."

"You didn't have any dinner? Why don't you fix yourself something now?"

"I'm not hungry, but I'll see what I can find if you are."

When Sean declined her offer, Stacey put the steaming cups of coffee on a tray, which he carried into the living room.

After they were seated on the couch he said, "I feel I owe you a dinner, since you missed yours on my account. How about tomorrow night?" He looked at his watch. "Tonight, actually."

"You don't owe me anything. It's the other way around."

He smiled. "I'm not liberated enough to let a woman pay the check, and since I dislike standing up while I dine, it would be simpler if you accepted my invitation."

Stacey was torn between a desire to accept and a strong feeling that it wouldn't be wise. She had no doubt that Sean expected an innocent date to lead to much more. He was undeniably exciting, and she found him physically attractive, but Stacey didn't indulge in casual affairs—which is what it would be to him.

"I don't believe either of us will feel like going out tonight," she hedged.

"You needn't make up your mind right now. I'll call you later this afternoon." He looked at her more closely. "You need some sleep. Why don't you go to bed?"

"I'm not that tired." Her statement would have been more convincing if she hadn't been struggling to suppress a yawn.

"It would be very disconcerting to have a beautiful woman doze off in the middle of our conversation," he teased. "You don't have to stay up to entertain me. Go ahead, get into bed."

"Well, maybe I will lie down for a few minutes, but I'm not going to sleep."

Sean chuckled at the veiled warning. "Don't worry. I've yet to take advantage of a woman while she slept."

Stacey's cheeks flamed. Was the curious vulnerability she felt around him that obvious? "I wasn't implying that you would," she muttered.

"On the other hand, I might make an exception in your case." He laughed at the expression on her face. "Just joking, honey."

Stacey really didn't expect to fall asleep. How could she with the most vital man she'd ever met right in the next room? Sean Garrison was definitely the stuff dreams were made of, but he wasn't meant to be taken seriously. He reacted instinctively to any presentable woman—and would run like a thief if one took him seriously.

Stacey tucked her hand under her cheek and sighed. What would it be like to have a man like that in love with you? Her eyelids drooped as she imagined his dark face just inches from her own, his arms reaching for her.

It was only a short time later that Sean appeared in the doorway. "Would you mind if—" He stopped when he saw she was asleep.

He walked over to the bed and stared down at her for a long moment. She looked small and fragile curled up like a child, but the contours of her slender body were those of a beautiful woman. Sean was used to beautiful women. He was also used to the rush of desire he felt. What startled him was the protectiveness that accompanied it.

He picked up the quilt lying at the foot of the bed and tucked it around her. When Stacey made a tiny sound of contentment, Sean gently stroked the silky hair off her forehead.

"If you're as innocent as you look, lady, you could very well mess up my life," he said softly.

Chapter Two

The sun coming through the open drapes woke Stacey at dawn. For a moment she couldn't understand why she was fully clothed on top of the bed instead of in her nightie under the covers. As memory returned she jumped up and tiptoed to the door. It was very quiet in the living room. When she peeked in she saw Scan sound asleep on the couch.

His long legs were crossed at the ankles, his mouth was firmly closed, and he was breathing quietly. Even caught off guard, Sean was in command of himself. It didn't surprise Stacey.

She went back into the bedroom and gathered some clean clothes, resisting the urge to select something feminine. She chose a pair of jeans and a white cotton turtleneck and took them into the bathroom.

After her shower Stacey dressed and then applied make-up sparingly, just a touch of mascara and a slick of lip gloss.

She let her hair float casually around her shoulders after a vigorous brushing.

There were sounds coming from the kitchen when she emerged from the bathroom. Stacey found Sean heating up the coffee.

"I'm sorry if I woke you," she said.

"I was just dozing." He gazed at her admiringly. "You look as though you'd had a full night's sleep."

Stacey had second thoughts about her choice of an outfit. Sean's comprehensive glance was traveling over the curves revealed by her tight jeans and clinging pullover.

"It's amazing what a shower can do to perk you up," she said lightly.

He ran a hand over his jaw. "I could use one, in addition to a razor."

"I have small electric razor," she offered. "You're also welcome to use the shower."

"You're a lifesaver," he declared fervently.

"No job too difficult for Mother Marlowe. I'll make breakfast while you're getting cleaned up."

After providing Sean with everything he needed, Stacey started breakfast. It was almost ready by the time he returned to the kitchen.

"You're right about a shower perking you up," he said. "I feel like a new man."

The new man was as wildly attractive as the old one. He'd rolled his sleeves partially up his muscular forearms and left the top few buttons of his shirt undone. The effect was casual and very macho.

"Drink your orange juice while I scramble the eggs," Stacey said.

He grinned. "Yes, Mother."

Stacey had relegated Mrs. Henderson's violets to the back porch without a twinge of conscience. There were certain priorities in life.

Sean seemed perfectly at home in the rather unusual situation, leading Stacey to wonder if this was really so unusual for him. Were his partners supposed to perform in the kitchen as well as the bedroom? Talk about equal rights for women! What was his contribution? Swift color warmed Stacey's ivory skin as her lively imagination supplied the answer.

Sean looked at her admiringly. "Your cheeks are nice and rosy this morning. You were pale last night."

She bent her head over her plate. "I'm a morning person."

"That's going to present a problem," he said thoughtfully.

"Not really." Stacey chose her words carefully. "You and I live in worlds as different as night and day—literally. You're rich, and I'm not. I work for a living, and you spend your time enjoying yourself. You—"

"Where did you get that idea?" he asked.

"You could scarcely live in that luxurious apartment if you were poor."

"I mean the part about my not working for a living."

"You sleep until noon. Don't try to tell me you're a night watchman."

"There are other nocturnal pursuits." He laughed at the disapproving expression on her face. "Besides the one you're thinking of."

"Okay, what do you do?" she challenged.

"I own the Alcazar and Majestic theaters."

Stacey's mouth dropped open. They were legitimate theaters that presented Broadway plays. Each program carried the announcement Garrison Enterprises Presents, but Stacey had never made the connection.

"Believe me, dealing with temperamental stars who don't like their dressing rooms is not enjoyment," Sean was saying. "Neither is sobering up a drunken stage manager right before curtain time."

"It must be very exciting, though. You get to meet all those famous people and go to glamorous parties."

He smiled at her animated face. "You wouldn't like it. You're a morning person."

She laughed. "With that kind of incentive, I could change."

"That's what I'm counting on," he said softly.

Sean reminded her suddenly of a sleek, stalking leopard. It made Stacey uneasy. What did it take to discourage him?

She looked at her watch. "I think you can make your phone call now."

Lobo had covered a couple of miles in his unexpected freedom flight. His pursuit of the cat had taken him into unfamiliar territory, and then he'd wandered in the wrong direction. He didn't seem upset by the episode, but he greeted Stacey and Sean with enthusiasm when they showed up to claim him, dividing his attentions equally between them.

"I found him in my garage when I came home last night," John Cuzak said. "I don't mind telling you I was a little scared at first. That's one big dog!"

"But very gentle," Stacey said in Lobo's defense.

"I discovered that when he licked my kid's face. I thought the wife was going to have a heart attack."

"We're very grateful to you for returning him," Sean said.

Stacey didn't see how much money changed hands, but the man was effusive with his thanks.

Sean's Lincoln Continental provided Lobo with a great deal more room than Stacey's compact car. He settled down in the back seat with a sigh of contentment. But when Sean stopped the car in front of Stacey's house a few minutes later, Lobo was ready to go with her.

"You've alienated my dog's affections," Sean said ruefully. "He's prepared to toss me aside like a dirty shirt."

"Not really. He thinks you're coming in, too."

Sean glanced at his watch. "This is really a good time to get some business taken care of, as long as it's so early."

"You see what you've been missing all this time? Morning is the best part of the day."

He raised one eyebrow. "A very famous playwright once said there was nothing you could see in the morning that wasn't improved by viewing it in the late afternoon."

"How about this glorious sunshine?" she countered.

"You can tell me tonight how it stacks up against a candlelight dinner."

Stacey paused with her hand on the door handle. "Sean, I really don't—"

"I thought we'd also catch a performance of *Adam's Folly*," he cut in smoothly. "If you haven't already seen it, that is."

Adam's Folly had been a huge hit on Broadway for months. The show had just gone on the road, and Los Angeles was its first stop. Tickets were almost impossible to get, especially since the touring company featured most of the original cast. Stacey would have jumped at the chance to sit in the topmost balcony. How could she turn down choice orchestra seats?

"We can have an early dinner before the play or a late supper after. It's up to you."

She gave in without a struggle. "I hate to eat with one eye on the clock."

"Supper it is then. I'll make a reservation at Chez Luis."

Chez Luis was a current favorite of the jet set and entertainment crowd. Less prominent people waited weeks for a reservation. It promised to be a very eventful evening, but Stacey didn't want Sean to think she was swallowing the bait without seeing the hook.

"Do you always use incentives to get what you want?" she asked dryly.

He smiled. "When my company isn't enough."

"It isn't that," she protested. He had neatly put her on the defensive. "I'm sure you have no trouble getting dates."

"It isn't quantity I'm interested in, it's quality."

"You must have that, too, with the kind of circles you move in."

"Do you subject every prospective date to this in-depth analysis?" he asked wryly.

"That's the whole trouble. I'm not sure it's a good idea for us to date. Under normal circumstances we'd never even have met. Maybe that's the way we should leave it."

"Or maybe our meeting was preordained." His voice was silky. "Did that ever occur to you?"

Stacey couldn't help laughing. "You mean Lobo's antipathy toward cats is part of some grand celestial scheme?"

He grinned. "I can't think of any other reason for the night we just put in."

Although Sean had had very little sleep, he didn't show it. In spite of his unconventional life-style, he was in excellent shape. His body was lean, with no fat padding his powerful frame. Somewhere in his busy life he found time to work out, Stacey decided. Bedroom calisthenics alone couldn't account for a physique like his.

"At least everything turned out happily," she said. "I would have been devastated if anything had happened to Lobo."

Sean scratched the dog's ear with affection. "He does tend to grow on you, doesn't he?"

"It's hard to believe I found him a little intimidating at first. Like you," she added in a burst of candor.

He chuckled. "I suppose I do have a rather short fuse at times. But you found out that Lobo and I share a common trait: we're all bark and no bite."

"*He* is anyway," Stacey remarked pointedly. "I wasn't so sure about you last night. You had steam coming out of your ears."

"A regrettable lapse, but I did have slight provocation," he reminded her. "Don't you have a temper? It's supposed to go with that beautiful red hair."

"I've been known to shout a little," she admitted.

"Good. I don't like passive women."

Conquests were probably so easy for this man that they became boring. "You prefer challenges, I take it?" she asked dryly.

"Not necessarily, but I don't let them discourage me." His eyes held hers. "Finding a lively, intelligent woman with spirit and warmth is a rare occurrence."

Stacey felt a rush of pleasure, even though she knew it was blatant flattery. "You have quite a way with words," she remarked lightly.

"And you don't believe one of them." He smiled.

"I recognize all the moves even though I don't play the game."

He scrutinized her face thoughtfully. "I wish I could believe that. It would be refreshing not to play games."

"That's the way I feel, too. I'll make a deal with you. Neither of us will say a single thing we don't mean tonight."

Sean's white teeth flashed in a wide grin. "Did you ever read that story about a man who had to tell the absolute truth for twenty-four hours? It was a disaster."

"Men have more trouble with the truth," she answered complacently. "*I* won't have any problem."

"We'll see."

Stacey suddenly thought of a few personal questions that could prove embarrassing. She would just have to steer him away from them.

"Besides, we'll only have to be candid for a few hours," she said hurriedly.

"You don't plan on inviting me to spend the night again?" he teased.

"I didn't invite you last night. You invited yourself."

"That's true, but I'd like one more try at getting comfortable on that sofa."

She raised an eyebrow. "Are you sure that's where you planned on sleeping?"

His eyes twinkled mischievously. "Has our truth fest started yet?"

"You've just answered my question." When she reached for the door handle, Lobo looked expectantly at her, but Stacey shook her head. "You're in the doghouse, buster. You can't come to my house again until you learn to behave yourself."

Sean laughed. "Which one of us are you talking to?"

"Both of you. Lobo is all yours. I'm taking the day off."

"That's your punishment for chasing around," he told the dog. "Women are hard on transgressors."

"Spoken from experience?" Stacey asked coolly.

"Just a general observation on the human condition," he answered innocently. "I'll see you at seven-thirty."

Stacey was filled with an unaccustomed excitement as she dressed for her date. Men had always been plentiful in her life. She had even imagined herself in love with a few in college, but not since then. It was a long time since she'd felt this singing in her veins.

Not that she was in love with Sean. Stacey realized that his attraction for her was purely physical. She had found herself looking at his firm mouth, imagining how it would soften against her lips. Or would it? Was he a tender lover or a demanding one?

Her speculation wasn't limited to a chaste kiss. Men didn't have a corner on erotic imagery. Doubtless they would be very surprised to learn that women fantasized over *their* bodies, too. Stacey had felt a compelling urge to run her hands over the tapering triangle of Sean's torso, to discover the taut muscles that lay beneath his smooth skin.

She drew a deep breath as her fantasies threatened to get out of hand. As long as she understood that her feelings were merely sexual, there would be no problem. All she had to do was face the fact and avoid getting involved with him. If he had more in mind than a pleasant evening, that was *his* problem.

Stacey put a lot of thought into selecting an outfit. After discarding several choices as too ingenue, she picked a simple black silk dress with a scoop neck and long sleeves. It hugged her slim midriff and hips flatteringly before flaring out in a skirt with a handkerchief hemline.

It was a sophisticated gown that called for a corresponding hairdo. She spent a long time twisting her hair into a complicated arrangement of curls that were piled high on her crown before cascading down to the nape of her neck.

The result was quite chic, especially after she clasped on the dangling pair of pearl earrings.

She had darkened her long eyelashes with mascara and deepened the color of her eyes with green eye shadow. A new silver lip gloss applied over her lipstick gave her curved mouth a sheen. When she glanced in the mirror as she was spraying herself with perfume, Stacey hoped Sean would find her as alluring as the glitzy females he was accustomed to.

His reaction when he rang the bell a short time later wasn't what she'd hoped for. His expectant smile dimmed as he looked at her.

"Is something wrong?" she asked, puzzled.

He recovered swiftly. "No, certainly not. You look charming."

"Our truth fest has started," she reminded him. "Something's bothering you, and I'd like to know what it is."

"It's nothing," he insisted.

"I expected you to have trouble telling the truth, but not in the first five minutes," she said disgustedly.

"Okay, you win. I was just surprised. You look so different."

"Of course I look different," she said indignantly. "Do you know how long this hairdo took? I thought you'd be pleased."

"I'm sorry, honey," he said contritely. "You look terrific. It's just that I had a mental picture of the way I saw you last."

"Did you expect me to go to the theater in jeans?"

"No, of course not. You're gorgeous. Everyone's going to turn around to look at you, and all the men will envy me."

His effusive praise didn't soothe Stacey's ruffled feelings. What was really wrong? Had Sean been attracted to her because she was a novelty, a freshly scrubbed milkmaid type? That wasn't very flattering. So much for his claim that warmth and intelligence were what counted.

Stacey's pique disappeared during the play. Their fifth-row-center seats were a treat, and the play was excellent. Her eyes were shining as she watched the performance, unaware that Sean's attention was focused on her. His expression was indefinable as he watched her unaffected enjoyment.

She clapped enthusiastically as the curtain went down on the last act. "Wasn't that marvelous? I can see why it was such a smash on Broadway."

"I'm glad you enjoyed it."

"Everybody did." Stacey sighed happily. "It must be wonderful to be the author of a hit play."

"That's an interesting observation," Sean remarked as they joined the crowd, inching their way up the aisle. "Most people want to star in one."

"I'm a writer," she explained.

"Is Mother Marlowe your pen name?" he teased.

"No, just a means to an end until I make my mark in the literary world."

"It isn't easy, is it?" he asked sympathetically.

"That's the understatement of all time!" Her mouth twisted ruefully. "My mother is constantly pointing out how high the odds are against my succeeding."

"It's the same in any profession. There's no instant formula for success."

"Tell that to my mother!"

"What does she want you to be?"

"Married." Stacey's green eyes danced with merriment.

Sean's gaze swept over her flawless features. "That shouldn't present a problem."

"You don't know her requirements."

He grinned. "I can guess—a rich young doctor."

"That would be her first choice, but she wouldn't be displeased by a lawyer. Almost anyone except another writer. Fortunately for her, I don't know any."

"Would you like to meet Michael Browning?"

"Could I?" Stacey exclaimed. He was the author of the play they'd just seen.

"I don't know if he's here tonight, but we can take a chance."

Sean guided her out of the theater and around the corner to the backstage entrance.

The narrow door led to a different world. Utter chaos reigned as people milled around, laughing and talking. They looked unreal in the theatrical makeup that exaggerated their features. Mixed in among the glamorous actors and actresses were stagehands in faded jeans, carrying props. A heady air of excitement permeated the atmosphere. These were the people who created the dreams.

Sean was besieged as soon as he stepped through the door. Everyone seemed to have a problem for him to solve. It was illuminating to see him in his professional capacity. None of the impatience that Stacey knew was part of his nature was evident. He dealt with every crisis, no matter how trivial, without a hint of annoyance.

Most interesting to Stacey was Sean's handling of the star, Magda Lugana. The instant she saw him the volatile actress launched into a tirade with flashing eyes. He used his charm shamelessly, and she wound up kissing him on both cheeks. If he could bottle that charisma, he'd make a fortune, Stacey thought cynically.

A young starlet waited to approach Sean until she was sure of his full attention. She was beautiful to begin with, and artful makeup made her breathtaking. A skintight leotard revealed a body as sensuous as her face.

Stacey was filled with an unaccustomed feeling of inadequacy as she watched from her position against the wall. She had gradually been eased out of the elite circle around Sean. He was looking down at the ingenue with amusement at her blatant seductiveness, but there was also male appreciation in his eyes.

The girl was smoothing his lapel in a subtle caress. "Did you have a chance to talk to Mr. Rheingold about me?"

"He's out of town, but I left a message for him," Sean replied.

"I'd do just about anything to get that part," she murmured.

"Yes, I know you would." Sean's voice was cynical.

"I'd be most awfully grateful to you." She left nothing to doubt, reinforcing the promise with a sultry look from under theatrically long lashes.

Two stagehands walked in front of Stacey carrying a large piece of scenery. Their loud instructions to each other prevented her from hearing Sean's reply to the young actress. When her view was unimpeded once more, the girl was smiling up at him radiantly.

"You're a real gent," she said with feeling.

He laughed. "That's not what I'm usually called around here." As the girl left he looked around for Stacey. "There you are! What are you doing over there in a corner?"

"Other people seemed to have priority," she answered quietly.

The scenes she'd just witnessed made Stacey realize how far out of reach Sean was. When she'd told him they lived in different worlds, she hadn't understood the magnitude of that statement. It was more than day versus night. He lived a life of glitter, easy sex and no commitments. He had his choice of exquisite females. How could any one woman expect more than a very special night or two?

The women in his life probably took what they could get without thinking beyond the moment, but Stacey knew that wasn't her nature. If she'd ever been tempted to ignore her better judgment and allow a relationship with Sean to develop, tonight was an eye-opener.

He had moved to her side. "You're my priority," he said, his voice deepening.

"You could have fooled me. You really should hand out numbers," she said lightly. "It must be very gratifying to be so popular."

"Not when everyone wants something."

"But there are rewards." Stacey couldn't keep the distaste out of her voice.

"Mr. Garrison, could you take a look at—"

"Not now!" Sean said sharply to the man who had approached him. It was his first flash of impatience. He turned back to Stacey. "What are you implying?"

"Nothing." There was no point in discussing it. "You were going to introduce me to Michael Browning," she reminded him.

Sean was far from satisfied with her answer, but he accepted it reluctantly, perhaps realizing that it was impossible to have an uninterrupted conversation in their present surroundings.

He looked around until he found the stage manager and beckoned the man over. "Is Browning here tonight?"

The man shook his head. "He called to say he was going to New York for a few days."

"I'm sorry," Sean said to Stacey. "When he comes back I'll try to arrange a meeting for you."

"It's all right." She smiled. "I'd be too much in awe to say anything intelligent anyway."

* * *

The restaurant was only a short distance from the theater, so they didn't have much opportunity to talk on the way. Then, after they were seated at their table, a constant procession of people intruded on them. The owner stopped by to greet Sean, the wine steward appeared to discuss vintages, and the waiter presented large glossy menus.

When everyone finally left them alone, Stacey said, "Is this what all your nights are like?"

"More or less."

"No wonder you sleep till noon," she said.

"You sound disapproving."

"I didn't mean to." She shrugged. "Different strokes for different folks."

"It wouldn't be your choice, though?"

"You lead a very fascinating life," she answered noncommittally.

"I suppose some people might see it that way, but I work at a job like anyone else."

"Come on!" Stacey said impatiently. "How many men are surrounded by gorgeous, accommodating women who will do *anything* to advance their careers?"

"You think I take advantage of that fact?" Sean's blue eyes were chilly.

"You don't have to make apologies to *me*."

"I'm not. I merely want to clarify the issue. You believe I bed down every ambitious actress who offers herself to me in the hope of getting a choice part. Is that correct?"

Stacey was sorry she'd started the whole thing. Nothing but unpleasantness would result from discussing personalities.

She chose her words carefully. "I merely meant that a man in your position has more opportunities presented to him. I wasn't implying that you took advantage of them."

Sean's lips curled derisively. "Now who's having trouble with the truth?"

Stacey fiddled with her silverware. "I don't know why you think I'm lying."

"Possibly because you can't look at me."

She forced herself to meet his gaze, but she couldn't hold it. Sean knew exactly what was going through her mind.

"If you have such a rotten opinion of me, I can't imagine why you accepted my invitation," he remarked smoothly.

"I wanted to see—" She stopped abruptly.

He seemed more amused than upset. "Now we're getting somewhere. You wanted to see *Adam's Folly*, and at the time it seemed worth spending an evening in my company. But after discovering that I'm a perverted satyr, you're having second thoughts."

"I didn't say that," she muttered uncomfortably.

"It's true, though, isn't it? I'm the worst kind of male chauvinist."

Stacey's temper flared. All right, if that's the way he wanted it! He had no right to put her on the defensive. "I gather you're denying it. After seeing you in action, I have a little trouble believing that."

He continued to smile, but there was a hint of steel in his voice. "What exactly did you see?"

"A tone deaf Hottentot would have gotten the message that actress was sending," Stacey said angrily. "If she was that grateful before the fact, I can just imagine her delirium after she gets the part."

"You don't believe in helping people?" he asked evenly. "You showed the same enthusiasm at the prospect of meeting Michael Browning."

"That was different!" Stacey exclaimed indignantly.

"Why?"

"Because it was a perfectly innocent response. I wasn't going to..." Her voice trailed off.

"Offer anything in return?"

"Yes, if you insist on putting it into words," she replied distantly.

"I do." Sean's amusement fled, leaving his face hard. "Brenda Cabot is a better actress than she gives herself credit for. She doesn't have to sleep her way to the top, but she's insecure. Acting is a tough business. Although I think she's misguided, it isn't up to me to judge. I promised to recommend her for the part she wants because she'd be very good in it. That's the only reward I want. If you choose not to believe me, that's up to you."

Stacey was startled by the controlled anger behind his words. Could she be wrong about Sean? Remembering the actress's last words to him, "You're a real gent," threw Stacey into further confusion. The woman could just as easily have been thanking him for making an offer without strings.

Sean was watching Stacey's mobile face. "If you have to think about it that long, I can only conclude that you *don't* believe me."

"I'm not sure what to think," she said slowly. "I've never known anyone like you."

"How many deep-sea divers have you known, or helicopter pilots or flamenco dancers? Is someone automatically suspect if he's in a business you're unfamiliar with?"

"I guess I sort of rushed to judgment," she answered remorsefully.

His face relaxed. "Recognizing it is a step in the right direction."

"You've made me ashamed of myself," Stacey said soberly. "I always faulted other people for being closed minded. Now I find that I'm just as guilty."

He smiled. "You're young enough to change."

"I intend to," she assured him.

"Does that mean we're friends again?"

"I don't know why you'd want to be," she answered ruefully.

The candlelight reflected in his eyes, making them glow. "I can think of several reasons."

Stacey was willing to give him the benefit of the doubt, but she still felt that Sean was out of her league. "I'm not going to change *that* much," she warned.

He looked at her curiously. "Correct me if I'm wrong, but I get the feeling that you're afraid of me."

"*Wary* would be a better word."

"All right, wary then. Why?"

"I think you expect more than friendship."

"Is the idea so repugnant?" He neither confirmed nor denied the fact.

"No," she answered honestly. "You're a very attractive man."

"Well then?"

How could she explain how she felt about love and commitment without sounding like a wide-eyed romantic, helplessly out of step with the times? "I think meaningless affairs are tacky," she said lamely.

"Dear little Stacey, if we ever have an affair, I assure you it won't be tacky." He didn't touch her, but his husky voice was a caress in itself.

She tried to ignore his magnetism. "I'll bet the first caveman said that to an early cavewoman before he dragged her into his den."

"Why are you so defensive with me?" he asked softly.

"Because you're like an ad man selling a product," she told him candidly. "Your line is too slick. I want a man to be honest with me."

"How much more honest can I be than to say I'd like to make love to you?"

"You can admit that's all it is without pretending to feel the same passion that Romeo felt for Juliet."

Sean sat back in the chair, his eyes narrowing slightly. "That's very illuminating. You're looking for true love?"

"I'm not *looking* for anything, but you make it sound as though it doesn't exist."

"Do you know of any cases?" he asked dryly.

"Of course I do! Don't you?"

"I presume you're speaking of real people, as opposed to the aforementioned Romeo and Juliet?"

Stacey gazed at his handsome, jaded face. Sean Garrison had everything—looks, wealth, position. Yet he was like the Tin Man in *The Wizard of Oz*. He didn't have a heart.

"I really feel sorry for you," she said slowly.

"Because I'm missing the joys of being miserable?" His mouth twisted sardonically. "Men and women have a special chemistry between them that can be quite wonderful. It's only when they start making promises that disillusion sets in."

She stared at him in sudden awareness. "I'm sorry if you've had a bad experience, but don't you think it's unfair to generalize about all women?"

He looked back warily. "What makes you think I've had a bad experience?"

"Your scars are showing." Her voice was gentle.

Sean was silent for a long moment, his expression guarded. Finally he said, "If you'll look more closely, you'll see that they've healed."

"Not if you've walled off every emotion except passion. You won't be truly cured until you can have a wholehearted relationship with a woman, not just a brief fling."

He smiled. "Are you propositioning me, or is this one of Mother Marlowe's sure-fire remedies?"

Stacey smiled back. "I give advice instead of chicken soup."

"I was hoping it was a proposition." His voice deepened.

"You weren't listening to me."

"I heard every word." He took her hand across the table. "You're partially right about me. I was burned once, and I suppose it left me . . . critical. The women I've known since haven't inspired trust. But I'm not as unprincipled as you think. I'm completely up front about my feelings."

"You don't want any entanglements," she stated flatly.

He stared intently into her emerald-green eyes, frowning slightly as though trying to see behind them. "I didn't think I did."

"You aren't going to insult my intelligence by telling me I'm different from all the rest!"

"I won't say it because it would sound like a line. The idea also scares the hell out of me," he added, almost to himself.

Stacey felt a rush of pleasure, which she knew was idiotic. This man had more approaches than a freeway! She wouldn't allow herself to think what it would be like if he were sincere.

"You don't have to worry," she told him. "There are some jobs Mother Marlowe turns down."

"That's not your motto."

"You just can't believe advertising anymore," she answered lightly.

"Why don't we take it slow and easy, and see what develops?" His voice had a silky quality.

"I can tell you ahead of time: nothing," she insisted.

"That's a pity. I would have enjoyed making love to you, and I would have seen to it that you enjoyed it, too. But if you've made up your mind, we'll just relax and enjoy each other's company."

Stacey wasn't sanguine enough to believe Sean would give up that easily. Did she really want him to? That was a hard question to answer. Common sense didn't always prevail when the man was as compelling as this one.

The arrival of their dinner lessened the sexual tension between them. Sean didn't return to the subject after the waiter left. They discussed the play and explored each other's preferences, discovering that they shared a lot of the same likes and dislikes.

"I knew we were soul mates!" he exclaimed after they'd agreed on a current movie.

"It was a big box office hit. Do you know how many other people liked that movie?"

"Statistics never interested me," he answered dismissively. "Now tell me how you feel about the L.A. Rams."

They laughed and talked and argued their opinions heatedly. It was the most stimulating date Stacey had ever had.

She was oblivious to the passage of time until their waiter coughed politely. He had been hovering nearby for several minutes.

Stacey glanced around in surprise at the nearly empty room. "They're closing."

"Not to worry. I know an after-hours place," Sean said, beckoning for the check.

It was almost morning before they drove up in front of Stacey's house. The entire neighborhood was hushed.

"I can see now why you hired me to walk Lobo," Stacey remarked as Sean took her key and opened the front door.

"He'll have to settle for a walk around the block with Mitch today."

"I'll take him out this afternoon," she said. "The poor dog shouldn't have to suffer because I had too good a time to come home at a reasonable hour."

Sean followed her inside and turned her to face him. "Did you really enjoy yourself, Stacey?"

She tilted her head back to smile up at him. "Would I have spent all night with you if I hadn't?"

"The night isn't over yet," he murmured.

"Yes, it is," she stated firmly. "It's morning now."

His hands slid up her neck to frame her face. "You said morning was the best time."

"Sean, I don't—"

His mouth cut off her protest, and his arms drew her close. Stacey stiffened as their bodies touched. The contact was everything she had imagined. Sean's hard, muscular frame was supremely masculine, from his broad shoulders to his flat stomach and taut thighs.

She was held prisoner by his strength, but his mouth was seductive rather than insistent. It moved gently over hers, suggesting limitless pleasure. A surge of warmth started in Stacey's midsection. It spread in all directions, undermining her will to resist. She was pliable in his arms, allowing him to mold her soft curves to his rugged angles until they were totally aware of each other.

Sean's arms tightened, and his mouth became more demanding. He parted her lips for a male invasion that left Stacey clinging to him. His probing tongue sent prickles of excitement racing through her veins. She could feel his own tension mount as he strained closer to her and pulled the pins out of her hair.

As it tumbled around her shoulders he ran his fingers through the silky strands, murmuring, "I've been wanting to do this all evening. And this." He nipped lightly at the delicate cord in her neck. "And this." His lips slid along the neckline of her gown to the hollow between her breasts, setting up a clamor in her blood.

The extent of her desire shocked Stacey. Never had she responded to a man so overwhelmingly. It was painful to remind herself that this was an everyday occurrence to *him*. Only the woman was different each time.

She disengaged his arms and moved away, taking a deep breath. "I'd like you to leave now."

"Be honest. That's not what you really want," he said softly.

"Yes, it is," she insisted.

He came over to stand very close to her. "Our truthfest is still in force, Stacey. You want me as much as I want you. Admit it. There's something very powerful between us— magic, magnetic attraction, call it what you will."

"I call it sex," she said bluntly.

"That's reducing it to basics, but at least you'll admit there *is* something there."

She searched his face without finding what she was looking for. "It isn't enough."

His expression hardened. "You want pretty speeches, is that it?" Before she could answer he said, "You're a beautiful woman, and I'd like to make love to you, but not under those conditions. Contrary to what you think, I do have principles."

How could she tell him that she wasn't asking for a declaration of love? It was too soon for anything like that. She wasn't in love with him either, but Stacey had a feeling she could be. That was why an affair with Sean would be self-destructive. He would retreat into his protective armor at the first sign of danger that his heart might become involved.

"You can't change, and neither can I," she said slowly.

"It's a pity." His eyes wandered over her bright, tousled hair, her velvety skin and slightly tremulous mouth. "I'd better go. Goodbye, Stacey." The words held a note of finality.

Chapter Three

After Sean left, Stacey undressed and got into bed. But sleep didn't come immediately, tired as she was. The events of the night she'd just spent were too stirring.

Sean had come into her life like a lightning bolt, and left in the same way. He had brought a quality of excitement she was going to miss, brief though it had been. Well, at least that was all she had to regret, Stacey told herself. It was cold comfort somehow.

She awoke a few hours later, unused to sleeping in the daytime. As she brushed her teeth, Stacey was in a quandary. Did last night's fiasco mean that Sean didn't want her to walk Lobo anymore? That didn't seem fair. Why should the dog be penalized just because his master was disappointed in her? Stacey was sure that wasn't his intention. Sean might have a lot of faults, but he wasn't a petty man.

Besides, only a one in a million chance had brought them together. They'd never have occasion to see each other again. She sighed unconsciously as she dressed in jeans and a loose-fitting pink cotton sweater.

Mitch greeted her jovially in front of Sean's apartment building. "When you didn't come back the other day I thought you'd kidnapped Mr. Garrison's dog."

"You wouldn't believe what happened!" Stacey exclaimed.

"The night man filled me in. He said Mr. G. was a mite upset. I told you Lobo was the apple of his eye."

"I know. I'm just lucky that he was willing to give me a second chance."

"He's a great guy," Mitch said admiringly. "But you found that out for yourself."

"Yes, he was...uh...very understanding." Stacey didn't really want to discuss Sean's virtues. "Will you get Lobo for me?"

Mitch returned a few minutes later, accompanied not only by Lobo, but Sean as well. Sean was dressed in cream-colored slacks and a matching turtleneck pullover that hugged his broad-shouldered torso. In spite of his scant amount of sleep, he showed no signs of fatigue.

Stacey looked at him in surprise as Mitch went back to his post. "What are you doing here?"

He smiled. "I live here."

"You know what I mean. Why aren't you asleep?"

His eyes admired her slender figure in the tight jeans. "I could ask you the same thing."

"I told you I was coming to take Lobo for his run," she reminded him. Suddenly Sean's unexpected appearance took on new significance. He *was* going to let their personal differences affect their working relationship. "You might have called and told me you'd changed your mind," she said stiffly.

"Where did you get that idea?"

"You mean you haven't?"

"Why would you think that? The matter was settled last night."

Stacey was reminded that they'd settled a lot of things. She held out her hand for Lobo's leash. "I'll take him now. You're probably in a hurry to get someplace."

"I had lunch in mind. Have you eaten yet?"

Stacey was thrown for a loss. Sean's farewell the night before had been very definite. She hadn't imagined his cool voice and set jaw. Why was he being so charming today?

"I know of a nice little place not far from here," he was saying. "How about it?"

When he smiled winningly, she was tempted, but nothing had changed between them. Better to let well enough alone.

Stacey shook her head. "Lobo's ready for his exercise." The dog barked eagerly on hearing his name, and she stroked his head.

"We can walk to the café," Sean suggested.

"Dogs aren't permitted in restaurants."

"I hadn't thought of that," Sean admitted. Suddenly he snapped his fingers. "I've got it! We'll have a picnic in the park. He can race around to his heart's content while we're eating."

"Dogs aren't allowed off their leashes in the park."

"Whose idiotic idea was that?"

"I don't know, but there are signs all over."

Sean frowned. "There are too many rules and regulations in the world. Pretty soon they'll have laws about what you can do in your own backyard!"

Stacey laughed. "There already are. Fences can't be over a certain height. If I'd had a higher one, Lobo couldn't have leaped it like Superdog."

Sean looked at her thoughtfully. "That's an idea."

"I couldn't raise the fence even if I wanted to. I'm only renting," she said hastily.

"I meant we could have our picnic in your backyard. I'll stop by Angelo's and have them pack us a lunch."

Stacey hesitated. "That's not a very good idea."

"Would you prefer something else? The Westside Deli makes good sandwiches."

"You know what I mean," she said quietly. "We've managed to stay on good terms. I think we should leave it that way."

"What are you afraid of, Stacey?" he asked softly.

"Nothing. I just try to avoid unpleasantness."

Sean chuckled. "If I didn't make a scene last night when you wouldn't let me make love to you, I'm not apt to make one over a chicken sandwich."

Swift color rushed into Stacey's cheeks as she looked over her shoulder to see if Mitch was within earshot. "Will you stop talking like that? Someone will hear you."

His smile broadened. "I'm the one who should mind. It wouldn't do my image any good if the news got out."

Stacey knew that Sean wasn't worried about his image. He didn't have to be. There were all too many willing women eager to bolster his ego. Why wasn't he taking no for an answer? Because he wasn't used to being turned down, which made her a challenge? That wasn't an acceptable reason.

"I won't tell anyone if you don't," she said grimly.

"Good. Now, what's it going to be, Angelo's or the deli?"

"Why do you want to have lunch with me when you must know it's going to be a waste of time?" she demanded.

"Since you can't have that low an opinion of yourself, you must be fishing for compliments." His expression was purely male as he gazed at her. "Shall I list your attractions?"

"No! Not here." Stacey lowered her voice hurriedly.

A couple had come out of the elevator and were standing nearby, waiting for Mitch to bring their car around.

Sean laughed. "Okay, we'll go into it later. Why don't you go on ahead with Lobo while I pick up the food? Unless you want me to bring you back here this afternoon to get your car."

"No, that would be foolish."

"All right. I'll see you shortly."

As she led Lobo to her car, Stacey had a feeling she'd been outmaneuvered. Why hadn't she put her foot down and told Sean she didn't intend to have anything more to do with him? Because she didn't want to, Stacey admitted to herself. Her better judgment couldn't prevent a rising sense of anticipation. Sean made everything special. He could elevate a simple picnic into an event.

Lobo had climbed into the back seat and was resting his head on her shoulder, his usual position.

Stacey reached up and patted him. "If you weren't so lovable, I'd be really annoyed at you. Do you have any idea how you complicated my life by chasing after that cat?"

He turned his head and licked her face.

"Sure, turn on the charm," she grumbled. "You and your master are two of a kind."

Stacey did hasty repairs to her makeup when she got home, then set the umbrella table on the patio with silverware and napkins. Sean arrived with two large paper bags just as she finished.

He had brought an elaborate assortment of food. On top of the first bag was a thick slice of paté wrapped in wax paper, and a jar of caviar. Under that was a bottle of chilled wine, a package of cocktail crackers and a round loaf of French bread.

The other bag held a roast chicken and two cartons containing pasta salad and marinated vegetables. A plastic bag was filled with grapes and peaches, and a cardboard box contained tiny cream puffs and chocolate éclairs.

"There's enough food here for a dozen people!" Stacey exclaimed. "What do you expect me to do with all the leftovers?"

"I could be persuaded to come back tomorrow."

She busied herself opening the crackers. "Don't make rash statements. Getting up before noon is bound to become tiresome sooner or later."

"I'm not so sure." He gazed at the firm outline of her slim body as she reached to an upper shelf for wineglasses. "It might turn out to be habit-forming."

"You don't really believe that."

"Don't be so sure. You've been wrong about me before," he warned.

"But not this time." She gave him a troubled look. "I'm really flattered by all the attention you're showering on me, but I wish you wouldn't."

"It doesn't obligate you to anything." Sean took a plate of paté out of her hands and set it on the table before framing her face between his palms. "You have nothing to worry about, honey. I'd never try to force you to do anything you didn't want to do."

That wasn't as comforting as it should have been. Sean didn't have to use force. He had much more potent weapons.

"Surely you know by now that you can trust me." His thumbs were making slow circles over her cheekbones, but a glint of laughter sparkled in his blue eyes. "How many men would have spent the night with you without trying to share your bed?''

She smiled back reluctantly. "You were too angry to even consider it.''

"Is that what you think?'' His voice deepened to a husky pitch.

As his dark head bent toward hers the telephone rang, startling them both. He released her reluctantly, and Stacey moved away quickly.

The caller was a close friend, Carla Winslow. From long experience, Stacey knew she was a nonstop talker.

As soon as she could get a word in Stacey said, "Can I call you later, Carla? I'm sort of busy right now.''

"I haven't told you my big news yet,'' the other woman protested. "I met the most fantastic man. I'm in love!''

Stacey sighed. "Not again. How many times have you been in love this year?''

"I know I've said it before, but this is the real thing.''

"You felt the same way about Peter and Dwayne,'' Stacey reminded her. "Not to mention a couple of others.''

"So I made a few mistakes.'' Carla's defensive tone changed to enthusiasm. "Tony's different. He's everything I ever wanted in a man—romantic, thoughtful, attentive. Wait till you meet him. You'll see.''

"I know exactly what I'll see,'' Stacey replied crisply. "A handsome guy who's stringing you along with a charming line. Your trouble is you're entirely too gullible.''

"And you expect a guarantee with every relationship,'' her friend complained. "There's such a thing as playing it *too* safe.''

Suddenly Stacey became aware of Sean watching her with an expressionless face. "We'll discuss it later, Carla,'' she said hastily. "I can't talk now.''

"You should stick to chicken soup," he said dryly after she'd hung up. "It's bound to be better than your advice."

"You don't know Carla. She changes boyfriends the way other women change lipsticks."

"Not everyone wants a commitment," he remarked evenly.

"But she does. That's the whole thing! She goes into every relationship thinking it's the love affair of the century."

"Your friend sounds very refreshing."

Stacey's lips curled. "Spoken like a true male."

"You think she has the wrong attitude?"

"Let's just say it hasn't worked out so far."

"But maybe someday it will. Have you ever thought of that? At least she's willing to take a chance."

Stacey knew that Sean's remarks were self-serving. But his criticism, coupled with the same sentiments from Carla, shook her confidence. *Was* she too wary? By refusing to accept Sean on his own terms, was she turning her back on something that could be quite wonderful?

His expression softened as he gazed at her mobile face. "I don't know about you, but I'm starving. Why don't you spread the caviar on some crackers for us while I open the wine."

Her somber mood dissipated when they carried the food onto the patio. Sean was at his most entertaining, and the lunch was delicious. Stacey didn't have to worry about what to do with the leftovers because Lobo was a bottomless pit. He devoured everything that was tossed his way.

"I never saw a dog eat pasta salad before," she commented.

"His stomach is ecumenical. He's equally fond of Chinese and Mexican food."

"You spoil him dreadfully," Stacey said, proceeding to do the same thing. She stripped the meat from a chicken leg and fed it to the dog, who took it out of her hand with great delicacy. "Is it true that Lobo sleeps on your bed?"

"Who told you that?"

"Never mind. Does he?"

Sean smiled. "You're welcome to find out anytime you like."

"A simple yes or no would answer the question."

"But it wouldn't be as much fun." Something flickered in the depths of his eyes. "How about tomorrow night?" Before she could refuse he said, "I spent the night at *your* house. The least you can do is let me reciprocate in kind."

"Somehow I don't think you'd expect to spend the night on the couch."

"You're right. I wouldn't." He cupped his hand around the back of her neck and drew her face close to his. "I want to make love to you for hours, and then I want to hold you in my arms and fall asleep with you curled up against me."

His low voice was hypnotic. Stacey could almost feel his hands and mouth on her sensitive skin. The quivering sensation that started in the pit of her stomach made her heart beat like thunder.

Sean's face was so close that his warm breath entered her parted mouth. His lips brushed hers in a feathery caress that was tantalizing. She closed her eyes and waited for him to deepen the kiss, knowing it was inevitable. The chemistry between them couldn't be denied.

As Sean reached for her, Lobo burst into frenzied barking. He was transformed from a mild animal into a fearsome, bristling creature as he dashed across the yard to get at the cat that was spitting at him from the top of the fence.

After one frozen moment, Stacey and Sean were mobilized. Sean got to him first and grabbed his collar.

As soon as the cat disappeared, Lobo reverted to his usual calm. He sat down and looked up at them, as though to ask what the fuss was all about.

"Shame on you!" Stacey exclaimed. "You're a very bad dog."

"Not to mention the fact that your timing is terrible," Sean said ruefully.

She avoided his eyes. "Do you think we ought to put him in the house?"

"No, I'll keep a closer watch on him." He smiled. "Unless you want to take up where we left off."

"I'd say the mood was kind of battered."

"I'll be happy to try to resurrect it," he offered. As the phone rang again, Sean added with resignation, "At some other time. This place is only slightly less eventful than the United Nations."

Stacey had brought the phone outside and plugged it into a jack on the patio. An unfamiliar man's voice greeted her when she answered it.

"Could I speak to Mother Marlowe?" he asked. "I'm calling about the ad."

"This is Mother Marlowe," Stacey replied.

"No kidding! You sound real sexy."

"The ad happens to be legitimate," she said austerely. "If you're looking for something kinky, you've reached the wrong place."

"Hey, wait a minute, don't hang up! I was just surprised, that's all. You sounded different than I expected, but my business is on the up and up if you're interested."

"What is it?" she asked cautiously.

"I need someone to pick up my shirts at the laundry. I never have time in the morning, and they're closed when I get off work at night. Your ad said you do things like that."

"I certainly do. My service is designed to make life easier for people," she said happily. Another client was very welcome. "Can I have your name and address?"

"The name is Mike Reynolds."

After he'd given her an address in Encino, a community in the valley not far from her, she quoted him a price.

"That sounds okay," he agreed.

"Do you live in an apartment house? Is there someone who can accept the shirts when I deliver them?"

"The manager will hold them for me. Unless you'd like to stop by around seven," he added casually. "We could have a drink and get acquainted."

"I have almost no contact with my clients, Mr. Reynolds," she answered primly.

"You mean we're never going to meet?"

"I doubt it seriously."

"That seems rather unfriendly," he complained.

"We aren't friends; we're business associates."

"Which means we aren't total strangers any longer," he pointed out triumphantly.

"Your shirts will be waiting for you when you get home tomorrow night." Stacey's voice held a note of finality as she prepared to end the conversation.

"Don't hang up," he said hastily. "I know it sounds as if I'm coming on to you, but I'm really not. I'm just an outgoing guy who'd like to know you better."

"Why?" she asked bluntly. "I could be fat and fifty."

"Not with that voice! What do you look like really?"

"It's completely irrelevant."

"We could meet at some public place," he persevered. "I don't blame you for being cautious, but I assure you I'm neither a sex maniac nor an oddball. I'm thirty-two years old, five eleven, blond hair and brown eyes."

"Mr. Reynolds, I really don't—"

"I have a rising career as an attorney in a well-known law office. I'm unmarried, frequent good restaurants and am considered a perfect gentleman."

Stacey couldn't help laughing. "You sound too good to be true."

"I can supply character references. How about it? Will you meet me somewhere for a drink? You pick the place."

"I'm sorry, but it's out of the question," she said firmly.

"I forgot to mention that I'm also persistent. I'll try again after you've gotten acquainted with my laundry and discovered I'm a man of impeccable taste."

"Modesty is apparently the only virtue you don't possess," she remarked dryly.

"That's very possible," he agreed.

"Well, it was nice meeting you, Mr. Reynolds, and—"

"Mike, please," he interrupted.

"All right . . . Mike. I'll see that your expensive shirts are delivered to your door."

Stacey was smiling as she hung up, but Sean's expression was forbidding when she returned to him.

"I'm sorry it took so long," she apologized. "That was a new client."

"Do you usually get that friendly with strangers?"

"I thought I was very businesslike," she protested.

"Not when you let him get that personal." Sean frowned. "You're entirely too trusting."

Stacey started to laugh. "You've certainly changed your tune."

"I'm serious, Stacey." His eyes were troubled as they rested on her lovely face. "There are all kinds of kooks out there. I don't like the idea of everyone having access to your phone number."

"They don't have my address, and I can always hang up if I get a crank call."

"I'm not worried about those. It's the people who hire you."

"Like you?" she teased.

"Something like that," he replied moodily. "You're a very beautiful woman, honey. I don't like to see you getting into situations that could be potentially dangerous."

He sounded really concerned about her. Stacey hid her gratification under a light tone. "You just want me all to yourself."

He stared at her fixedly. "You might very well be right."

The intensity behind his words made Stacey's heart beat faster. Maybe it was part of a smooth line, but just maybe he was starting to feel more than desire for her.

"That young man I just spoke to was probably harmless, but I'm not going out with him," she said quietly. "I'm not that naive."

"I hope not," Sean muttered. "But I'd feel better if you got a conventional job."

She smiled. "What would Lobo do without me?"

"I'll make a bargain with you. We'll both take him out on weekends."

"No deal. You'd get involved with one of your glamorous actresses, and I'd be deprived of visitation rights," she answered with calculated carelessness.

He cupped her chin in his hand and looked deeply into her eyes. "Would that bother you?"

She gazed back impishly. "Of course. I'd miss Lobo terribly."

"You sure know how to flatter a guy." Sean laughed and ruffled her hair playfully.

"Stacey!" Her mother's voice sounded outside the gate. "Are you back there? I rang the bell, but—" Eileen Marlowe's words ended in a gasp as she entered the yard and

Lobo came bounding toward her. "Good heavens, what's that?"

"He's harmless, Mother." Stacey went over and hooked her fingers under Lobo's collar.

"Even so, I'd prefer that you put him back in his cage."

Stacey laughed. "That was my first reaction, too, but you'll get used to him."

"It isn't on my list of priorities. Where did you get him?"

"He isn't mine, unfortunately. He belongs to Sean Garrison. Come over, and I'll introduce you."

Sean stood politely to meet Stacey's mother, who eyed him speculatively.

"I don't believe I've heard Stacey mention your name. Have you two known each other long?" she asked.

"Not very," he answered noncommittally.

Stacey tried to head off her mother's imminent inquisition. "We just finished lunch, but there's plenty left. Would you like something?"

"No thanks, I had lunch at the club," Eileen replied.

"An éclair or a cream puff then? They're marvelous."

"They look delicious, but I really shouldn't," Eileen said reluctantly. "Every bite has a million calories."

"Neither you nor your daughter have anything to worry about," Sean observed.

"Stacey always did have good taste in men," Eileen said approvingly.

"What brings you out this way?" Stacey interjected hurriedly.

"I brought you a bag of avocados. Our trees are loaded with them."

"How nice. I'll walk out to the car with you and get them," Stacey said, hoping she'd take the hint. If her mother stayed, she wouldn't rest until she discovered everything there was to know about Sean.

Eileen saw through Stacey's transparent effort to get rid of her, but she had no intention of cooperating. It merely whetted her curiosity. Was this the special man—finally?

She settled comfortably into a chair under the umbrella. "There's no hurry. I believe I will have an éclair. And a cup of coffee, if it isn't too much trouble."

"Wouldn't you prefer some wine?" Stacey asked despairingly. She didn't want to leave her alone with Sean.

"No, I'd like coffee," her mother stated firmly.

After Stacey had gone into the house Eileen turned her full attention on Sean. "How did you and my daughter meet, Mr. Garrison?"

Sean was tempted to tell the older woman that he came home and found Stacey in his apartment, but he resisted the urge. "I answered her ad," he said. "Stacey walks my dog for me."

Eileen frowned slightly. "Then you two have a business relationship."

"I like to think we've also become friends," he answered smoothly.

"I see." It was clear that she didn't, but she intended to. Her glance swept over the food on the table. "I do hope I didn't interrupt your lunch."

"Not at all. I'm delighted at the opportunity to meet you."

Eileen gazed discreetly at his well-tailored slacks, the cashmere pullover and obviously expensive thin gold watch on his wrist. So far, so good. She proceeded to the important step of finding out his occupation.

"It's such a lovely day to eat outdoors, isn't it?" Eileen remarked innocently.

Sean was having trouble containing his amusement. He knew what she was after, but he didn't know how she was going to accomplish it.

"You doctors are so fortunate to be able to take an afternoon off in the middle of the week," she commented.

The corners of his mouth twitched. "I'm even more fortunate. I have every afternoon off."

Eileen was startled. Of all the answers she'd expected, that wasn't one of them. "I hope you don't think . . . I mean, I just assumed you were a doctor. I'm sorry."

"It's all right." He smiled. "I've learned to live with it."

Stacey came out of the house carrying a tray. "I thought that pot would never boil," she muttered. "I wish you'd drink instant, Mother."

"It isn't the same," Eileen commented absently.

"There was no hurry. Your mother and I were having an interesting talk," Sean said with a broad grin.

His amusement was a dead giveaway. "I'll bet she found out more than your name, rank and serial number."

"Stacey!" Eileen exclaimed indignantly.

"It was just a joke, Mother."

"Not a very funny one. You'll give Mr. Garrison the wrong impression. If I asked any questions, it was merely to make conversation."

"I understood that," Sean soothed. "I was flattered to be mistaken for a doctor."

"You didn't!" Stacey gasped.

"It was a natural assumption," Eileen said defensively.

"Perfectly natural," he agreed. "I wish I could have qualified."

"I'm sure whatever you do is equally useful," Eileen said graciously, seeing another opening.

"Would you like some coffee?" Stacey asked Sean, her mouth a straight line. "I made a full pot."

"No thanks. I have to be going." He stood up.

Eileen glanced uneasily at Stacey. "I hope you're not leaving on my account."

"Not at all. I have an appointment downtown." He whistled to Lobo.

"I'll walk you to the door," Stacey said. "Don't go away, Mother." Her voice was ominous. "I want to talk to you."

When they were in the house out of earshot, she said, "I'm sorry Mother put you through the third degree."

Sean laughed. "I thought she was charming."

Stacey sighed. "She really is when she isn't being the protective mother hen."

"Who can blame her? Someone has to protect you from men like me."

Her mother had scared him off, Stacey decided. Sean was skittish enough to begin with. All these questions had tipped the balance.

At least he didn't know she cared. Stacey lifted her chin. "In case neither of you have noticed, I'm a big girl now. I can take care of myself."

To her surprise he said, "In that case, how about tomorrow night?"

She looked at him warily. Was this another invitation to spend the night at his apartment? "What did you have in mind?"

Sean's white teeth flashed in a grin. "You ought to know by now."

Stacey had made up her mind that she wanted to go on seeing Sean, even though it would have to be his way. She had even faced the possibility that they might become lovers, given the potent alchemy between them. But to set up an appointment to make love was distasteful. It should be something beautiful that just happened.

His laughter died as he looked at her clouded face. "I was only teasing, sweetheart. I don't know what it is about you, but I think you've reformed me." He gently smoothed the soft hair off her forehead. "You've awakened feelings I didn't know I still had."

His tenderness moved her. She gazed into his strong face with a kind of wonder. "You've awakened feelings in *me* that I didn't even know I had."

"Sweet, dear little Stacey." He gripped her shoulders and pulled her closer. "Are you always this honest?"

"I try to be. I'm not good at playing games, Sean."

He smiled. "I found that out."

She wanted to be sure he understood. "I wasn't playing hard to get last night. When I discovered how you felt about women, I made up my mind not to see you again."

His face was expressionless. "How do you think I feel about women?"

"You want to enjoy yourself with no strings attached."

"That's been my pattern up until now," he admitted.

"You don't have to qualify it. I realize you probably won't ever change."

"Yet you're willing to go on seeing me?"

"Yes."

"Why?"

Her mouth lifted at the corners. "So I don't have to give up Lobo?"

His hands tightened. "Why, Stacey?"

She examined his face, finding strong emotions. His blue eyes burned with intensity; even the planes of his high cheekbones seemed sharper. That was the thing about Sean. He wasn't passive about anything. He met both problems and passions head on. Anyone lucky enough to share his life, even briefly, would be enriched by the experience.

She tried to put her feelings into words. "You make me feel alive, as though I could parachute out of a plane or swim the English Channel. There's a whole world out there, and I don't want to sit on the sidelines anymore."

"I want to show you that world," he said huskily. "I want to see it through your eyes. You can give me so much more than I can give you."

"I don't think so, but I'll try," she whispered.

Sean's arms closed around her convulsively, but he released her after a brief hug, glancing toward the patio. "Do you think we'll ever have any time together without other people, animals or telephones?"

She sighed. "I wouldn't count on it."

"Think positively." He bent his head and kissed her sweetly. "Tomorrow night at eight?"

She nodded.

Stacey refused to acknowledge the brief pang that assailed her when she wondered what Sean was doing that evening. From now on she was going to take what came her way without questioning the donor.

Eileen greeted her with raised eyebrows. "Well, that was certainly a lengthy farewell. Can I assume you're serious about this man?"

That was something Stacey wasn't prepared to admit. Not the way things stood between Sean and herself.

"If I were, you certainly would have ruined everything. Mother, how could you?"

"What did I do?" Eileen tried to sound innocent.

"Well, I'll admit you didn't ask him if he'd prefer to be married on a Saturday or a Sunday, but only because you didn't get around to it."

"You're being ridiculous, Stacey! I was just trying to be polite."

"Like asking him if he was a doctor?"

"I didn't actually put it that way. It was just a little mix-up, that's all. What *does* he do?" Eileen couldn't contain her curiosity any longer. "He was terribly secretive about it."

"Possibly because no one likes to be interrogated."

"Nonsense! A person who has nothing to hide doesn't mind a little friendly interest."

"Otherwise known as prying," Stacey commented dryly.

"You're being as evasive as he was. I knew it! He's unemployed." Eileen sighed dramatically.

"Would that make him any less of a person?" Stacey demanded. "You liked him, didn't you?"

Eileen frowned, ignoring the question. "He certainly didn't look indigent. I know good clothes when I see them, and that watch was wildly expensive."

Stacey realized that her mother would worry the problem until she solved it, so she said reluctantly, "Sean was probably too modest to tell you what he does for a living. I guess you could call him an impresario. He brings Broadway plays to Los Angeles and stages them at the theaters he owns."

"How exciting!" Eileen's eyes lit up. "I'm so happy for you, darling."

"Wait a minute," Stacey protested. "Sean and I just met. There's nothing between us."

"I saw the way his eyes followed you," Eileen said confidently. "And you have a kind of glow about you."

"That's sunburn. Don't order the wedding gown, Mother. Sean isn't the marrying kind."

"No man thinks he is. It's up to the woman to convince him."

"Not in this case." Stacey's eyes were shadowed. "Sean can have his pick of women. He happens to be attracted to me at the moment, and I enjoy his company, but that's all it is."

Eileen looked searchingly at her. "Are you sure that's all it is, Stacey? For you, I mean."

"I just said so." She couldn't quite meet her mother's eyes.

"Maybe he's too worldly for you," Eileen said hesitantly.

"I can't believe you're advising me to let this one get away," Stacey joked. "He fills all your requirements. He's healthy, wealthy and wildly handsome. Sean's even a celebrity of sorts."

"I'd like you to marry well," Eileen said quietly. "It's more comfortable to be rich than poor. But above all, I want you to be happy."

"I know that." Stacey's voice was muted. Underneath her mother's scatterbrained behavior was a warm, caring human being.

"Even after such a brief meeting, I could tell that he's a fascinating man," Eileen said. "Maybe too fascinating. He could be one of the rare ones who light up your life like a shooting star and then leave it in darkness."

"That's very poetic, Mother." Stacey pinned a bright smile on her face.

She couldn't allow her mother to know that the same doubts had occurred to her. The alternative was to play it safe, but Stacey knew that would only bring regrets.

Why were they both being so serious anyway? She wasn't in love with Sean. He was just a very exciting man to be with. And when it was over, it would be over.

"Let's get the avocados out of your car before we both forget them," she said.

Chapter Four

Stacey was ready and waiting when Sean rang the bell at eight o'clock the next night. Anticipation fizzed like champagne in her veins as she opened the door.

This time his smile didn't falter when he saw her. "You look lovely," he said warmly.

She had left her hair loose around her shoulders the way he preferred it. Her outfit wasn't as sophisticated, either. She'd chosen a white knit, two-piece dress with a straight skirt and a loose-fitting top that had little bows embroidered in silver thread.

"You look pretty nifty yourself," she commented. "You could get a job modeling something expensive."

He grinned. "That rules out Jockey shorts."

"I was thinking of designer suits," she answered reprovingly. "Yours are elegant."

He was wearing a dark suit with a muted narrow stripe. His silk tie picked up the subtle shade and contrasted strikingly with his stark white shirt.

"When a beautiful woman pays me such lavish compliments, I can't help thinking she has an ulterior motive."

The words were joking, but she sensed the truth behind them. Sean's encounters with women had made him distrustful. Instead of being annoyed, Stacey felt a tug at her heart. If nothing else came of their relationship, she was going to give him back his faith in the female sex.

"I do want something, but I doubt if you'd give it to me," she remarked casually.

His look of disappointment was swiftly masked by a cynical smile. "Don't underestimate your charms."

"Okay, you can give me Lobo."

Sean was speechless for a moment as he adjusted his thinking. "Would you settle for a string of pearls?" he asked with a smile.

"Nope, it's Lobo or nothing."

"Don't I have anything else you want?"

"You've used up your quota of compliments," Stacey answered crisply. "Are you taking me out to dinner, or was that just an idle promise?"

"I never go back on my word," he declared. "Would you like to go to the Trianon?"

"That would be lovely." Like all the restaurants Sean frequented, it was both expensive and exclusive.

"I'll phone and tell them we'll be there in twenty minutes."

"Don't you have a reservation?"

"I wanted to leave the choice up to you."

"There goes the Trianon." Stacey sighed. "We'll never get in at this hour."

"Trust me." After a brief phone conversation, Sean secured a table.

"How on earth did you do that?" she exclaimed. "You must practice blackmail as a sideline."

"Nothing that sinister." He helped her on with her coat. "The owner owes me a favor."

"So you do collect sometimes."

"Only for a beautiful woman, not *from* one."

"Now who's tossing around compliments?" Stacey asked as they walked out to the car.

"I was just stating an obvious fact. Don't tell me men haven't told you how beautiful you are, because I won't believe it." He turned her toward him and playfully traced the pure line of her profile. But as the moonlight illuminated her upturned face, his smile vanished. "You're almost too perfect to be real," he muttered.

His long fingers outlined the shape of her mouth, sending a shiver up Stacey's spine. "Nobody's perfect," she whispered.

The light went out of his face like a cloud passing over the moon. "I suppose you're right." He reached for the door handle.

From inside the car Stacey watched Sean walk around to get in the driver's side. Her comment had obviously struck a nerve. It reminded him of the duplicity of women—or at least, one woman. What had she done to make Sean like this? He must have loved her very much. The burning question was, did he still?

His mask of sophistication had slipped back into place by the time Sean got into the car. He also changed the subject deftly. "Did your mother have anything to say about me after I left yesterday?" He sounded amused.

"Nothing I'd tell you."

He grinned. "Was it that good, or that bad?"

"I don't know which you'd consider it. She thought you were too worldly for me," Stacey said in a burst of candor.

He slanted a glance at her. "Do you agree?"

"I don't know. But that isn't what—" She stopped short. How do you tell a man that you don't want to play stand-in for a lost love?

"What does *worldly* mean anyway? That I've been around more? It's natural, since I'm older than you."

Stacey gave a tiny laugh. "I think she's afraid you'll give me a slick line like a used-car salesman, get me to fall in love with you and then trade me in for a newer model."

Sean's face was austere once more as he stared through the windshield. "I thought we'd discussed that."

"We did! I understand perfectly, but you know how mothers are."

"I don't want to hurt you, Stacey," he said slowly.

"Not to worry. I don't fall in love with every handsome man I meet."

That brought an unwilling smile. "You're doing the compliment thing again."

"Just stating an obvious fact." Stacey grinned as she repeated his words to her.

Sean was like a skittish horse, she mused, determined not to have a bridle slipped over his head. He was wary of every word, every implied suggestion. Was he really worth the effort?

Stacey turned her head to examine his strong profile. Sean was moody; he had a quick temper and an irritating habit of lumping all women together. On the other hand, he could be warm and tender, he was exciting to be with and he made her feel alive.

The answer to her question was yes. Sean's credits far outweighed his debits. They could have a wonderful relationship once he realized she had no intention of falling in love with him.

Sean was aware of her scrutiny. He laughed a little self-consciously. "I'm not sure what to say. Women don't usually tell men they're handsome."

"I'm a very unusual woman," Stacey answered calmly.

His hand covered hers. "I knew that the minute I saw you."

People were waiting for tables when they arrived at the Trianon, but Sean and Stacey were seated immediately at one of the upholstered booths that lined the room. These were considered choice because the occupants were far enough from the dance floor to enjoy the music and still carry on a conversation.

Sean appeared more relaxed in his normal element. He was his old charming self. They talked and laughed through dinner, completely at ease with each other.

When she noticed that he'd pushed his vegetable to the side of his plate, Stacey said, "You should eat your zucchini. It's good for you."

"So's liver, but I don't eat that, either."

"Actually liver isn't that healthful. It has a lot of cholesterol."

"Don't tell me doctors are finally warning against something everybody hates!"

"I know what you mean. It does seem that everything you like is either high caloric or causes sterility in laboratory rats."

"I've given up worrying about it," he said carelessly.

"Does that mean you don't care if you get fat, or you don't want children?"

A shadow seemed to pass over his face, but his smile remained. "Fat men are supposed to be jolly."

"How about children?" she asked casually. "Every dog ought to have a boy to play with."

"Lobo's too used to ruling the roost, and I'm getting too old."

This time Stacey was sure she wasn't imagining it. Sean's joking tone was forced. Had he wanted children with the shadowy woman in his past? He would make a wonderful father. She had a swift image of Sean romping with a small boy. When Stacey realized that her imaginary child had auburn hair, she drew in her breath sharply.

"Let's dance," Sean said abruptly.

They threaded their way silently toward the dance floor. Stacey felt slightly constrained, but when she moved into Sean's arms, the constraint vanished.

Her body merged with his as pure sensation took over. She was aware of every inch of his lithe frame. Her own body was pliable, conforming to his hard angles with ease, as though assuming a remembered position.

They danced wordlessly for a time. Sean seemed as bemused as Stacey. His hands stroked her back in a slow rhythm that was subtly erotic, combined with the play of their bodies against each other.

Sean's lips were resting on her temple, his warm breath feathering her soft hair. "I feel as though I'm dancing with a cloud," he said huskily.

Stacey's reply died on her lips as she raised her head and their eyes met. It was a magic moment, needing no words to convey the feelings that engulfed both of them.

When the music stopped, Sean's lips brushed Stacey's in a caress that was filled with promise. He released her reluctantly, keeping possession of her hand as they walked back to their table.

Stacey had trouble shaking off his spell, even when the contact was broken and they were seated. She looked blankly at the waiter who asked if she wanted coffee.

Sean ordered for both of them. He was more in command of himself than she, but he, too, seemed distracted. His instruction to the waiter was a conditioned response.

"I'm sorry," Sean apologized right after the man left. "I didn't ask if you wanted dessert."

"No thanks. Coffee will be fine."

As their polite exchange registered, Stacey realized how ludicrous it was. Only minutes ago Sean had been practically making love to her on the dance floor, and now they were acting like casual acquaintances.

"If I indulge in too many desserts, I won't feel like a cloud anymore," she remarked. "You'd have to steer me around the dance floor like a two-ton truck."

He stared intently at her for a long moment before matching her light tone. "I think you need a special license for that."

"It's possible. The long arm of bureaucracy is everywhere."

They were at ease with each other again, but when the music resumed playing he didn't ask her to dance. Sean called for the check as soon as they'd finished their coffee.

Since it was still fairly early, Stacey thought they'd go on to one of the many clubs that offered late-night entertainment.

When he headed west on Wilshire Boulevard, away from Beverly Hills and the Sunset Strip, Stacey tensed. This was the direction of Sean's apartment. It appeared he hadn't been joking about her spending the night.

Was that what she really wanted? On a purely physical basis the answer was clear, but shouldn't there be something more? Did she want to be just another warm body in Sean's bed?

Stacey was so involved in soul-searching that she didn't notice he was equally silent. His face wouldn't have enlightened her anyway. Sean was staring enigmatically at the road. It wasn't until he turned onto the Sepulveda entrance to the freeway that she realized they had passed his apartment. He was taking her home.

That didn't solve the problem; it only changed the locale. Did he feel she'd be less self-conscious in her own surroundings? That showed sensitivity at least.

"I hope you don't mind going home this early." He finally broke the long silence between them.

"No, I . . . it's all right."

"I'm taking your advice and mending my ways." His smile looked slightly sardonic in the dim light from the dashboard.

"Are you sure you can change?" She tried to make it sound like a joke.

"I'm not sure about anything," he muttered.

That was one point they were in total agreement on. Stacey's nerves were wound tightly as the car slid to a stop in front of her house. She fumbled in her purse when they reached the entry.

Sean took her key and opened the door. His hand closed over hers when he gave it back. There was an odd note in his voice as he said, "Thank you for a wonderful evening."

"Isn't that supposed to be my line?" She laughed self-consciously.

"It isn't a line." The pressure of his hand increased as he bent his head to kiss her briefly. "Good night, little one."

Stacey watched in complete amazement as he walked quickly down the path. She stared after the departing car until the red taillights disappeared in the darkness. Of all the things she was expecting, this wasn't one of them.

She turned on the lights in the living room and sat down on the couch, trying to figure out what was going on in Sean's mind. Was he playing some elaborate kind of game? But why would he? She hadn't imagined the flame of desire that had scorched both of them when their bodies merged. He wanted to make love to her. He'd been saying so all along. Then why this abrupt departure?

Stacey couldn't help feeling rejected, although she told herself it was better than making love with a man who felt only passion for her. Was Sean really acting unselfishly? He was very perceptive. Sex was a way of life for him, but he may have realized it wasn't a casual thing to her.

On the other hand, that might have been why he beat such a quick retreat when his feelings threatened to overwhelm his better judgment. He didn't want to get involved with someone who might become too intense.

Stacey sighed heavily. Sean was entirely too complicated. Why couldn't he just accept their attraction as inevitable? She would just have to put up with his wild mood swings until he realized she wasn't trying to trap him into anything.

Stacey half expected Sean to be waiting for her in the lobby again, as he had before. She'd even rehearsed a casual greeting. Nothing in her manner would indicate their date had ended anticlimactically. Her preparations proved to be unnecessary. Lobo was waiting, but Sean wasn't. Mitch held the dog's leash.

After a brief conversation with the doorman, Stacey drove off, feeling subtly let down.

She was disappointed, but it never occurred to her that Sean wasn't going to call. It wasn't until several days had passed that she began to get the message.

Incredulity was her first reaction. Through all their brief ups and downs there had been an invisible bond between them that often frayed yet didn't break. When she accepted the reality of the situation, Stacey became angry. All the noble traits she'd ascribed to him were in her own mind. Sean Garrison was the shallow playboy she'd first suspected. He wasn't worth a second thought.

But mixed in with her high indignation was a monumental sense of loss.

Fortunately that week was a busy one. Mother Marlowe's business picked up considerably. Stacey was hired to address two hundred wedding invitations, water someone's yard once a day for a week and market for an old lady who'd sprained her ankle.

Mike Reynolds was another small but steady source of income. She took his shirts to the laundry and picked them up once a week. The task didn't require discussion after their original agreement, but he phoned often, making good his claim of being persistent.

Although Stacey continued to turn down all his invitations, Mike wasn't discouraged. After the first couple of times they settled into a routine. He would ask her to meet him somewhere, she would refuse and then they'd talk about a variety of things.

Stacey got to know quite a lot about him. At first she thought he was the typical male on the make, but at least he wasn't offensive about it.

"Why are you wasting your time with me?" she asked one day. "You can't be hard up for girlfriends."

"No, there are plenty of willing women around." He sighed.

Stacey couldn't help laughing. "Shouldn't you be dancing for joy?"

"The sexual revolution has inhibited a lot of men," he remarked plaintively. "Maybe I'm a dinosaur in the twentieth century, but I still believe in romance. When a woman says 'Your place or mine?' before you've even asked her, it turns me off."

"Poor baby!"

"I suppose I can't expect sympathy from the opposite sex," he said in resignation.

"Because that's what you men have been doing to *us* for years."

"Not all of us."

"Oh, no? You're born with the hunter's instinct. Why else would you keep calling me when it's obvious I'm not one of your eager admirers?"

"You've just answered your own question," he said quietly. "The kind of woman I'm talking about would have accepted my first invitation and shown up with a toothbrush in her handbag. I'd like to go out with someone just for the pleasure of her company."

If it was a line, it certainly was a novel one. "Well, hang in there, Mike. They say for every man there's a woman."

"Not you?" he asked wistfully.

"I'm afraid not."

"Have you already found your man—is that it?"

Stacey had consciously avoided thinking of Sean. Now his face arose in her mind's eye, dark and brooding the way she'd seen him last. That wasn't the way she wanted to remember him. It wasn't the way he appeared in her dreams.

"I have neither the time nor the inclination to discuss my personal life," she said coolly, hoping to discourage Mike once and for all.

She was surprised when he phoned again the next day, but the call wasn't personal.

"Could you pick up my tuxedo and take it to a cleaner that gives one-day service?" he asked. "The senior partner of my firm is having a black-tie dinner at his home tomorrow night, and my jacket needs cleaning."

"You must have known about the party before this."

"I did, but I forgot," he admitted.

"You aren't very well organized."

"Don't scold, Mother. If you'll do this one thing for me, I promise to wash behind my ears and hang up my towel."

Stacey laughingly promised. Any constraint she'd felt with Mike disappeared. It was impossible to stay angry at him.

The manager of Mike's building let her into his apartment and left her alone there. Before going into the bedroom, Stacey looked around the living room with interest. It was slightly untidy, which wasn't unexpected. What did surprise her were the quantities of books, so many that they filled the bookcase and overflowed onto tables.

Stacey walked over to look at the titles. Mike's tastes ran the gamut from bestsellers to scholarly works on a variety of subjects. He wasn't the hedonist she'd supposed. Many evenings must be spent reading in that big leather chair. There was also an excellent stereo set and stacks of cassettes showing the same wide range of taste as the books.

The bedroom was in wild disarray. Mike was evidently a chronic oversleeper. An alarm clock on the nightstand was overturned, his pajamas were at the foot of the unmade bed and the closet door was open wide.

After locating his tuxedo and draping it over the only uncluttered chair, Stacey made the bed and hung up Mike's clothes.

"This is on the house," she said to a snapshot stuck in a mirror frame. "Penance for misjudging you."

She picked up the snap for a closer look. A pleasant-looking blond man smiled engagingly, his arm around a beautiful girl. Mike Reynolds was about the way Stacey had pictured him, but apparently appearances were deceiving.

Stacey was reading in bed the next night when the phone rang a little after eleven. In the split second before she answered it, Stacey was convinced it was Sean. She'd been thinking about him all day.

By now he should be yesterday's news. Maybe going to his apartment every day was what kept memories alive. The wisest course would be to quit, but she couldn't bring herself to do it.

Her heart was beating rapidly as she reached for the phone, preparing to be coolly distant. No! That might indicate she cared. Yet she certainly didn't intend to be friendly. Courteous disinterest would be the better course.

She didn't articulate these thoughts. They flashed through her mind with the speed of lightning.

When Mike's voice greeted her instead of Sean's, Stacey felt like a punctured balloon. Disappointment made her waspish.

"Do you know what time it is?" she demanded. "I don't run a twenty-four-hour service."

"I'm sorry. I know it's late," he apologized.

"Why did you call then?"

"I need someone to talk to, Stacey."

She uttered an exasperated sound. "What is it this time, your love life or your laundry?"

"I'll pay for your time," he said tentatively.

That brought remorse. She'd been so wrapped up in her own problems that she hadn't realized Mike had some of his own. He sounded completely unlike his normally carefree self.

"You don't have to pay me, Mike. I'm sorry I was so snappy. What's wrong?"

"Everything!" He groaned. "Tonight was a disaster!"

"What happened?"

"I went to that dinner at my boss's house in Holmby Hills. Mr. Pennington is a very dignified man, and his wife is one of those grande dames who probably goes to bed in an evening gown—alone."

Stacey grinned, knowing the type he was describing. "With a dog collar of ten-millimeter pearls."

"Exactly."

"Well, you couldn't have expected the party to be exactly stimulating."

"Oh, it was stimulating all right! My date saw to that."

"Don't tell me she made a play for your boss!"

"Just as bad. As you guessed, the party wasn't a barrel of laughs. After dinner there was a lot of legal talk and plenty of brandy. Cindy sopped it up like a sponge and then disappeared."

"I wouldn't dwell on it, Mike. Sometimes people drink too much when they feel out of their element. I'm sure everyone understood. Did she pass out in one of the bedrooms?"

"I wish she had!" he said fervently. "She went skinny-dipping in the pool with the chauffeur."

"You're putting me on! He wouldn't jeopardize his job that way."

"He would after they finished the bottle of brandy she smuggled outside."

Stacey started to laugh. "Well, at least he didn't get his uniform wet."

"Will you find it equally amusing when I get fired?"

"Lighten up, Mike. You won't get fired—the chauffeur maybe, but not you. The worst thing they can blame you for is your terrible taste in women."

"And she was one of the better ones."

"Good Lord, you do need help! The next time one of these business things comes up, you'd better let me get you a date."

"Preferably a frigid spinster who doesn't drink and can't swim. Although my chances of getting invited to anything but a hanging are slim."

"Just win a lot of cases, and you might work your way back up—in five or ten years," she teased.

"You sure know how to reassure a guy," he said, although he sounded a lot more cheerful.

"That's some of Mother Marlowe's free advice."

"Do you think it would help if I sent Mrs. Pennington flowers?"

"With your luck, she'd be allergic to them. Diamond earrings would make more points."

"I don't think my unemployment check will cover the payments."

By the time they hung up, both Mike and Stacey felt better. His problem had been put into its proper perspective, and hers was unsolvable anyway, so why dwell on it?

Stacey was working at her typewriter the next afternoon when the phone rang. She answered absentmindedly, her thoughts on the characters in her book. Sean's voice drove them completely out of her head.

"What are you doing?" he asked.

"Working," she answered automatically.

"Watering Mrs. Henderson's violets?" Amusement filled his voice.

"No, she took them back, thank goodness." Stacey pulled herself together. Why was she acting as though everything was dandy between them? For that matter, why was he? "Is something wrong with Lobo?" That would be an explanation.

"No, he's fine."

"Then why are you calling?"

"I wanted to hear your voice."

"Is this a sudden yen, like a pregnant woman craving pickles?" she asked acidly.

"The craving part is right anyway." His voice had a husky catch.

"I can't imagine what you mean."

"You're angry, and I don't blame you," he said regretfully.

Stacey had her pride to salvage. Sean mustn't think she cared one way or the other about his defection. "I'm not angry, just busy." She kept her voice matter-of-fact. "What can I do for you?"

"I want to see you."

"About what?"

"Have dinner with me tonight."

"I don't see my clients socially," she answered coolly. "I believe you were the one who gave me that advice."

"You made an exception in my case," he said softly.

"And it proved to be a mistake—one I don't intend to repeat."

"Give me another chance, Stacey. I can explain everything."

"I don't doubt it for a minute. The only thing I can't understand is why you want to." Bitterness crept into her voice in spite of all her efforts.

"I hurt you, and I regret it deeply."

"I wasn't hurt, just a little . . . surprised."

"That makes two of us."

She could almost see the wry twist to his mouth. "Well, there was no harm done."

"I'm afraid I did a great deal of harm," he said quietly. "I damaged something very lovely between us."

"It might have been," she admitted. "But we had too many strikes against us from the start."

"I can't accept that!" Frustration filled his voice. "Can't we at least be friends?"

Mike Reynolds was a friend. Sean was in an entirely different category. Still, they might as well be civilized about the thing. She stifled a deep sigh. "Sure, why not?"

"Then you'll have dinner with me tonight?"

"No, we're better off being phone pals."

"I want to see you, Stacey," he insisted.

"You don't know *what* you want, Sean. Call me in a decade or two when you have a clue."

"If you won't have dinner with me, can I come with you tomorrow when you take Lobo out?"

"What would be the point of paying me if you're there to take him yourself?"

"He looks forward to his time with you. Can I come along?" he repeated persuasively.

Stacey knew it wasn't a good idea. But if she said no, Sean might think she was angry that he'd dropped her so abruptly—or worse, that she minded because she was more than casually attracted to him. It wouldn't be a comfortable hour, but she'd survive. Her self-respect demanded as much.

"It's up to you," she said carelessly. "If you feel it's worth getting up that early."

"I can't think of anything *more* worthwhile," he answered. "I'll see you at ten."

After a restless night debating her decision, Stacey arrived at Sean's apartment house at a quarter to ten. She planned to leave without him if he wasn't ready. After all, he couldn't expect her to stand around waiting for him. That plan was scotched when she found him in the lobby with Lobo.

Stacey frowned unconsciously. "You're early."

"I thought *you* might be." He smiled.

She had an uncomfortable feeling that Sean had seen through her. "I got up early," she mumbled. "My clock was fast."

"No problem. Lobo's primed for action."

The dog proved his statement by trotting eagerly beside Stacey to her car. Sean's Lincoln was parked in the driveway. He had evidently expected them to use it, but after a moment's hesitation he meekly followed her.

Stacey suppressed a grin as Sean folded his long frame into the passenger seat of the small compact. His head just cleared the roof, and his legs were cramped at an awkward angle. Buckling his seat belt was difficult.

"Are you comfortable?" Stacey's eyes held a mischievous glint.

"I feel like the middle olive in a tightly packed jar," he grunted.

"You can change your mind if you like."

"I already did that once—with dire results." He turned his head to examine her delicate features broodingly.

Stacey started the car and stared straight ahead.

"Besides," he continued when it was clear that she wasn't going to reply, "I'm growing accustomed to getting up early."

"I might have outsmarted myself," she commented carelessly. "Pretty soon you won't need me anymore."

"A provocative statement if ever I heard one," he answered.

Stacey refused to let the conversation become personal. "I'd miss Lobo terribly, of course," she said quickly. "But at least my income is a little more stable. I've gotten a lot of new clients."

"Did Mrs. Henderson recommend you to all her friends?"

"No, she wasn't one of my satisfied customers, unfortunately."

"Don't tell me she really did miss that leaf I broke off?"

"Possibly. Her lips moved when she examined all two dozen plants." Stacey grinned. "I don't know if she was counting or cursing."

"You'd better stick to animals instead of plants," Sean advised.

"Preferably male animals. I hate to admit it, but men are easier to deal with than women."

"You've decided to specialize in men?" he asked casually.

"Not necessarily. I simply said they were less demanding."

"The one you were talking to the day I was there sounded *very* demanding."

"Mike?" Stacey laughed reminiscently. "He turned out to be something of a surprise."

Sean's face darkened. "That sounds as though you've progressed to more than a business relationship."

She had been driving mechanically, winding up into the hills that were still largely uninhabited except for rabbits and squirrels. She stopped the car on a bluff overlooking the ocean.

"I don't think that concerns you," she said crisply before opening the door and pulling back the seat so an eager Lobo could leap out.

Sean followed as she strolled after the dog. He seemed on the verge of saying something but thought better of it after a glance at her remote profile. They walked in silence to the top of the hill.

The sun sparkled on Stacey's windblown hair, turning it to tongues of flame that darted in all directions. She gathered the tumbled curls in both hands and held them back from her face, then released them quickly when she became aware of the molten expression in Sean's eyes as he gazed at her unguarded features.

The sexual tension between them was as strong in broad daylight as it had been in a romantic, candle-lit setting. Stacey turned away and whistled for Lobo.

"Let him run," Sean said. "This is what he looks forward to."

"I'm always afraid he'll get lost."

"Lobo and I are like bad pennies. We both keep turning up."

In Sean's case the question was, why? Stacey had no intention of asking, however. Lobo came crashing through the underbrush in answer to her whistle, defusing the atmosphere.

"That's a good boy." She pulled some weeds out of the dog's ears. "You always come when I call you."

"He'd be crazy not to," Sean murmured.

Stacey refused to let the tension mount again after Lobo ran off down the path. "I read in the paper that *Adam's Folly* is closing soon," she remarked. "What's your new project?"

"The theater will be dark for a short time while we do some renovating. After that I'll go to New York to negotiate for a Broadway musical."

"My, you do lead an exciting life."

"Fascinating," he said dryly. "Would it surprise you to know that I came home alone the last five nights, right after the performance?"

She hadn't seen him for *ten* nights. Stacey hated herself for asking, but she couldn't help it. "How about the five nights before that?"

"I had dates with five different women."

That was what she'd suspected, but hearing it confirmed caused unexpected pain. "Why are you telling *me*?"

"Because you asked."

Stacey bit her lip and stooped down to pick up a stone. She threw it at a tree with unexpected force. "I was only making conversation. I don't want to hear about your love life."

His mouth twisted sardonically. "You've effectively fouled that up."

"Most men would think five women in ten days was a pretty good track record," she answered indignantly.

"You weren't listening very carefully. I said I spent the last week alone."

Stacey's green eyes sparkled with anger. "I suppose even a machine overheats eventually!"

"I was trying to forget you, but it didn't work," he said quietly.

"You want me to believe you were just dying to be with me? That's the reason you took out other women and didn't even phone *me*?"

"It was stupid of me." He reached out to touch her hair, but when she jerked back sharply he dropped his hand. "I can't expect you to understand."

"Oh, I understand all right! You were scared to death that I'd take you seriously!"

"I'm afraid I wasn't concerned with your feelings—only my own," he answered somberly. "It's a confession I'm not proud of."

"Don't insult my intelligence! I know why you've stayed away. I just don't understand why you came back. Unless your sophisticated life-style has worn thin and you feel the need for a few quick laughs again. Well, sorry, pal. Cinderella doesn't want to waltz with the prince anymore."

His face was stern. "You don't believe any of that!" He pinned her arms to her sides and held on firmly when she would have pulled away. "I don't blame you for being hurt and confused, but you must have some idea of how I feel about you. And you're not exactly indifferent to me, either! Try to tell me you don't feel the excitement when we're together."

Stacey lifted her chin to deny it, but she couldn't. Not when his hands were burning their brand into her skin, and his blazing eyes were looking into her very soul. What Sean said was true, anyway.

"Okay, you're right," she said slowly. "But where does that leave us? For some reason you've placed me out-of-bounds."

"No! Not anymore." He gathered her into his arms and cradled her head on his shoulder, stroking her silky hair. "I've been the world's biggest fool. I can only hope you'll forgive me."

Stacey tilted her head back to look up at him. "It isn't a question of forgiveness. You have to explain. I can't spend my life waiting for the phone to ring."

"You'll never have to." He cupped her chin in his palm and smiled down at her. "If you'll give me another chance, I'll put in a direct line from my place to yours."

Stacey smiled back unwillingly. She shouldn't let him off the hook this easily, but righteous indignation was a poor substitute for the happiness that suddenly welled up inside her.

"I had something more visual in mind," she commented.

He kissed the tip of her nose. "From now on you'll have to watch where you walk so you don't trip over me. I'm going to pop up oftener than a toaster."

"Are you sure, Sean?" She looked at him searchingly. "I don't want to pressure you into anything."

His face sobered. "If I could have stayed away from you, I would have."

"That's not very flattering," she said haltingly.

"Dear heart, we have to talk." He led her over to a flat rock and sat down with his arm around her shoulders. "I don't know where we're heading. I can't make any promises. No, let me finish," he said when she started to interrupt. "The only thing I guarantee is that I'll always play straight with you, no tricks, no lies. If you're willing to put up with me, I'll try to see that you don't regret it." A smile lightened his solemn expression. "And if you don't say yes, I'll camp on your doorstep until you change your mind. So, how about it? Will you take me back?"

Stacey laughed out of pure happiness. "I don't see what other choices I have."

Sean's warning meant nothing to her. He was worrying about problems that would never arise. They didn't have to fall in love to enjoy each other's company. Just being together would be enough.

Chapter Five

Stacey bloomed like a rare hothouse flower after Sean came back into her life. Happiness gave her an inner glow.

Stacey was unaware of it, but her mother wasn't. On one of her frequent visits, Mrs. Marlowe questioned her guardedly.

"What have you been doing with yourself lately? We never see you anymore. Your father says he wouldn't recognize you."

"Tell him I look the same except I'm putting on weight." Stacey patted her flat stomach.

"Since you almost failed home ec in high school, I gather you've been eating out a lot."

Stacey regretted giving her mother a clue. An admission would lead to questions about whom she'd been out with, and she didn't want to discuss Sean.

"I don't know why you always criticize my cooking," she said to distract Eileen. "I make fantastic fudge. I even thought about marketing it before I decided to become Mother Marlowe instead.''

"I can't believe you're still running errands for people." The subject was changed, as Stacey had hoped, but not necessarily for the better.

"I should think you'd be proud of me," she complained. "I'm running a successful business."

"A precarious one. What happens if no one calls for a week or two?"

"I have steady customers. It wouldn't be a disaster."

"Are you still walking that man's dog?"

"Yes, he…uh…I'm going to pick him up shortly. Lobo, I mean."

Eileen probably wouldn't have thought twice about it if Stacey hadn't gotten so flustered. She inspected her daughter's flushed face more closely. "Are you still going out with his owner—what's his name?"

"Sean Garrison." Stacey carefully brushed some cookie crumbs into a neat pile. "I see him now and then."

"Are you sure that's a good idea?" Eileen asked quietly. She knew now what had put the sparkle into Stacey's eyes.

"Why not? He takes me to marvelous places."

"That never induced you to date any of the other rich men who would have done the same thing," Eileen commented dryly.

"I'm not going out with Sean for his money! He's a tremendously exciting man. When I'm with him, I—" Stacey came to an abrupt halt.

"That's what I was afraid of." Eileen sighed. "You're falling in love with him."

"No! It isn't like that at all. We don't even talk about love."

"That isn't one of the requirements."

"You've got it all wrong, Mother," Stacey said earnestly. "Sean and I have a very special relationship. I can tell him all my hopes and ambitions. We talk about everything and laugh a lot together. He's like a best friend."

"That's not what nature intended when the sexes were clearly defined," Eileen stated crisply. "If Adam and Eve had merely been friends, we wouldn't have a population explosion today."

"You're being utterly ridiculous!"

"All right, look me straight in the eye and tell me that all you want from this man is friendship."

Stacey's lashes fell before her mother's shrewd gaze. "Maybe something will develop in time. It's too early to say."

"Which means he hasn't given you any encouragement."

Stacey stood up and carried their coffee cups to the sink. "Are you still worried that I'll be an old maid?"

Eileen's heart sank as she gazed at her lovely daughter. Stacey had so much to offer. Out of all the men in the world, why did she have to fall in love with one who didn't appreciate her?

"I hope that's my biggest worry in life," Eileen answered gently. Then her voice returned to its former asperity. "I'd just like to have some grandchildren while I can still get down on the floor to play with them."

"If I don't get married, I'll adopt some for you," Stacey promised with a grin. "You can even come along and pick them out."

"Like puppies or kittens?" Eileen asked disgustedly. "Where did I go wrong?"

Stacey laughed. "You should have had more than one child."

Eileen picked up her purse, preparing to leave. "I hope you have at least one yourself. That will be my revenge."

Stacey's laughter faded after her mother left. She didn't like to be reminded of the impermanence between Sean and herself. Most of the time she didn't give it a thought. Life was too full. Eileen's talk about babies had struck a nerve, though. That was something Stacey didn't allow herself to think about—like marriage.

She put both of them out of her mind as she prepared to pick up Lobo. They would have a marvelous romp in the woods, and that night she had a date with Sean.

Their plans suffered an abrupt revision when he called at six-thirty.

"I don't know how to tell you this, sweetheart, but all hell's broken loose around here. The male lead is sick, and his understudy doesn't know the lines."

"Isn't that the idea of an understudy?"

"Tell me! But what can I do? I have to give him a crash course."

"That's too bad," she said neutrally.

Stacey struggled to contain her disappointment. But it was the second night in a row this had happened. The night before, Sean had been forced to cancel because the fire inspectors had found some supposed violations. Sean said he suspected they just wanted to see the performance from the wings, but he had to humor them.

What with one thing and another, Stacey hadn't seen Sean in almost a week. That would have been merely frustrating if it hadn't been for Eileen's visit that morning. She had raised doubts that Stacey had resolutely suppressed until now.

Was Sean growing tired of her? Was it only coincidence that he'd broken two dates in a row, after being inexplicably busy the nights before that? Stacey set her jaw firmly. Well, she'd known the score going in. Sean might have had the decency to level with her, but she wasn't going to call him on it. Never complain, never explain.

"I hope you understand, darling," he was saying.

"No problem," she answered with forced cheerfulness. "Give me a call if you ever get things straightened out."

"What are you talking about? We have date."

"You just broke it."

"I was hoping you'd come down to the theater. I know it's a big bore to hang around backstage, but I'll get away as soon as I can. We can at least have a late supper together."

Stacey's heart bounded back to its accustomed place. "That would be super!"

"Great, honey. I'll leave word at the stage door."

Stacey was ashamed of her suspicions. Why had she let her mother upset her? Maybe her relationship with Sean wasn't what Eileen would have preferred, but it suited Stacey just fine!

She waited until the first-act intermission to arrive at the theater, hoping Sean would have more time then, but that proved to be a mistake. He was nowhere in sight. The usual chaos reigned backstage, and everyone was too busy to answer her questions. In addition, she was constantly in someone's way.

"Watch it, lady," a stagehand grunted as he edged past her with a heavy prop.

"Sorry," Stacey murmured. She backed into another stagehand and apologized again.

A sleek blonde in a provocative black sheath and stilt heels was regarding her with amusement. Her makeup, while elaborate, wasn't the exaggerated kind that many actresses wore. She didn't appear to be in the play.

"You're new in the business, aren't you?" she asked.

Stacey made a wry face. "I really stick out like a sore thumb, don't I?"

The woman looked condescendingly at Stacey's simple beige silk dress and matching hand-knit sweater. "You're a little…um…ivy league, even for an ingenue. Don't tell me, I'll bet your name is Muffie."

Stacey usually gave everyone the benefit of a doubt, but she made an exception in this woman's case. Smiling sweetly, she said, "How clever of you. But then, I've always heard witches are clairvoyant."

"Why you little—!" The blonde's face turned an ugly red.

"Have you been here long, darling?" Sean came up in back of Stacey and kissed her cheek. "Nobody told me. I'm going to chew out a few people."

"Don't do that. Everyone was busy. I knew you'd find me sooner or later."

He framed her face in his hands and gazed down at her with a glow in his eyes. "I don't want you wandering around alone. Someone will steal you away from me."

"Still pouring it on, Sean?" the blonde asked derisively.

His eyes cooled as he glanced over at her. "What are you doing here, Francine?"

"The same thing as your little friend," she drawled. "I just hope Kenny will be as poetic."

Grim amusement crossed Sean's face. "You and Ken? I didn't know he was old enough for post-graduate work."

Her eyes narrowed dangerously, but before she could reply, Sean put his arm around Stacey's shoulders and turned away. "You'll have to excuse us," he said. "I promised Stacey a late supper."

Francine watched them go, her chest heaving with fury. "I'll get even with you, Sean Garrison, if it's the last thing I do," she muttered.

"Who was that woman?" Stacey asked as Sean guided her out the exit.

"Nobody important..."

"I guessed that, but who is she?"

"The girlfriend of the second lead. I didn't realize it till tonight."

"You knew her before, though."

"Yes."

After a look at his stony face, Stacey decided to drop the subject. She wasn't going to let the unpleasant blonde spoil their evening.

They went to a quiet restaurant, not one of the glitzy ones that reverberated with noise generated by celebrities and their faithful followers.

"I hope you don't mind, honey," Sean said. "I don't feel like being pestered by a lot of headwaiters and wine stewards."

He looked tired for the first time since Stacey had met him. "I like this place," she assured him. "We don't always have to travel the star trek."

He reached out and stroked her cheek. "What did I ever do to deserve you?"

"You're a very nice man." She smiled.

"Is that the best you can do?" he teased.

"What do you want me to call you?"

His eyes sparkled with laughter. "How about sexy? Or irresistibly charming?"

"You'd better settle for nice. You look too tired to live up to any of those other things."

"You'll rejuvenate me."

"No, honestly, Sean, you look beat. We should have postponed our date."

"No way! I haven't seen you in days." He sighed. "It's been a real dog and pony show lately—Magda and her fits of temperament, Ken trying to pad his part. A few good notices and he thinks he's Robert Redford."

"Is Ken the blond man who plays the next-door neighbor?"

"That's the one."

"Isn't he a little young for that Francine person?"

Sean grinned. "I suppose I could have gone all day without saying as much, but it wouldn't have mattered. I'm not exactly her favorite person."

Anyone could tell that from their brief exchange. Was it love turned to hate? Was she the one?

Stacey slanted a glance at him. "Did you two—" She stopped abruptly. There was no delicate way of asking.

"Never!" Sean answered her unasked question. "I'd sooner bed down a snake. She was a friend of—" Now it was his turn to pause.

Stacey felt as though she'd stumbled into a mine field. Sean had the brooding look in his eyes she'd come to dread. Although she was dying to know the story, raking up the past was dangerous. The future was what mattered, anyway.

Sean looked around irritably. "Where's the waiter? The service around here is atrocious."

It was so unlike him to complain that Stacey was convinced he was tired. "You're going home to bed as soon as dinner is over," she told him.

He covered her hand on the table. "Sorry to be such a grouch, honey. Maybe you're right, but I'll make it up to you. The theater is dark on Sunday. How would you like to spend the whole day together?"

"That sounds nice." She tried to control her eagerness, but her voice betrayed her. It was breathless.

"Where would you like to go?"

"I don't care."

"Pick someplace," he urged.

"Well, let's see—someplace where we can take Lobo."

"That rules out a whole spectrum of things, from museums to horse racing," he pointed out.

"We could go swimming," she suggested. "Even waterskiing. Does Lobo like boats?"

Sean grinned. "He needs something larger than a motorboat, and you can't ski behind a yacht."

"That's true. Okay, scratch the waterskiing. We'll just go down to Santa Monica."

"I have a better idea. What about driving to Laguna for the day?" It was a lovely seaside resort town not far from Los Angeles. "Bring a change of clothes, and we'll stay for dinner and dancing in the evening."

"What will we do with Lobo?" Stacey asked doubtfully. It sounded like a heavenly outing, but the dog was a real problem. She was almost sorry she'd suggested including him.

Sean kissed the tip of her nose. "Leave the details to me."

Southern California is noted for its weather, but that Sunday outdid itself. The sun blazed like a golden ball suspended in the clear blue sky. As they drove down the coast all traces of smog disappeared. The air was clean, with a bracing tang of salt.

"This was an inspired idea," Stacey said.

Sean smiled at her animated face. "We aren't there yet."

"Isn't getting there supposed to be half the fun?"

"I think that was a slogan dreamed up by an airline. It didn't work for the people who landed in Paris and found their luggage had gone to Hong Kong."

"It was a bus line, I believe, and I never realized you were such a cynic. Besides, I have my luggage right here." She patted her overnight case. "You can't spoil my enjoyment."

"I never want to do that." He became unexpectedly serious. "I want to add to it."

"You do! I like being with you," Stacey said impulsively.

He squeezed her hand so tightly that it was almost painful. "If I thought it could always be like this . . ." His voice trailed off.

She wouldn't have chosen this perfect day for things to come to a head, but a confrontation had been building between them. No matter how relaxed their days or nights, the tension always built when Sean took her home.

His kisses and caresses aroused Stacey unbearably, but Sean seemed to have a built-in warning signal. He always left her aching and unfulfilled. It didn't help matters that she knew he was suffering the same way.

They were both shaken by the encounters. Sometimes Stacey despaired of his ever working through his problems, yet she couldn't give up. There was too much at stake.

"Guarantees aren't worth the paper they're written on," she said now, her voice muted.

"God knows I'm aware of that!" he muttered.

"Then why do you keep looking for them?" she asked in frustration.

A muscle worked in his jaw. "Because I'm a damn fool!" With a conscious effort he forced himself to relax and smile at her. "Today is *one* thing I can count on to be perfect.

Anyone with problems is out of luck. I didn't even put my answering machine on. How about you?''

"No, I didn't either," she answered slowly.

Stacey realized that Sean was donning his protective shell again. She considered forcing the issue, then rejected the idea. He had to come to terms with himself without any persuasion from her.

Sean was shying away from intimacy because he knew it wouldn't be a casual affair for her. He felt that would imply an obligation on his part, one he wasn't willing to assume. Under those circumstances, what could she say? That she wouldn't hold him responsible if her heart became involved? That was no basis for a healthy relationship.

If Sean was aware of her introspection, he chose to ignore it. He continued to make light conversation, as though they'd never skated on cracking ice. "Mother Marlowe's clients can just fend for themselves today, right?''

"I rarely get a call on Sunday. People do their own errands on the weekend."

"That's when most of my crises and calamities occur."

"My clients are nice, normal people—except for Mike." Stacey couldn't help laughing as she recalled his bizarre date.

Sean frowned. "You're amused by abnormality?''

"Mike's not a weirdo," she protested. Her lips twitched again. "He might be a little far out, but in a nice way."

"I'm not sure I understand what that means. Perhaps you can enlighten me."

She was too busy explaining to notice the ominous note in Sean's voice. "He pretends to be a crazy, wild guy—like wearing those ghastly shorts with the little red hearts on them—while actually he's really a very conventional man."

When dead silence fell in the car, Stacey realized how that might have sounded. How could she explain that she'd seen

Mike's shorts on the floor in his bedroom? That would only make things worse!

"I pick up his laundry every week," she said hastily.

"Doesn't it usually come wrapped in a package?"

"Well, yes, but I—"

"No need to explain." Sean turned his head to look at her with eyes that were devoid of their usual warmth. "As you once pointed out, it doesn't concern me."

"That's correct." Stacey lifted her chin, feeling anger rise.

What right did Sean have to act like a betrayed husband? He didn't want her, but he didn't want anyone else to have her, either. Hell could have a snowstorm before she'd tell him she wasn't having an affair with Mike!

They finished the short trip in silence. Sean concentrated on his driving, and Stacey made an elaborate show of looking at the scenery. Only Lobo enjoyed the ride.

The Ritz Plaza was a lovely hotel sitting on the brow of a hill overlooking the ocean. A high, white wall surrounded carefully tended grounds dotted with palm trees and colorful flower beds. When Sean turned into the wide driveway that led to the hotel, Stacey was startled.

"Where are you going?" She broke the long silence.

"I booked a room for us."

"What for?" she asked bluntly.

His face was emotionless. "So we'd have a place to change and somewhere to leave Lobo while we had dinner."

Stacey hadn't thought ahead to the evening. Getting through the day was going to be difficult enough. She thought of telling Sean to take her home but decided that would be even more awkward. Even if everything was over between them, surely they could be adult about it.

"Maybe we should skip dinner," she remarked casually. "After a day in the sun I'm usually zonked."

"Whatever you say," he answered indifferently.

When he continued up the driveway and stopped in front of the entrance, Stacey thought he was going to cancel the room.

A smiling bellman opened her door. "Checking in?"

Before Stacey could set the man straight, Sean said, "Yes, you can take the lady's bag." Sean helped her out as impersonally as though he, too, were paid to do so. "We still need a place to change," he said, anticipating her protest.

That was true. Stacey was annoyed at herself for not wearing her bathing suit under her sundress, but regrets were futile now. She held Lobo's leash while Sean registered.

"Another fine mess you've gotten me into!" she muttered, glaring down at the dog, who gazed back at her happily.

A king-size bed with a pretty flowered spread dominated the room they were shown to. What a waste, Stacey thought sardonically. A fleeting expression of mockery passed over Sean's face, as if he appreciated the irony also.

His voice was elaborately polite, however, when he asked, "Would you like to change first? I'll carry your suitcase into the bathroom for you."

"I can manage," she said with dignity. "It isn't heavy."

Not nearly as heavy as her heart. How would she ever live through this day, with Sean treating her as a stranger he was saddled with? Stacey took a deep breath and opened her suitcase.

She'd bought a new outfit just for today, a rose-colored caftan made of a soft, gauzy material. The matching high-heeled slides were an extravagance because they wouldn't go with anything else in her wardrobe, but she'd wanted to look special for Sean.

Stacey emerged from the bathroom feeling a little self-conscious. The semisheer material lightly veiled her body, giving a provocative glimpse of her rounded curves. The gown was a trifle long, so she lifted it a bit, waiting nervously for Sean's reaction. For all the interest he showed, she could have been wearing a Mother Hubbard.

He frowned as his eyes traveled down to her feet. "Will you able to walk in those things?"

Stacey's nails bit into her palms. "I learned to walk at an early age."

His smile was unpleasant. "I'll bet you were a precocious child."

"Not very. There were a lot of things I didn't learn," she answered curtly. "Are you going to change? I'd like to go down to the beach."

When he rejoined her, Stacey treated him to the same indifference he'd shown her, but her lack of interest was feigned. Sean was a sight to raise any woman's blood pressure. His brief navy trunks allowed a dazzling view of muscular thighs and calves. His snug dark blue pullover made his broad shoulders even more impressive.

After a brief look, Stacey turned away to pick up her purse.

The beach could be reached by an elevator from the ground floor or a flight of steep wooden steps leading to the sand. When they went down to take the elevator, it was filled with workmen.

"We'll have this thing fixed in a few minutes," one of the men assured them.

"If you believe that, you believe in the tooth fairy," Stacey whispered.

Sean smiled naturally for the first time. "I think you're right. Shall we walk down?"

The stairs were no problem for Lobo. He took them two at a time and was out of sight before they were halfway down. Stacey and Sean proceeded more cautiously. He walked ahead of her while she clutched her caftan in one hand and held on to the railing with the other. Her thin spike heels had an annoying way of sinking into the cracks.

Sean was already on the sand when Stacey's heel caught and didn't come loose. She lost her balance and pitched forward, clutching at air. Sean had just turned to face her. He held out his arms instinctively, but he didn't have time to brace himself. As she hurtled into him, he tumbled backward onto the sand, cushioning her fall.

"Are you all right?" she asked as soon as she could get her breath. When he just stared at her in a kind of daze, she panicked. "Please tell me you're not hurt!"

"I was, but I'll get over it," he said in a husky voice.

"Oh, good Lord, you have a concussion." She smoothed the dark hair off his forehead distractedly. "Don't move, darling. I'll get help."

His arms tightened around her as she started to get up. "I don't need help. I know exactly how to do this."

His hand cupped the back of her head while his legs imprisoned both of hers. She struggled to get free, convinced he'd hit his head on a rock. What else could account for this behavior? Then his lips touched hers, and Stacey knew Sean was in possession of all his faculties.

His mouth almost sucked her breath away with its urgency. He was like a starving man offered food. Stacey was powerless to resist. All their problems were washed away in a flood of mutual desire.

"I'm sorry, sweetheart," he muttered against her throat. "I'm always telling you that, but say you forgive me."

"I'm sorry, too." She framed his face in her palms and looked down at him despairingly. "Oh, Sean, why do we do these things to each other?"

"You didn't start it. I did." He groaned. "I'm as jealous as a teenager with his first crush, but I can't help myself. The idea of you with another man—'' His hands pressed he body more firmly against his.

Stacey suddenly became aware that they were on a pop ulated beach. She slid onto the sand, in spite of his effort to stop her.

"I haven't been with another man," she said quietly "Mike is just a friend."

Sean sat up, avoiding her eyes. "You don't owe me an explanations."

That was what she had told herself earlier, but it was im portant to erase the unhappiness from his face. "I don' have any reason to lie about it."

His pain only deepened. "No, you don't, do you?"

"How can I convince you?" she asked hopelessly. "Can' you trust *any* woman?"

When he didn't answer at first, looking searchingly at her Stacey returned his gaze unflinchingly. After a nerve twist ing moment he folded her in his arms and crushed her s tightly that she could feel his heart thundering.

"My beautiful angel," he muttered into her hair. " didn't believe women like you existed."

Stacey wanted to cry. Instead she drew back and smile up at him. "I won't if you don't stop squeezing the life ou of me."

Before he could answer, Lobo came bounding over. H had been swimming. When he shook himself, water flew i all directions. Stacey and Sean leaped up as the cold drop landed on their heated skin.

"Someday I'm going to make a rug out of that dog," h swore.

"You said he was like one of the family," she teased.

"Yeah, the problem child," Sean said disgustedly.

"All that fuss about a few drops of water."

"Is that what you think I'm complaining about?" He raised her chin in his palm and stared down at her with glittering eyes.

"That's quite a dog you've got there." A man had come up to them. "He's an Irish wolfhound, isn't he? How much does a dog that size eat a day?"

The mood was broken. Stacey stood by quietly as Sean answered the man's questions. If they hadn't been interrupted, would Sean have taken her upstairs and made love to her? Was that really his intention when he'd reserved the room? Would she have belonged to him now if they hadn't had that stupid argument over Mike?

After a few moments Stacey moved away and walked down to the water's edge, where she removed her shoes and caftan. Sometimes it seemed as though fate was conspiring against them, but even fate had to run out of obstacles eventually. A current of happiness ran through Stacey, as deep as the one in the ocean. She and Sean had finally reached an understanding. Their love would be all the sweeter for having been postponed. She walked out a little farther before diving into a wave.

Stacey was floating lazily, her face turned up to the sun, when she felt a tug on her ankles.

She gasped as Sean surfaced beside her. "You scared the daylights out of me! I thought you were a shark."

"What makes you think you're any safer?" He bit her shoulder gently.

She curled her legs around his waist. "Don't you dare make marks. How would I explain it to my mother?"

"Tell her you have a gentleman friend who's a were-wolf."

Stacey lifted her chin. "You'll have to bite me on the neck."

"Never say I didn't oblige a lady." He nipped along the delicate cord in her neck until he reached her ear, which he nibbled on.

"Werewolves aren't partial to ears," she observed faintly. His mouth was lighting a fire that even the cool water couldn't douse.

"Then they're crazy." Sean's hands caressed her body, lingering over her breasts before moving down to fit her more closely against him. "Every part of you is delicious."

"Enough!" Stacey summoned the strength to put her hands against his chest. She untwined her legs. "I can't take you anywhere," she scolded with mock severity. "You're making a spectacle of us. We'll never be able to come back to the Ritz Plaza again."

"I'll find someplace else."

He reached for her once more, but Stacey twisted away and struck out for shore. "I'll race you in," she called over her shoulder.

Sean tempered his powerful strokes to hers, swimming alongside instead of trying to beat her. When they reached shallow water he let her pull away.

"You win," he proclaimed, standing up and starting to wade ashore.

"Don't patronize me!" In a surprise move, Stacey pushed him hard. "When I beat you it will be fair and square."

Sean was caught unawares. He went under with a startled look on his face. By the time he surfaced, sputtering, Stacey was a slim figure running for the blanket Sean had spread on the sand. He had left Lobo there with instructions to stay.

Sean approached deliberately, hands on his hips. He was a daunting sight. Water trickled down his sleek body, emphasizing the rippling muscles beneath his smooth skin. He was like a well-coordinated jungle cat moving confidently on his prey.

"You're about to pay for that dirty trick," he stated.

She eyed him warily. "What are you going to do?"

"Give you a lesson in ethics."

As he scooped her up in his arms and started back to the ocean, Stacey shouted, "Lobo, kill!"

The dog looked up, thumped his tail briefly and then went back to his fascinated scrutiny of a small sand crab.

Stacey struggled in Sean's arms. As they reached the water's edge she tightened her arms around his neck, their laughter mingling.

He grasped her long hair in one hand and tugged her head back. Whatever he was about to say went unspoken as he looked down at her, his expression changing.

"Do you know how beautiful you are?" he asked in a voice hoarse with emotion.

"Tell me," she whispered.

A little girl poked Sean in the thigh. "My ball went in the water, mister. Will you get it for me?"

He looked at the child without really seeing her.

"I want my ball." She started to cry.

Sean lowered Stacey gently to the sand and waded in to get the brightly colored ball. He returned to Stacey and led her back to the blanket.

"You sit there, and I'll sit here." He put her large beach bag between them. "If I touch you one more time, I won't be responsible for the consequences."

"At least you're not an exhibitionist," she answered lightly, although her hands were shaking as she reached for the suntan lotion.

Stacey gradually relaxed as the afternoon wore on. They swam and ate hot dogs from the snack bar, laughed and joked together the way they did at the best of times.

Only when they went upstairs at the end of the day did the tension return. The lazy, restful afternoon had relaxed Stacey, but now she felt suddenly shy.

"I'll take the first shower," she said without looking at him.

He started to say something and then stopped, concealing a smile.

Was he going to suggest joining her? Stacey wondered as she shampooed her hair. Maybe he was waiting for an invitation. That wasn't like Sean, though. When he wanted something he took it. Perhaps he didn't want to rush her.

Stacey's nerves were stretched tautly by the time she'd towel dried her hair to a mass of soft ringlets, then wrapped herself in another towel.

"It's all yours," she said as normally as possible, indicating the bathroom.

"I'll bet you used all the hot water," he teased.

"Hotels don't run out of hot water."

Something flickered deep in his eyes as he looked at her flushed cheeks and bare, creamy shoulders. "How about towels?" he murmured, tracing the curve of her breasts where they swelled over the tightly wrapped bath towel.

"I left you one," she mumbled.

"I'd rather use yours."

He tugged at the edge that was tucked inside, and the two ends came apart, opening in the front. Stacey grabbed for them instinctively, but he held her hands. As the towel fell to the floor Sean's eyes devoured her. Then he touched her almost reverently, his fingertips feathering over her breasts, her stomach, her hips.

"I knew you'd be perfection," he said in a husky voice. "Your skin is like warm velvet."

His slow exploration was tantalizing. The arousing caresses visited each erotic zone of her body, lingering where she was most vulnerable.

"Oh, Sean, Sean." She murmured his name over and over, reaching out for him blindly.

His mouth covered hers, fueling the flames, while he gathered her against his hard body. The sensitive tips of her breasts stiffened into little rosebuds when they came into contact with his chest. Stacey was melting inside, drenched with desire for this man she loved so dearly. The revelation came to her as he lifted her into his arms.

"You're like an obsession with me. I have to have you." His voice was thick with passion.

He was turning toward the bed when a knock sounded at the door. They looked at each other incredulously.

The knock sounded again. "Room service," a cheery voice called.

"Tell him it's a mistake," Stacey whispered.

When a look of almost comic dismay crossed Sean's face, she knew it wasn't. She scrambled to her feet and hurriedly picked up the towel.

"I ordered dinner for Lobo," he groaned.

"You didn't!"

"I forgot to bring his dog food," Sean answered helplessly.

Lobo trotted expectantly after the waiter as he wheeled in a table filled with silver-lidded dishes. The man removed the covers with a flourish.

"One steak and two hamburgers," he said. "Just push the table outside when you're finished, sir."

Stacey felt hysterical laughter rising as Sean silently signed the check. His face was a study of conflicting emotions.

After the waiter left, Sean said, "What can I say?"

"*Bon appétit* is about all I can think of." She started to laugh as a sort of safety valve.

"I'm glad you can see the humorous side," he replied grimly.

"Well, one of us is pleased, anyway." She nodded at the dog, who was shifting impatiently. "Is all of that for Lobo, or are we having dinner in the room?"

"You deserve more than a hamburger for putting up with me," Sean muttered as he started to cut the steak.

Stacey inspected the table. "Is he going to eat the potatoes, too?"

An unwilling smile curved Sean's mouth. "Need you ask? You've seen what he puts away."

She popped an olive into her mouth and took one of the french fries. "You owe me that," she told the dog.

"He's in hock up to his ears," Sean agreed fervently. "I hope he enjoyed himself today, because it's his last outing with us."

"Don't be too hasty. If we run across a female poodle, we can double date."

"You're a very rare lady," Sean said, gazing at her with deep feeling.

Stacey was warmed by the respect and affection she saw in his eyes. It meant as much somehow as his passion. To cover her own feelings she said, "While you're feeding the bottomless pit, I'll get dressed."

He cupped her cheek tenderly. "Maybe it's better this way. I don't want our first time to be rushed."

Chapter Six

Stacey and Sean had dinner in the hotel dining room. It was very elegant, with softly shaded lights and a single, perfect rose in a crystal vase on each table. A small orchestra played for dancing.

"This has been a wonderful day," Stacey remarked softly as she glided around the floor in Sean's arms.

"It's a tribute to your patience that you can say that," he answered wryly.

"Do you think all I want is your body?" she teased.

He gave her a slow smile. "I was hoping that was part of my attraction."

"You *are* rather spectacular," she admitted.

"I hope you'll think so," he murmured with his lips against her temple.

The familiar magic was building when the music came to a stop. They reluctantly returned to their table just as the waiter was bringing dinner.

The huge steak that covered her plate was more than Stacey could possibly eat. "Lobo's going to get a midnight treat," she remarked. "Be sure to ask for a doggy bag."

"He thinks he's died and gone to heaven since he met you," Sean said. "You've changed his whole life."

"That's only fair." She looked deeply into Sean's eyes. "He's changed mine, too."

They were staring wordlessly at each other when a man came over to their table. He was younger than Sean, about Stacey's age.

"Stacey?" When she looked up he said, "I thought it was you! I'd know that gorgeous red hair anywhere."

"Hello, Walter." Her voice was devoid of warmth as she said, "What are you doing here? I thought Beverly Hills was your beat."

"For pleasure, but this is business. I'm in food supplies with my father, and the Plaza is one of our customers. I have to make the rounds for goodwill."

Since he didn't seem in any hurry to move on, Stacey was forced to introduce the two men.

"Won't you join us?" Sean asked politely.

"I thought you'd never ask," Walter Caldwell answered, to Stacey's dismay. He snapped his fingers at a waiter. "Bring me a Scotch and soda," he ordered before returning his attention to Sean. "I hope you know what a lucky guy you are. I would have killed to get a date with Stacey in college."

"You went to school together?" Sean asked neutrally.

"We went to the *same* school," she interposed sharply.

"She was something else—head cheerleader, editor of the school paper, you name it," Walter said reminiscently.

Stacey realized he'd had several drinks. "That's ancient history, Walter."

"Best years of my life," he replied solemnly. "Except for this beautiful girl here. She wouldn't give me the time of day."

"I can't understand that." Sean slanted an amused glance at Stacey.

"I wasn't a macho football player like Tyler Cassidy," Walter explained, as though Sean's observation had been genuine. "But you broke his heart, too, didn't you, Stacey? When Tyler found out she was two-timing him with his best friend, he damn near blew the big game."

"There's not a word of truth in that!" she exclaimed angrily. "Besides, it's rather rude to discuss people Sean doesn't know and couldn't possibly be interested in."

"You're right, doll," Walter said penitently. "I get carried away when I remember all the fun times we had."

"Those were the good old days," Sean remarked sardonically.

"Right. So tell me, what business are you in?" Walter asked.

After what seemed like an interminable time, he left. When they were alone once more, Stacey was aware of a subtle change in Sean.

"Walter was always a jerk, and he hasn't changed," she said apologetically.

"He's still rather Joe College, but it was interesting to get a glimpse into your background."

"You didn't," she answered succinctly. "Walter never let the truth get in the way of a good excuse for himself."

"You didn't go with the college football star?"

"I dated him, but it was nothing heavy," she explained carefully. "Anything more was strictly in his own mind."

"Men have a habit of jumping to conclusions," Sean conceded, a little too agreeably. "They also tend to overreact when the relationship ends. Especially when they lose out to their best friends."

"It wasn't like that at all!"

"I'm sure it wasn't. And anyway, people change. Is that what you're saying?"

"I haven't changed! I mean, a person's basic qualities remain the same."

Sean's smile didn't reach his eyes. "I quite agree with you."

Stacey had the frustrated feeling that he was agreeing for the wrong reasons. "What I was trying to say—"

"I understand perfectly," he interrupted smoothly. "No need to explain."

The waiter appeared at their table. "Can I get you something else? More coffee?"

When Stacey shook her head, Sean said, "Just the check." After the waiter had gone he said, "Would you excuse me?"

She watched him thread his way toward the exit, wondering what had gone wrong. Surely Sean couldn't be jealous of the men she'd dated in college. They had been mere youths! But something was bothering Sean. She was too closely attuned to him not to realize that he was retreating into his shell again.

The mask was still in place when he returned and said, "I'm afraid we'll have to start back. I thought I ought to check in, so I called the general manager. Fortunately, as it turns out. He says there's a problem with the lighting system."

Stacey stared at his closed face, unable to believe Sean was shutting her out once more. She wanted to pound on his chest and shout, demand an explanation, tell him he couldn't do this to them! But she didn't.

Keeping herself tightly in check, Stacey rose to her feet. "It's always something, isn't it?" She fought to keep her voice level.

"It does seem to be," he answered with the same control.

The trip home was a nightmare. They both tried very hard to make casual conversation, but uncomfortable silences fell. They didn't usually have to talk to communicate, but their present situation wasn't normal. They both knew it.

When Sean pulled up in front of Stacey's house she got out almost before the car stopped. "Thank you for a lovely day," she said. "Don't bother to walk me to the door." She was gone before he could reply.

Sean watched her walk up the path, a brooding look in his eyes, but he didn't attempt to follow her. When she was inside, he put the car in gear.

Stacey was tense until she heard the car drive away. Then she dropped onto the couch and stared into space. They'd had their ups and downs. She'd told herself it was over before, but this time it was final. She couldn't take any more.

When it was only unfulfilled desire between them, she could hang in there. But once Stacey realized she was in love with Sean, everything changed. She didn't expect him to love her in return, yet without even trust, what did they have? She would have given herself freely, but not to provide mere sexual gratification. A hundred other women could perform the same function.

After a long time she got up and went to bed, feeling decades older than her twenty-five years.

Stacey knew even before she opened her eyes the next morning that there was some reason she didn't want to wake up. When memory rushed back she turned over and buried her face in the pillow.

An old platitude occurred to her: today is the first day of the rest of your life. The days would have to improve a great deal to be merely bearable!

Pushing Sean firmly out of her mind, she showered, dressed and sat down at her typewriter.

When the phone rang in the middle of the morning, Stacey jumped like a startled doe. There was no reason to suppose it was Sean. His behavior the night before told her that he, too, had written off their relationship. Sean had changed his mind in the past, however, and Stacey no longer wanted any part of him. He'd succeeded in making her as mixed up as he was!

She counted the rings, waiting for them to stop. When they did, she turned on her answering machine. That would allow her to get important calls while avoiding Sean's.

Her precautions proved unnecessary. He didn't phone.

Other people did, though. During the next few days, she picked up a number of new clients, which filled the gap in her income.

When her contact with Sean was severed, she'd given up Lobo as well. The decision wasn't a happy one, but Stacey realized every cord had to be cut. There was always the danger of a chance meeting with Sean, or the necessity to confer with him about something concerning the dog.

She'd written a short note claiming she could only take care of clients who lived in the valley, since she'd gotten so busy. When even that didn't bring a response, Stacey knew everything was truly over.

Toward the end of the week she received a call from a woman who gave her name as Claudia Jennings. She wanted Stacey to wait at her apartment for some moving men.

"They won't even tell me whether they'll be here in the morning or the afternoon." Claudia's voice was filled with frustration. "I can't take a whole day off from work."

"I'll be happy to accept the job, but I work by the hour. It could be kind of costly," Stacey warned. "Isn't there a manager who could let the men in?"

"No. I'm moving into a duplex." Claudia sighed. "Whatever it costs, I'll just have to pay it."

"Well, keep a good thought," Stacey consoled her. "Maybe they'll break an unwritten rule and show up at a reasonable hour."

They didn't, however. Stacey spent the whole day in the empty house. It was the kind of place she wouldn't have minded living in herself if she hadn't been lucky enough to find her house. Older buildings, completed before construction costs became so prohibitive, had such nice, spacious rooms.

Stacey wandered through the house, admiring the separate dining room and large kitchen. The place should be quite attractive once it was furnished. She wondered about Claudia's taste. Would everything be starkly modern? She'd sounded young, but voices could be deceiving. Stacey's eyes darkened when she remembered thinking that about Sean.

Since memories only caused pain, she tried to banish them by going outside and weeding a flower bed.

It was a long, boring day. True to some mysterious fraternal oath that decreed furniture couldn't be delivered until it was too late to put anything away, the moving van arrived at a quarter to five. Stacey was directing the men when Claudia returned, not much later. She was a very attractive young woman with short chestnut curls and big hazel eyes.

"They just got here?" she exclaimed. "I could have taken off work an hour early and been here myself!"

"I know. It's a shame," Stacey sympathized.

"That buffet goes in the dining room," Claudia called to the two men who were carrying it toward the bedroom. A moment later she uttered a cry as a third man dumped a carton on the living room floor. "That goes in the kitchen. It's marked *dishes* right on it," she muttered under her breath.

"Would you like me to stay to help you?" Stacey asked. "No charge," she added hurriedly.

"Would you? I'd be eternally grateful!"

After the men had gone, leaving everything helter-skelter, Stacey and Claudia started to unpack boxes in the kitchen. The resulting disorder was monumental. Dishes and cutlery covered every tabletop and counter space, while the floor was an obstacle course cluttered with unwieldy objects.

Finally Claudia sagged against the sink. "I'm fading fast. If I could find the coffeepot, I'd make us a cup of coffee— if I could find the coffee, that is," she added wearily.

"You need a break," Stacey decided. "Let's knock off for a while."

"There's no place to sit down." All the chairs were piled high with more cartons.

"Listen, you're not going to get everything done tonight anyway, so why don't you come over to my house for dinner," Stacey suggested. "After a hot meal you'll feel more like tackling this mess."

"That's awfully nice of you." Claudia looked at her curiously. "Why are you doing this? I'm a total stranger."

"I've been through moving day myself. I know what a pain it is."

"You're the first person who's offered a helping hand," Claudia said slowly. "Sometimes I've felt like chucking the whole thing and going back home."

"Where are you from?"

"A little town in Ohio that's only a speck on the map compared to Los Angeles. But the people are friendly, and all my family is there."

She sounded so forlorn that Stacey asked, "Why did you come out here?"

"I'm a computer operator, and there's more opportunity in a big city. I was offered what sounded like a lot of money—until I discovered the cost of living in this town."

"You have a lovely home, though," Stacey consoled her.

Claudia sighed. "I hope it will be someday."

"Sooner than you think. Come on, we're wasting time. You can follow me to my house."

Claudia looked a lot more cheerful after she'd had a glass of sherry and kicked off her shoes. She was curled up on the couch, gazing around admiringly.

"This room is charming. I hope my place will feel as warm and welcoming."

"I'm sure it will. I liked your things." Stacey laughed. "At least what I could see of them."

"I suppose I was foolish to ship my furniture across the country, but I thought it would make me feel less alone to have familiar things around."

"You won't be alone long," Stacey said confidently.

"I don't know." Claudia's expression was doubtful. "I haven't met many people."

"Perhaps you should have rented in one of those apartment complexes that cater to singles."

Claudia made a face. "I looked at those. The apartments were cramped, and the people were dreadful! When the manager took me out to show me the pool area, all the guys looked me over as though I were a piece of merchandise at an auction."

"I know what you mean," Stacey murmured. "But sometimes you can find a decent one among the flakes." She was thinking of Mike.

"No thanks. I got their message, and it wasn't what I wanted to hear."

"That reminds me. I'd better check my answering machine. Back in a minute." Stacey stood up and went into the bedroom.

She sat on the bed and wrote down the numbers of the people who wanted her to call back. Some were clients, and some were friends. Toward the end of the tape a deep voice made her heart leap into her throat. It was Sean. He sounded urgent.

"I have to talk to you, Stacey. Call me as soon as you get in." Not please, or will you? Just do it!

She stared at the phone as though it could tell her what he wanted. Not that it mattered. She had taken her last roller-coaster ride. Could something have happened to Lobo, though? Sean would know she'd want to hear. Stacey rejected the idea immediately, recognizing it for what it was— a desperate excuse to return his call.

She went back to the living room, trying to compose herself. But the effort wasn't wholly successful.

Claudia looked at her curiously. "Is anything wrong?"

"Just a small problem. Nothing important. Are you getting hungry? I'll start dinner."

"Let me help." Claudia followed her into the kitchen. "Don't go to any trouble. Whatever you were going to have is fine," she said when Stacey stared blankly into the refrigerator.

"What?" Stacey was having difficulty dragging her thoughts away from Sean. "Oh...well, actually, I forgot to defrost anything. My offer of dinner might have been premature."

Claudia joined her and peered into the refrigerator. "You have eggs and cheese and tomatoes. If I can find a few more ingredients, I can make *Huevos Rancheros*."

"How would you know about Spanish-style eggs, coming from the Midwest?"

"Cooking is my hobby. I read cookbooks the way other people read mysteries."

"I'm in awe," Stacey said. "You're looking at a person who would starve to death if the can opener hadn't been invented."

Claudia laughed. "Then maybe I'd better cook dinner."

Stacey sat on a stool and watched while Claudia prepared dinner. The result was delicious. She was as good as she'd professed to be.

The easy camaraderie between them gradually relaxed Stacey. Sean was only a dim shadow in the back of her mind—until the shrilling telephone brought him to the forefront.

"Aren't you going to answer it?" Claudia asked when Stacey sat rigid.

She began to mop up the coffee she'd spilled. "It's probably no one important. The machine will pick it up."

At that moment Mike's voice came from the machine. "Hi, Stacey. I called to tell you about my latest disaster. You're not going to believe *this* one!"

Stacey jumped up and ran to pick up the phone. Mike was just what she needed. "I'm here, Mike."

"Thank the Lord! I need someone sane to talk to."

She grinned. "Did you lose your latest girlfriend to the butler?"

"I wish! This one wants to move in with me."

"Don't worry. When she sees how messy you are, she'll move out."

"A wrecking ball in the bedroom wouldn't discourage her! Aren't there any nice, normal girls around anymore?" he asked plaintively. "You're the only one I know, and you won't go out with me."

Stacey glanced over at Claudia, who was trying not to listen. Thick lashes feathered her smooth cheeks as she gazed down at her plate.

"What are you doing tomorrow night?" Stacey asked Mike.

"Don't tell me you're finally going to weaken!"

"Not exactly, but I think it's time we met. I'm helping a friend move into a new house, and we could use a clever pair of hands to hang pictures." She ignored Claudia, who was shaking her head so violently that her soft curls bounced.

"What you really want is a strong back to move furniture," Mike grumbled.

"You can always say no."

"And miss the chance of convincing you what a splendid fellow I am? You knew I'd say yes."

Stacey smiled. "I don't think you're going to regret it." She gave him the address. "Be there at six o'clock. I'll even throw in dinner as an inducement."

Claudia faced her indignantly after she'd hung up. "How could you do such a thing? You gave my address to a man you don't even know yourself!"

"Relax." Stacey grinned. "I know more about Mike than I do about men I've dated for months. He's really nice."

"If he's so nice, why are you meeting him for the first time at *my* house?"

"I just thought he could lend a helping hand," Stacey answered innocently.

Claudia's eyes narrowed. "You'll be there, too, won't you?"

"You heard me offer to bring dinner."

Claudia started to laugh suddenly. "What's it going to be, three cans of chili?"

"An excellent idea. I'd better bring my own can opener, too, in case we can't find yours."

Claudia's face sobered. "Seriously, Stacey, I wish you hadn't done that. I've told you how I feel about the guys in this town."

"I couldn't agree with you more, but Mike's different. Trust me. Would I steer you wrong?"

Claudia laughed again, helplessly. "How do I know? We just met a few hours ago."

It didn't seem possible. There had been an instant rapport between them. It grew as they discovered more about each other while they lingered over dessert. Stacey had taken ice cream from the freezer and chocolate sauce from the pantry, ignoring Claudia's teasing.

By the time Claudia left, Stacey was in a cheerful mood. She was even looking forward to the following night, something she hadn't done all week. Unless her instincts were wrong, Claudia and Mike were made for each other. She was exactly what he was looking for.

Stacey was getting into bed when the phone rang again. A sixth sense told her it was Sean. She turned out the light and slipped under the covers, waiting for the machine to switch on.

"Stacey? Where the devil are you? You must have gotten my messages by now." He sounded annoyed and impatient. *"Call me back!"*

She remained in the same position for a long time, staring into the darkness.

Stacey was up and out of the house early the next morning. She had some legitimate errands to do, and when those were completed she invented others to avoid going home.

Her mother was delighted when Stacey dropped in unexpectedly.

"What a nice surprise!" Eileen smiled. "I'll tell your father you haven't forgotten our address after all."

Stacey returned her smile. There was a genuine fondness between them. "How could I? You stitched it in big numbers on that needlepoint pillow you made for me."

A buzzer sounded, and Eileen said, "Come into the kitchen with me. I'm making Hello Dollies." They were a sinfully rich combination of chocolate, butterscotch and nuts.

Stacey sniffed appreciatively. "My timing was perfect."

"You're the only person I know who can stuff herself on these things and not gain an ounce." Eileen looked critically at her daughter's delicately boned face. "You've lost weight."

"My new diet must be working," Stacey replied lightly.

"Since when have you had to diet?"

Stacey never had and still didn't. The long days and restless nights had taken their toll.

"You're not eating right," Eileen scolded. "You'd better stay for a home-cooked dinner tonight."

"I can't. I volunteered to provide dinner for a couple of friends. Do you have any suggestions?"

"Outside of taking them to a restaurant, you mean?"

"Come on, Mother, be helpful. What can I make that isn't too complicated?"

"I knew you came with an ulterior motive." Eileen opened a well-stocked freezer. "How about a tuna casserole and some corn bread? You can put them in the oven together."

"Great! I really didn't come for that, but I won't turn down blessings from heaven. Thanks a million."

"I'm doing it for your friends—so you'll keep them," Eileen replied.

Stacey returned home with just enough time to change to working clothes—jeans and a plaid shirt. She tied her long hair back with a ribbon, ignoring the red light that meant messages were waiting on the answering machine.

It was most unprofessional. She might lose clients that way. A cloud of despair engulfed Stacey. Sean was bound to destroy her one way or another. She rejected the thought and set her jaw grimly. No way! This time he'd met his match.

Claudia had made headway with the kitchen. Although the rest of the rooms were still in shambles, the dishes and cooking paraphernalia had been put away.

"You're moving right along," Stacey said approvingly.

"If you don't go into the rest of the house."

"With three pairs of hands we'll get everything straightened up in no time."

Claudia's face clouded. "I still wish you hadn't asked Mike."

"Too late—there he is," Stacey said as the doorbell rang.

He did a double take when she answered the door. "Wow! You didn't tell me you were a knockout."

"You didn't ask me. Come and meet Claudia."

Mike's smile broadened when he saw the other woman. "A gorgeous redhead and a beautiful brunette. What did I do right?"

Stacey wanted to tell him to tone it down. He was coming on like the men Claudia detested. He looked the part, too. His tight jeans and chest-hugging T-shirt seemed to have been chosen to show off his masculinity.

"Claudia just moved to Los Angeles," Stacey said hastily.

"I would have met the plane with a brass band if I'd known," he said.

When Claudia's lips curled and she didn't answer, Stacey said, "We asked you over here to work, not to stand around throwing bouquets."

"*We* didn't ask you; Stacey did," Claudia remarked coolly.

"What's the matter with *her*?" Mike asked with raised eyebrows after Stacey had pulled him into the living room.

"She isn't one of your ever ready, toothbrush-in-the-pocketbook girlfriends. Back off," Stacey scolded.

"Gladly. That's one thorny female," he rasped.

Well, so much for her skill as a matchmaker, Stacey thought wryly. The evening was going to be a disaster. All she could do was try to minimize the damage.

"Claudia's really a nice person. She's just homesick and lonely."

"I'm not surprised!" Mike shook his head. "How can a girl that beautiful be such a pain in the ankle?"

Stacey slanted a speculative glance at him. "She could have been more polite, I agree. But at least you won't have to worry about combing her out of your hair. You're obviously not her type."

"The feeling is mutual!"

"Even if she secretly found you attractive, Claudia's not the kind of woman who runs after a man," Stacey remarked innocently.

"That's a relief." His voice was firm, but his eyes were thoughtful.

"I won't hold you to your word if you want to cut out."

"Oh, what the heck. I'm here now." Mike's good humor returned. "Besides, you promised me dinner."

Sometime later, Claudia stuck her head out of the kitchen. "Stacey, the timer just buzzed."

"That means we can eat. Turn off the stove, and come in and see what we've done to the living room."

Stacey and Mike had worked a minor miracle. He had pushed all the furniture into place while she'd put the empty cartons outside and connected the lamps. The room finally looked livable.

"You're fantastic!" Claudia gasped. "How did you do all this so fast?"

"Most of the credit goes to Mike," Stacey said. "He did the heavy work."

"The furniture might not be where you want it," he remarked hesitantly.

"It's perfect just where it is. Thank you," Claudia answered softly.

"My pleasure." His wary expression changed as he glanced at her shining eyes and flushed cheeks.

That was the turning point. They were both tentative with each other at first, but the ice was broken. Dinner was a festive affair. They all sat around the kitchen table, talking as though they'd been friends for years.

Stacey commented on it. "Who would believe we don't actually know anything about one another?"

"I know you're a great cook," Mike said, helping himself to another cookie.

"You really are," Claudia agreed. "I didn't realize you were putting me on last night."

Stacey laughed. "I wasn't. What you've just eaten was courtesy of my mother's freezer—except for the Hello Dollies. She baked those this morning."

"They're divine! Do you think she'd give me the recipe?" Claudia asked.

"Don't tell me you can cook?" Mike exclaimed.

Claudia grinned. "Everybody can, except Stacey."

"Don't you believe it," he said. "The women I know think a stove is an ancient artifact."

Claudia's eyelashes lowered slightly as she gave him a tiny smile. "Maybe you've been running with the wrong crowd."

Stacey decided it was time to leave them alone. She stood up. "I have to feed one of my client's birds. Sorry to leave you with the dishes, Claudia."

"I'll stay and help her," Mike offered swiftly.

Stacey drove home feeling the glow that comes from doing a good deed. She hadn't been wrong about them. The vibes were there when they met; they'd just gotten deflected slightly. They'd be good for each other. Claudia would tone Mike down, and he'd liven her up. She was fun when she stopped being so reserved.

Stacey's glow faded as she got closer to home. Another long evening of trying to concentrate on a book or TV. She really should put out the word that she was available again. Most of the men she'd dated had gotten discouraged when she kept turning them down. Another way Sean had disrupted her life.

He wasn't really responsible, though. She hadn't wanted to see anyone else. One evening with Sean had kept her happy for days. Stacey laughed bitterly. It was ironic that he thought she was running around with other men.

Stacey had forgotten to turn on the porch light when she left. The house was dark and unwelcoming. That added to her somber mood as she fumbled on the doorstep for her key.

Her heart leaped into her throat when she sensed, rather than heard, movement behind her. The tall, shadowy figure had moved as silently as a cat.

"It's about time you got home," a deep voice growled. "Where the hell have you been for two days?"

She gazed up speechlessly into Sean's dark face.

"Answer me, damn it!" His fingers bit into her shoulders.

"I . . . I've been out," she said breathlessly.

"With whom?" Even in the dim light she could see the fire in his eyes.

"That's none of your business," Stacey replied, pulling herself together. "Go away, Sean. We have nothing to say to each other."

"You know better than that." He took the key out of her clutching fingers and unlocked the door, then pushed her inside impatiently.

"You can't come in here as if you own the place," she stormed. "I want you to leave this minute!"

Her words fell on deaf ears. Sean was staring at her like a man who'd just found salvation. "God, how I've missed you!"

The look in his eyes was molten enough to melt her bones. Stacey felt a familiar weakness in her knees, but she refused to give in to it.

"It's over, Sean," she said firmly. "No more compliments, no more kisses, no more fighting and making up."

"That's what I told myself," he answered quietly. "But it was like giving up breathing. I can't live without you."

"That's unfortunate, because you'll have to. I don't want any part of you anymore."

"I could prove you're wrong," he said softly.

She stood her ground as he moved toward her. "All you could prove is that you're skilled at seduction. I'd hate you afterward."

His face paled. "You already do, don't you? I've destroyed any feeling you had for me."

He looked so desolate that Stacey's heart twisted. She'd never seen Sean this way. He was always the god figure, in charge of himself and everyone else. No matter how Stacey told herself he deserved to suffer, she couldn't bear his pain.

"I don't hate you, Sean," she said more calmly. "I'm just being sensible for both of us. We can't go on tearing each other apart. Each time it's harder to put the pieces back together. They just don't fit anymore."

"Will you at least listen to my explanation?" he pleaded.

"I already know what it is. You can't bring yourself to trust a woman."

"It never prevented me from sleeping with any of them. Why do you think I always stopped short of making love to you?"

"Because you knew I—" Stacey's lashes fell. "You thought I'd make demands on you."

"No, darling! Because I fell in love with you, and it scared me to death. I knew if I ever possessed you completely, I'd never be able to let you go, but I was afraid the time would come when I had to. You'd leave, and it would destroy me. In my own stupid way I've made us both miserable."

Stacey barely heard anything beyond the fact that Sean loved her. "This isn't some kind of joke, is it?" she asked uncertainly.

"Can you look at me and ask that?"

She gazed at the lines in his strong face, at the sharpness of his cheekbones. Sean had lost weight, too. He met her eyes steadily, conveying deep longing yet not pressuring her.

"I don't know what to say." She stared at him incredulously. "Why would you think I'd leave you? I haven't even dated anyone else since we met."

He looked surprised. "I didn't know. You talked about that Mike." A vein throbbed in Sean's temple. "I had a preview of what it would be like to lose you."

"I *told* you Mike was just a client. You don't believe me, do you?" she asked when he didn't respond.

"It doesn't matter." He took both of her hands and held on tightly. "I'm willing to take whatever you'll give me—for as long as it lasts."

"You really are an idiot," Stacey said with a mixture of love and impatience. "I think it's time we straightened out a few things between us." Her face sobered when they were sitting on the couch together. "First of all, you have to tell me why you're so suspicious. I can't fight shadows anymore."

"I realize you deserve an explanation, but it concerns an episode in my life that I don't like to talk about." Sean's reluctance was evident. He paused a moment before continuing, "I was married once, and it didn't work out."

After the initial shock, Stacey waited for details. When it became apparent that he wasn't going to supply them she said, "People get divorces without becoming emotionally crippled. Are you still in love with her?"

"God, no! I don't think I ever was."

His response was satisfying but hard to believe. "Then why did she destroy your faith in half the population?"

"I'd prefer not to discuss her."

"This is no time for chivalry!" Stacey exclaimed. "Either we clear the air, or we forget about us."

Sean hesitated for a moment, then sighed. "All right, but it's a sordid story." He chose his words carefully. "Gwen and I...went together...for several months. We were...very compatible."

Stacey supplied the information his pauses implied. They lived together and were great in bed.

"She professed to want children, so we got married," Sean was saying. "The children never materialized. Once she was legally my wife and financially secure, Gwen began to indulge her hobby—which was men. She was discreet at first. And terribly penitent when I found out." He smiled sardonically. "We had some rousing reconciliations. My patience ran out when I found her in our bed with one of my supposedly good friends."

"I'm sorry," Stacey faltered. "It must have been horrible for you. But all marriages aren't like that."

"Mine wasn't an isolated case," he answered grimly. "Promiscuity seems to be the norm nowadays."

Stacey could see how he would get that impression. Women fell in and out of his bed willingly. Why should he think she was any different? Her perfectly innocent remark about Mike's shorts could easily be misconstrued. Walter's babbling that night at the Ritz Plaza hadn't helped, either. Sean would be especially put off by Walter's false assertion that she'd cheated on a man with his best friend.

"I told you once that we came from different worlds," she said slowly. "I don't think I could live in yours. The people in mine still believe in the old-fashioned virtues: love and trust and honesty."

He looked deeply into her eyes. "Let me into your world, darling. I'm so lonely in mine."

How could she deny him what she wanted so desperately herself? There would be problems. It was mainly a matter of trust, but surely she could teach him that. Suddenly Stacey was supremely confident.

"Welcome home, darling," she said softly.

His face blazed with joy as he reached for her. "You won't regret it, my love," he said hoarsely. "I'm going to be a changed man. I'll be anything you like, do anything to make you happy."

She smoothed the harsh lines in his face. "Anything?" she murmured.

His tortured expression vanished as he gazed into her eyes. A smile curved his lips, and he lifted her in his arms wordlessly.

Chapter Seven

Stacey clung tightly to Sean as he carried her into the bedroom. She'd imagined this moment over and over, but nothing compared with the reality. Her whole body pulsed with yearning when he placed her gently on the bed and bent his head to kiss her tenderly.

"My beautiful love." His voice had a husky throb. "I've waited for this all my life."

"I have, too," she whispered, clasping her arms around his neck.

Sean's lips were warm and undemanding at first, savoring the sweetness of her mouth. He traced its contours with his tongue, and when her lips parted he entered the moist opening slowly.

Desire built in Stacey as his tongue probed deeply while his hands began a minute exploration of her body. He stroked her neck and shoulders, then cupped the fullness of both breasts. When they swelled in his hands as she drew in her breath, he transferred his tongue to one straining peak. The warm wetness penetrated her thin shirt, sending shivers down her spine.

"I've dreamed of making love to you like this," he murmured. "With all the time in the world."

Stacey uttered a wispy little sigh. "I can't believe it's really happening."

Sean's chuckle was deep and male as he unbuttoned her shirt. "Does this convince you?" He lowered his head and trailed a circle of tiny kisses around each breast.

When she arched her body at the tantalizing feeling, his hands slipped underneath her, supporting her hips while he kissed the smooth skin of her stomach.

"Your body is exquisite." He sat back on his haunches and gazed down at her with glowing eyes.

The glow turned to a raging fire when he unzipped her jeans and slid them down her legs. His hands were slightly unsteady as he stroked her thighs, lingering where they joined her body.

The flames he'd kindled inside her were threatening to burn out of control. Stacey sat up and tugged his shirt out of his slacks.

"I want to touch you, too," she whispered.

"Before this night is over you'll know every inch of me," he promised as he unbuttoned his shirt and tossed it aside. He pulled her against his chest, tangling his fingers in her hair. "I'm going to be part of you in every way."

She moved against him, burying her breasts in the mat of dark hair that cushioned his hard chest. "This is what I've wanted to do for so long."

"My sweet angel!"

He held her tightly for a moment before getting up to fling off his clothes. Sean's urgency was apparent when he returned to take her in his arms. Stacey quivered with expectation as he lowered his body onto hers.

The experience was all she had anticipated and more. Sean was a masterful lover. He fueled the flames that were devouring her, driving them higher and higher with his thrusting force. He gave her pleasure unlike any other. He led her and then waited for her, making her enjoyment a priority.

When he sensed that she had reached the breaking point, Sean gave her satisfaction. He carried her over the brink of yearning to fulfillment. Wave after wave of sensation swept through Stacey until her tense body was at peace.

She clung to Sean for a long time afterward. No words were necessary. Her eyes were closed, but his face was engraved on her eyelids. Just as his body had left its brand on her. She stroked his back slowly, enjoying the tactile feeling of his smooth skin.

"Mmm, that feels good," he murmured lazily with his head on her breast.

"One good turn deserves another," she teased, laughing softly.

Sean tilted his face to look up at her, his eyes dancing. "Always happy to oblige."

"Don't think I won't hold you to it."

His face filled with tenderness. "You won't ever have to ask. I'll never get enough of you."

"Considering the difference in our schedules, you might very well be right."

"I'll adjust my hours to suit yours," he promised. "I'll sell the theaters if they take up too much time."

"I was only joking," she said hastily. "We'll manage to see each other, and we can talk on the phone every day."

"There's a simpler solution." He stroked her cheek lovingly. "You could move in with me. Or I could move in here."

Stacey's long lashes fell. The thought of marriage evidently never crossed his mind. Perhaps it was too soon for that. But it was too soon to live together, also. Sean had married Gwen because they were great in bed together.

Making the comparison was painful, but she had to be realistic. Sean said he loved her, but he wasn't ready to make a commitment. Until she was on surer ground, Stacey didn't want to take such a big step.

She forced a smile. "My mother and father would have a collective heart attack. I think we'd better leave our living arrangements the way they are for now."

"Will you at least spend the weekend with me?"

She grinned. "That's the best offer I've had all week."

"You little devil. It darn well better be!"

The phone rang, startling both of them. Who could it be at this hour? Stacey was shocked when she looked at the clock and discovered it was only ten-thirty. With all that had happened, she thought it was the middle of the night. As she reached for the phone Stacey hoped it wouldn't be Mike.

Claudia's voice greeted her, however. She sounded slightly breathless. "I hope I'm not calling too late."

"It's okay. Is anything wrong?"

"No, I just wanted to thank you. For dinner and all, I mean."

Stacey began to smile. She could guess what the "all" meant. "I'm sorry I had to leave you with the dishes. Did Mike flake out, too?"

"No, he was very helpful. He's really quite nice."

Stacey's green eyes sparkled with mischief. "For a guy who wears shorts with little red hearts on them," she said deliberately.

Claudia's sharp intake of breath conveyed the same dismay as Sean's face. "How do you know that?" she asked. "I didn't think you two were...close."

"We aren't. I saw them on the floor when I went to pick up his dinner jacket." Stacey was speaking into the phone, but she was talking to Sean.

He groaned softly and buried his face in her throat.

"Do you have company?" Claudia asked suddenly.

"No, that was the television." Stacey smoothed Sean's hair. "So now you know that Mike is up for grabs."

"I wasn't asking for any reason," Claudia answered defensively. "I was just surprised. If you and he were..."

"We're not. You're welcome to him. Mike's a dear, but he's not my type."

Sean raised his head, and they exchanged a long look.

"I have to admit I'm glad," Claudia was saying. "He's the first man I've met out here who isn't God's little joke on the female sex. He asked me out for tomorrow night."

"That's nice." Stacey was having trouble concentrating with Sean's hand caressing her body. "Keep me posted, Claudia. I have to go now. There's...um...someone at my door."

"At eleven o'clock at night?" he asked after she hung up. His eyes were brimming with amusement.

"I couldn't very well tell her I want to make love to the most exciting man in the world."

"Why not? I'd like to publish it in the paper." His voice was like dark velvet.

Stacey moved suggestively against him. "Okay, let's rehearse what we're going to say."

The days that followed were glorious, capped by her weekend at Sean's. His housekeeper didn't come in on the weekend, so they had the apartment to themselves. Except for Lobo, who was filled with joy at seeing her again.

"Poor baby, did you miss me?" she asked.

"Not half as much as I did," Sean commented.

She ignored him. "Come on, sweetie pie," she said to Lobo. "Stacey will get you a dog biscuit."

"This must be what it's like to have a baby," Sean complained. "The breadwinner doesn't get any attention."

The mere idea of having Sean's baby was breathtaking. Was there any meaning behind the flip remark? Stacey was afraid to attach too much importance to it.

"You've had more than your share of attention," she remarked carelessly.

"But never enough of yours." He put his arms around her and kissed her sweetly. "Do you know what heaven it is to have you all to myself for two days?"

"One and a half," she said between kisses. "You have to go to the theater tonight."

"We have all afternoon," he answered in a husky voice.

"That's true." She slid her fingertips inside the back of his waistband. "How shall we spend it?"

Much later, Stacey was asleep with her head pillowed on Sean's chest. Her bright hair spilled over onto his shoulder. He gazed down at her tenderly for a long time, resisting the urge to kiss her awake. She looked so trusting in his arms that he was overwhelmed with a protectiveness he'd never experienced before.

She awoke instantly when he gently eased his arm away. "Is it time to go to the theater already?" she asked.

"No, darling. I was going to surprise you with a glass of champagne."

"What are we celebrating?"

He kissed the tip of her nose. "What a foolish question."

They sipped champagne and talked softly. And then they made love again. Each time was more wonderful than the last. They reached a state of ecstasy and descended to total happiness.

Finally Sean stirred regretfully. "I'd better take a shower and get dressed."

"Can I shower with you?"

He laughed. "I'd never get out of here."

"Well, if you don't have any willpower..." she pouted.

He bit her shoulder gently. "I'll remind you of that when I get home."

Stacey had refused his invitation to go to the theater with him. She'd seen the play, and she was always in the way backstage. Sean had promised to get away in a couple of hours and take her to dinner, but Stacey secretly planned to make dinner at home.

She didn't attempt anything too complicated, just steak, baked potatoes and a salad. Anyone could do that. But the candles on the dining room table and Sean's best china made the meal festive.

His eyes lit up when he saw the beautifully set table. "What a nice surprise. You're enough to come home to. I didn't expect anything like this."

"I wanted to show you I'm not just a pretty face," she answered mischievously. "I do know how to cook, contrary to some base lies going around about me."

"Tell me who's spreading them, and I'll deck the villain."

"My mother, for one."

"That complicates matters a bit," Sean admitted. He had followed her into the kitchen. "Would you like me to toss the salad?"

"It would be helpful. And then you can open the wine."

They worked side by side, as though this was their normal routine. Stacey suspected that Sean wasn't accustomed to doing anything around the house, but he seemed to be enjoying himself.

She looked complacently over the table when they were seated in the dining room. "Not too shabby, if I do say so myself."

"Too bad *Gracious Dining* magazine isn't here to take a picture," he agreed. The candlelight turned his eyes incandescent. "I could get used to doing this every night," he said softly. "How about it?"

Stacey's breathing quickened. "You're just trying to make me feel good."

"No, I'm trying to make us both feel good. What do you say?"

Was it really that simple? Had the mere fact of seeing her in his home—the rest of the house as well as the bedroom—made him realize they had more than just sex binding them together?

"Think of all the things we could do together if you moved in," he coaxed.

Stacey's bubble of happiness burst with a bang. "I thought we'd settled all that," she said curtly. "Eat your steak before it gets cold."

Her naturally ebullient spirits didn't stay down for long. Patience would pay off, she decided confidently. Sean would see they were meant for each other.

The weeks that followed seemed to bear out her prophecy. They spent golden days and romantic nights together, falling more and more in love. Sean begrudged any time away from her. He constantly renewed his urging that they live together.

Stacey was secretly hurt that marriage never seemed to occur to him as an alternative. Finally at her house one night she brought up the subject herself. Sean had just expressed his love in every possible way.

"I never knew anyone could mean this much to me." He stroked her bare body with sated appreciation. "You're mine, aren't you, darling?"

"Every way except legally," she answered quietly.

His caressing hand stilled. "Does that bother you?"

She hesitated. "It bothers me that you never even considered marrying me."

Sean removed his arm from around her shoulders and sat up against the headboard. "What gave you that impression? We never discussed it."

"That's what I mean."

"I didn't realize it was important to you," he said carefully. "If that's what you want, we'll get married."

Hurt and anger sliced through Stacey. "That isn't the most romantic proposal I've ever received."

"It's been a long time since I've proposed." His lips moved in a travesty of a smile.

"You didn't this time. *I* did." She stood up and reached for her robe. "Don't be alarmed, though. It was just temporary insanity."

Sean got out of bed and tried to take her in his arms. "I've been an insensitive clod, honey. I should have known what you wanted."

What *she* wanted, not what he did. Stacey felt tears threaten, but she held them back. "I really don't, Sean. I don't even know why I said it."

"I meant it when I told you I'd do anything to make you happy." His hands slipped under her robe.

He was just making things worse. She pulled away. "Can we drop the subject, please?"

"I think we'd better talk about this," he said slowly.

"Not tonight! Would you mind going home, Sean? I have a slight headache."

"Don't send me away, Stacey. We can't let a misunderstanding ruin what we have together."

"I understand you perfectly. Look me straight in the eye and say you want to marry me."

He stared at her helplessly. "This will make you angry, but I never thought of it. Matrimony is associated in my mind with bitterness and recriminations. Our relationship is pure joy."

"Married life doesn't have to be like yours was," she said, her voice faltering.

"I know that!" He folded her in his arms almost desperately. "We'll make it work. I can't give you up. I *won't* give you up!"

Stacey was passive in his arms as he rained frantic kisses over her face and neck. She'd won the battle, but at what cost? Sean would always feel, at the back of his mind, that she'd manipulated him. Until marriage was what he truly wanted, it wouldn't work.

"I'll get the license tomorrow," he promised.

"No. It's a big step for me, too. I'd like to think about it for a while."

"You evidently have been," he said soberly.

She mustered a smile. "Every girl thinks about getting married. I was just kind of testing the waters, but now I have cold feet."

He stared at her with mixed emotions warring on his strong face. "I have the damnedest feeling that we ought to go down to city hall tomorrow before any more misunderstandings can come between us."

"None will," she assured him.

Sean's explanation had made her feel better. The circumstances were wildly different in their case, but his failure to consider marriage was understandable. The seed had been planted, though. All she had to do now was wait.

It seemed to Stacey that all the world was in love. Claudia and Mike phoned her often with progress reports on their romance. They were cautious at first, but their language soon grew lyrical.

"She's wonderful," Mike enthused. "I thought women like Claudia had disappeared with slate records. I've torn up my little black book."

Claudia was equally effusive. "Mike is the dearest man I've ever known. He makes me feel so...so special!"

"Chalk up another one for Mother Marlowe." Stacey was smiling as she hung up the phone and returned to Sean. They were eating popcorn and playing backgammon in her living room. "I might take up matchmaking as a sideline."

"Don't get overly confident," he advised. "They haven't known each other long enough for the bloom to be off the rose."

"What a cynical thing to say!" she exclaimed.

"But accurate. Part of the charm of a new romance is the excitement of someone new."

"You think knowing another person really well spells the end of romance?"

Stacey had tried to keep her question casual, but something in her voice alerted Sean. He reached over and scooped her into his lap.

"Only for people who aren't truly in love—like us." His deep kiss dispelled her hidden fears.

Sean had more free time after *Adam's Folly* closed. The theater would be dark for two weeks while the renovations were being done; then he would have to go to New York.

Stacey and Sean used the time to full advantage. They were together constantly. They went to movies in the afternoon and took Lobo for long walks. They went bowling in jeans and dressed elegantly to go to the ballet. It was a magical time. They lived in a state of perpetual happiness, which made Stacey vaguely uneasy. Nothing this perfect could last.

One night they tried a new restaurant that had gotten excellent reviews. While they were waiting to be seated, Stacey noticed someone trying to get Sean's attention.

"That man is waving at you," she said. "He looks vaguely familiar."

Sean glanced over the crowded room. "It's Ken Pomeroy. He was the second lead in *Adam's Folly*."

"Shouldn't you go over and say hello?"

"No. He'll make a pitch for a part in the new play. I'm on vacation."

Sean acknowledged Ken with a nod, but when the headwaiter led them past the actor's table, they were forced to stop and say hello. The woman with him had had her back to them. When Sean saw it was Francine Wilson, his polite expression became strained.

"Good to see you, Sean." Ken was all smiles. "Enjoying your time off?"

"Yes. It's been a treat," Scan replied.

"Not for me." Ken's laugh was high-pitched. "I miss that old curtain going up at eight o'clock every night."

"I'm sure you'll get another part soon. Now, if you'll excuse—"

"I was wondering if you'd have anything in your new production," Ken interrupted quickly. "The word is out that you're bringing in *Saints Alive*."

"Nothing's settled yet," Sean answered noncommittally.

"He wouldn't tell you if it was," Francine drawled. "Sean doesn't like to part with anything, even information."

Sean's smile resembled that of a tiger baring its teeth. "I didn't know you knew me that well."

"I was Gwen's best friend, wasn't I?" Francine's eyes flicked to Stacey, then back to Sean's rigid face. "Be sure to say hello for me."

"That would be a little difficult, since she's in Europe." Sean took Stacey's arm, preparing to leave.

"I had a letter from her. She's coming home." Francine took malicious delight in catching him off base. "But of course you knew that. You two have always been close, in spite of everything," she purred.

Sean's fingers tightened unconsciously on Stacey's arm. "Our table is waiting." He turned away abruptly.

Stacey's head was buzzing with questions. Sean clearly hadn't known about Gwen's imminent return. Was his reaction good or bad? The sudden, painful grip on her arm had indicated strong emotion. Was it anticipation? Anguish? What? One look at his stormy face told her not to ask.

Sean tried to shake off whatever was bothering him, but the attempt wasn't successful. Stacey knew him too well to be fooled by mechanical smiles and automatic compliments. Finally she approached the problem from another direction.

"You were right about Francine," she said casually. "You certainly *aren't* her favorite person."

"The feeling is entirely mutual," he bit out.

"I suppose her reaction to you is normal."

He raised a sardonic eyebrow. "Thanks a lot!"

"I merely meant that since she was your wife's best friend, you'd have to expect her to blame you for everything," Stacey explained carefully.

"Francine is a perfect example of Gwen's perception about people."

"You mean they weren't best friends?"

"Let's just say Gwen thought they were."

From the contempt on his face, Stacey got a glimmering of the truth. Had Francine wanted an affair with Sean and been rejected? That would account for his revulsion and her venom. But it didn't answer Stacey's question about Gwen. Sean obviously still felt deeply about her. But in what way?

Conversation was desultory on the drive back to her house. Stacey had indicated that she wanted to go home rather than to his apartment.

When Sean walked her to the door she said, "I'll talk to you in the morning."

"Are you trying to get rid of me?" he asked.

"No, of course not. I just thought we could both use a little rest."

"From each other, you mean?" He followed her inside.

"What gave you that idea?"

He turned her toward him. "What's bothering you, Stacey? You've been very quiet all evening."

"You were a little withdrawn yourself—ever since you found out Gwen is coming home," she couldn't help adding. But maybe it was for the best. They couldn't keep pretending she'd never meant anything to him.

"So that's it. Gwen! When will you believe there's nothing between us?"

"When you believe it yourself," Stacey answered sadly. "Can you deny that you were thinking about her all through dinner?"

"Not pleasantly." A muscle twitched in his square jaw. "These past weeks I'd forgotten Gwen even existed. It was just a shock to be reminded of her."

"Why is she coming back?"

"How should I know? There could be a hundred different reasons."

And Sean could be one of them. "Will you see her while she's here?" Stacey asked in a small voice.

"Not if I can help it," he answered grimly.

"That's not what Francine indicated." Stacey was powerless to stop escalating her own pain.

"Francine is a vicious, vindictive woman. She was trying to cause trouble between us. Are you going to let her succeed?" he demanded.

"No." Stacey's long lashes fell. "I just can't help wondering. I mean, can you ever be completely indifferent to someone you were once married to?"

Sean ran his fingers through his thick hair in frustration. "It wasn't a marriage; it was a legalized affair. How can I convince you that she left me with only bad memories?"

"I believe you." Stacey tried, and failed, to put conviction into her voice.

He sighed. "No, you don't, and I can't understand it. Haven't these last weeks meant anything to you?"

"They've been wonderful," she said softly.

"But not enough to make you trust me."

"I do trust you, Sean." Stacey was frightened by the coldness in his face. "I just need reassurance every now and then. It still seems like a miracle. Sometimes I can't believe you really love me."

His expression softened as he cupped her face between his palms. "I don't know what else I can do. I've shown you in every way I know how."

"I know." She put her arms around his waist and rested her cheek on his shirtfront. "I'm just so afraid it won't last."

He kissed the top of her head. "You couldn't get rid of me if you tried."

"You said all the excitement was over when couples got to know each other," she reminded him.

"Why do you remember all the negative things I say and none of the positive?" He raised her chin and looked deeply into her eyes. "I also said I can't live without you. That you make my life joyful. I wake up every morning with a smile when you're in my arms. And when you're not, my day doesn't begin until I talk to you."

Stacey had tears in her eyes. "Oh, Sean, I feel the same way."

"Then why are we arguing?" he teased gently.

She smiled through her tears. "Because it's so much fun to make up?"

"You started it, so I think you should be the one to make amends."

"You're right." She reached up and slowly untied his tie.

"I'm going to expect something special in the way of an apology," he warned with mock sternness.

"I'll do the best I can," she murmured, unbuttoning his shirt.

"A man can't ask any more than that." He smiled as she slid his jacket off his shoulders and removed it along with his shirt.

But when he turned toward the bedroom she stopped him. "This is my apology, and I'm going to make it in my own way."

Taking his hand, she led him over to the fireplace and pushed him down onto the fluffy white rug that carpeted the floor in front of the hearth. While Sean watched with a mixture of amusement and anticipation, Stacey placed a pillow under his head and then struck a match to the bundle of kindling in the fireplace.

"Can I help?" he asked when the match sputtered out.

"No, this is my production."

She waited until the wood started to crackle, then stretched out next to him, propping her head on one hand so she could look down at him.

"I've always wondered what it would be like to seduce a man." Her fingertips made feathery circles over his flat nipples.

Sean's breathing quickened. "Any man?"

Stacey's long hair draped over his chest as she bent her head to brush her lips lightly across his. "No, only one very special man."

She unbuckled his belt and slid his zipper down. Sean lifted his hips so she could remove his slacks, but when he reached for her, she pinned his arms firmly to his sides.

"Isn't this where I tell you how beautiful your body is?" Her palms outlined the tapering triangle of his lean torso and continued over his flat stomach and narrow hips.

"I don't think 'beautiful' is the correct word." He was remaining motionless with an effort.

She slipped her hand between his rigid thighs and gently pushed them apart. "Your body really is beautiful in a wonderful, manly way," she murmured, stroking him lingeringly.

He groaned and reached down to guide her hand.

Stacey laughed softly and kissed the hollow in his throat. "Is it getting warm in here?"

"I'd call it a little more than warm," he answered in a strangled voice.

She stood up and unzipped her dress. Sean watched her without moving, although his eyes reflected the leaping tongues of the fire. The silk sheath slithered to the floor, leaving her clothed only in a lacy bra and panties. He made a sound deep in his throat as the firelight turned her skin to gold.

Stacey sank down gracefully beside him once more. She smiled into his ardent eyes and brushed against him as she leaned down to whisper in his ear while she removed his briefs.

Sean rolled over and pinned her to the rug. His face was dark with passion as he tangled both hands in her hair and stared down at her.

"If you're trying to drive me out of my mind, you've succeeded," he muttered.

Her smile was bewitching. "Not yet. The best is yet to come."

"I know." His mouth possessed hers fiercely while he stripped off her undergarments.

Stacey let him take over. All self-control deserted her as Sean's mouth devoured hers, and his thrusting body brought indescribable pleasure. She was an equal partner in their striving, arching her body to meet his surges. They were insatiable, feeding each other until a powerful burst of sensation brought release from hunger.

The light from the fireplace highlighted the sheen of moisture on their intertwined bodies as they lay very still.

Finally Sean rolled over onto his side without releasing her. His mouth rested on her temple. "Where did you learn so much about the fine art of seduction? You're fantastic!"

"I've been taking lessons from a master."

His chuckle had a deep masculine sound. "I think the pupil surpassed the teacher."

"That's because you inspire me." She tilted her head to smile up at him mischievously. "Does this mean you accept my apology?"

A shadow crossed his face. "I don't ever want anything to come between us again."

She smoothed away his frown. "Nothing did—or at least it turned out all right."

"But next time it might not," he replied somberly.

"There won't be a next time."

"I wish I could be sure," he muttered.

The specter of Gwen was in the room, poisoning the air. Stacey shivered slightly at the woman's awesome power. The mere mention of her name tonight had almost caused a rift between Sean and herself.

There was a slight hint of despair in Stacey's voice as she whispered, "I love you so much, Sean."

"Dear heart!" His arms tightened fiercely. "Let's get married, darling."

Her pulse started to race as she drew back to look at him searchingly. "Are you serious?"

"Can't you tell?" He strung tiny kisses over her face. "I want you to belong to me completely."

"I already do." She felt like laughing and crying at the same time.

"I want it settled. Let's get married right away!"

"The marriage bureau is closed now," she teased.

"You know what I mean. We love each other, so what's the point in waiting? You don't want a big wedding, do you?"

Everything was happening so fast that Stacey felt slightly dazed. "I always expected to have one," she said slowly. "I guess I owe it to my parents. I'm an only child. Mine is the only wedding they'll ever give."

The urgency went out of Sean's face. "You're right, honey. I was being selfish."

Stacey grinned. "I'll say one thing for you. When you make up your mind, you don't fool around."

She was too happy to notice the shadow that lurked in his eyes when he smiled back. "I'm a man of decision."

"That's what I like about you." Her face sobered slightly. "You don't really mind waiting, do you? All my mother's friends got a chance to cry at their daughters' weddings. It doesn't seem fair to cheat her out of the opportunity."

"As long as that's the only reason she's crying."

"She'll be absolutely ecstatic! Dad, too. I can't wait for you to meet him."

"I already owe him a debt of gratitude," Sean said fondly.

Stacey sat up and hugged her knees to her chest. "My cousin has two darling little children. One can be the flower girl, and one the ring bearer."

"It sounds as though you're planning quite a production."

"You only get married once," she answered happily. Her face was stricken as realization struck. "I'm sorry, Sean."

"It's all right, honey. This is your day, anyway."

That wasn't entirely comforting. It was his day, too. But a second marriage had to be something of an anticlimax, no matter how splendid the trappings.

"Maybe we should settle for a quiet ceremony," she said slowly.

"I don't want you to *settle* for anything." He took her in his arms and stroked her hair tenderly. "Book the church and alert the bridesmaids. You deserve the best."

"I already have it," she whispered with a full heart.

Sean left shortly after, saying he had something to do early in the morning. Stacey was a little disconcerted, but she told herself this was no time to look for things to worry about.

Besides, there *was* nothing. Sean loved her! Everything had worked out exactly as she'd hoped. Stacey banished the nagging little reminder that it was Gwen who was responsible.

Although it was late, she got out a pad and pencil and started writing down names.

Stacey overslept the next morning, after staying up half the night making lists. The phone woke her.

"You sound funny," Claudia said uncertainly.

Stacey yawned. "I was asleep."

"I'm sorry. I thought you got up early."

"I usually do, but I was up late. It's okay, though. I have a million things to do." Stacey's eyes started to sparkle as she thought about the previous night's events. "Isn't it a wonderful day?"

"How do you know? You aren't up yet."

"*Every* day is wonderful!" Stacey declared joyously.

"I'm glad *somebody* thinks so."

"What's wrong, Claudia?" The other girl's moody voice was starting to register.

"I've just been a prize idiot, that's all."

"In what way?" Stacey asked cautiously.

"Men are all alike! You can't trust one any farther than you can throw a bull—which is what they do!"

"I presume you're talking about Mike."

"He's the absolute worst! I should have known better than to believe anything a lawyer told me. They know all about twisting words around to say something different from what they really mean."

"What did he tell you?"

"He said he loved me."

"What makes you think he doesn't?"

"Because he's a liar and a cheat!"

"That doesn't sound like the Mike Reynolds I know," Stacey said slowly. "He conned you, too. He's very good at that," Claudia remarked bitterly.

"Why don't you tell me what happened?"

"We had a date last night, but Mike broke it at the last minute. He said he had to prepare for a case that was unexpectedly dropped in his lap that afternoon. The other attorney got sick."

"Things like that happen," Stacey said tentatively.

"That's what *I* thought." Claudia's laugh was sardonic. "I spent the evening baking a chocolate fudge cake, Mike's favorite. About ten o'clock I decided to take a piece over to him. I hoped he might be home by then, but if he wasn't, it would be a nice surprise when he did return."

"You have a key?" Stacey was learning the extent of their involvement.

"I used to," Claudia answered shortly. "No more."

"What happened when you went over there?"

"The lights were on, but that didn't mean Mike was home. He never remembers to turn them off when he leaves. When I got to his front door, though, I heard voices inside. One was a woman's voice," Claudia said dramatically.

"So what? It could have been his maiden aunt, or a cousin from Hoboken," Stacey said impatiently.

"He said he had to work," Claudia reminded her.

"Well, maybe it was a colleague."

"They were *laughing*!"

"Listen, Claudia, there are many things a man and a woman can do to break the law, but so far laughing isn't one of them," Stacey said crisply. "Your evidence would never stand up in court."

"I haven't told you the rest. I waited in my car outside his apartment building. It was almost midnight when he came down with a gorgeous brunette. She drove away in a little sports car."

"It couldn't have been anything heavy. She didn't stay all night," Stacey pointed out.

"Am I supposed to be happy they just had a short fling?" Claudia asked caustically. "Why are you defending him?"

"Because I haven't heard his side of it." Stacey knew the perils of jumping to conclusions. "Why don't you just ask him about it?"

"I did. After she left I told him precisely what I thought of him for lying to me!"

"That's not exactly asking for an explanation. What did he say?"

"He said that love implied trust, and if I could think him guilty of what I was accusing him of, we didn't have any basis for a relationship."

That struck a chord in Stacey. "He's right," she said quietly.

"How can you say that? If he had an excuse, he would have given it to me."

"Not necessarily. Men have their pride, too. You automatically assumed he was deceiving you."

"I thought you'd be more understanding," Claudia said stiffly. "I'm sorry I bothered you."

"I could agree that Mike is a low down two-timer. That would make you feel better, but it wouldn't solve the problem. As a good friend, I'm going to give you some advice. Call Mike and tell him you're sorry for spouting off."

"Never!"

"Tell him you were hurt and confused," Stacey continued inexorably. "Say that you're willing to listen if he wants to explain."

"What if he doesn't?" Claudia asked in a small voice.

"Then you have a lot of make-up work to do."

"You really believe there's a simple explanation?" Claudia asked wistfully.

"Have you had any problems lately?"

"Oh, no!" Claudia's fervent disclaimer described a picture of bliss in two short words.

"Do me a favor," Stacey said fondly. "Stop being such a dummy."

Stacey shook her head as she hung up the phone. Women in love were an irrational lot. They made their own troubles. Her face softened as she picked up the phone again to dial Sean's number.

Chapter Eight

Stacey was dying to tell her parents the earth-shattering news, but they'd gone away and she didn't know where to reach them. Her father liked to escape from the pressures of business by just wandering from one resort to another, stopping wherever they pleased.

Stacey felt mildly frustrated with no one to tell her good news to. She hadn't wanted to inform Claudia while her friend was so down. The prospect of seeing Sean that night was compensation, though. She could discuss plans for the wedding with him.

They spent a gala evening at the theater—someone else's. Stacey protested that it was a busman's holiday for him, but Sean said it was different when he wasn't responsible for the performance.

The play was an excellent comedy that left them in a happy mood. They talked animatedly all the way back to

Sean's apartment, where they intended to scramble some eggs instead of going to a restaurant.

The lights were on when they entered the foyer.

"You're as bad as Mike," Stacey scolded. "The electric company gets rich on people like you."

Whatever answer Sean was about to give was frozen on his lips. A beautiful blond woman in a chiffon caftan rose gracefully from the couch. Her hair was perfectly arranged in a short, chic style, and her figure, under the revealing gown, was alluring.

"Surprise, surprise, darling." She walked toward Sean with outstretched arms. He stood rigid as she put her arms around his neck and kissed him on the mouth.

Stacey didn't need to be told who the woman was. This was Gwen, Sean's wife. It was a measure of Stacey's distress that she didn't think of her as his former wife. Perhaps because Gwen wasn't acting like one.

Sean managed to pull himself together after a shocked moment. "What are you doing here?" he asked in a choked voice.

"I've had warmer welcomes in my day." Her pouting face cleared when she glanced at Stacey. "Oh, I see. How thoughtless of me not to have given you advance notice. I should have known you'd bring home a little friend." Her trilling laughter indicated that Sean often did but it wasn't important.

"I asked what you're doing here." His voice was ominous.

"Where else would I go, darling?" Gwen linked her arm in his as she turned to Stacey. "Hello. I'm Sean's wife."

He jerked his arm away. "*Ex*-wife!"

"Well, I suppose technically. But I always think of you as my husband." She turned to Stacey and explained, "I'm not ere much, but when I am we always...keep in touch, so to peak."

Sean held himself in with an effort. "The only contact we ave is the check I send you every month."

"Such a generous one, too," she purred.

"Is that why you're here? You need more money?" he demanded.

"You're such a lamb, always worried about my welfare."

"I'd better leave," Stacey murmured.

"No! You're not going anywhere," Sean stated.

"Of course not," Gwen agreed graciously. "I realize this s a bit awkward, but you mustn't let me spoil your date."

Stacey felt ill. Did the woman actually expect them to act s though she weren't there?

Sean felt the same revulsion. "Stacey is more than my ate," he said coldly. "She's my fiancée."

"I didn't know." Gwen was clearly startled. Her brittle hell of sophistication cracked for the first time. "Nobody old me."

"We just got engaged last night," he said.

"That changes things," she murmured, almost to herelf.

"Yes, I thought it would." His voice was sardonic. "I'll hone downstairs for a cab."

"But I have nowhere to go, darling." Gwen opened her ig blue eyes wide. "I always stay here."

"I'll get you a hotel room," he answered grimly.

"All my things are put away," she protested. "Besides, I ate hotel rooms. They're so cramped and impersonal. I'm ure Stacey won't mind if I stay here."

"If she doesn't, *I* do!" Sean said.

"Are you telling me you don't trust yourself with me?" iwen laughed merrily.

"As a matter of fact, I don't." A muscle jerked in his jaw. "I might do what I should have done when we were married."

"That sounds naughty." Gwen winked conspiratorially at Stacey. "Why don't you fix us all a drink, Sean? Stacey and I have a lot to talk about."

As she walked toward the couch, Sean said in a low voice, "I had no idea she was coming here."

"I know, but I still think I should leave," Stacey said miserably.

"I won't let her drive you away!"

Stacey tried to lighten the atmosphere. "I'm not sophisticated enough for a ménage à trois, and it's pretty clear she's not leaving."

"I'll get rid of her, I promise. Just stay with me."

Gwen patted the cushion next to her. "Come sit here," she called. "I want to hear all about you."

Stacey could feel her feet dragging as she walked into the living room and took a chair across from Gwen, not beside her.

"How did you two meet?" Gwen prompted.

As Stacey reluctantly explained about Lobo, it occurred to her that the dog was missing. He usually greeted them boisterously when they returned from a night out.

"Where is Lobo?" she asked.

"I closed him up in the den," Gwen said. "He's such huge hulk."

Stacey frowned at the thought of Lobo's being cooped up needlessly. "He won't hurt you."

"I'm not afraid of him," Gwen answered calmly. "I just prefer not to have dog hairs all over my clothes."

Sean exchanged a look with Stacey. "I'll go get him," he said.

Lobo came bounding in and made a dash for Stacey. She petted and cooed over him with extra fervor. Lobo's devotion was the only thing she could count on.

Gwen's eyes narrowed, noticing the expression on Sean's face as he watched the affection between Stacey and the dog.

"He is rather a love, isn't he?" She snapped her fingers. "Come here, boy."

Lobo trotted over obediently, but after sniffing at Gwen's hand, he returned to Stacey.

"What an unusual business you're in." Gwen took charge of the conversation again. "And what a novel way of meeting men."

"I'm not surprised that's the first thing you'd think of," Sean remarked. "You haven't changed."

"Temper, temper." Gwen turned to Stacey. "Is he as wildly jealous of *you*?"

"I haven't given him any reason to be," Stacey answered steadily.

Gwen gave Sean an amused glance. "Have you been telling tales out of school?"

"We have other things to talk about," he replied.

She wasn't perturbed by his austere tone. "Like the wedding? I adore weddings! When is it going to be?"

"We haven't set a date yet," Stacey answered for both of them.

"I see." Gwen quickly masked her look of satisfaction. "Do you plan on living here? I've always loved this place."

It had never occurred to Stacey that Gwen had lived here. Had they been making love in the bed she'd shared with Sean?

Sean was aware of Stacey's dismayed conjecture. His response was directed as much to her as it was to Gwen. "You never lived here. I bought this apartment after we were divorced."

"It seems like home to me after all the time I've spent here," Gwen answered demurely.

"Why are you deliberately giving Stacey the wrong idea?" he demanded.

"I certainly didn't mean to." Gwen was all wide-eyed innocence. "You're just overreacting, darling. We both made mistakes during our marriage, but that doesn't mean we aren't still friends."

Sean looked frustrated. Gwen's very presence seemed to confirm her statement. Any disclaimer on his part wouldn't carry much weight.

"I knew I was always welcome to stay here," she said.

Since Gwen's remark was directed at her, Stacey felt some comment was necessary. "Do you get back to California often?"

"Not as often as I'd like." Gwen glanced at Sean.

"Living in Europe must be very exciting," Stacey remarked, not knowing what else to say.

Gwen stifled a sigh. "It was a place to go...after the divorce."

"You found plenty of reasons before that, also," Sean observed tautly.

"How true. I'll never forget those trips." Gwen's voice was very soft. "Remember the New Year's we spent in Madrid?" Her eyes sparkled with laughter as she turned to Stacey. "Sean was feeling very delicate. We had arranged for a car and driver to take us to Toledo, and I convinced him the drive would do him good. He just wanted to stay in bed all day. Remember, Sean?"

"How could I forget the worst hangover of my whole life?" There was a stirring of amusement behind his curt words.

"Poor baby. That ghastly car didn't help, either. We were expecting a limousine," Gwen continued. "But the driver arrived in a car so ancient that shock absorbers hadn't even been invented in its day. We felt every pothole in the road. I don't think Carlos missed a one. Wasn't that his name, darling—Carlos?''

"It isn't what *I* called him." Sean smiled faintly in remembrance.

Stacey's chest felt constricted as she listened to them reminisce. Their marriage had obviously not been the complete disaster he'd described.

Gwen was reliving the experience with glee. "The man was a genuine character. I was starving, but Carlos wouldn't take us to a restaurant until he'd shown us every church and museum on the way to Toledo. He did make up for it, though. Eventually he took us to a very colorful little cantina."

"Where he undoubtedly got a kickback," Sean remarked dryly.

"But the food was marvelous," Gwen reminded him. "Or maybe I just remember it that way because it was such a wonderful day," she added wistfully.

Misery washed over Stacey at this evidence of the happy times Sean had shared with Gwen—and the certain knowledge that he was still in love with her. He was shaken to his very core at seeing her again.

Stacey remained frozen in her chair, wishing herself a million miles away.

Sean suddenly became aware of her huddled stillness. "I doubt if Stacey finds this very interesting," he said quickly.

"You're right. We're being rude," Gwen agreed. She smiled apologetically at Stacey. "Sean and I go back such a long way that everything reminds us of something we did together. We tend to forget anyone else is present."

His mouth thinned dangerously. "Your memory has convenient lapses."

"I never dwell on the sad parts, darling. I prefer to remember the exciting, crazy, wonderful times we had."

Stacey couldn't bear to hear any more of them. She stood up. "I really must be going."

"Maybe you're right," Sean muttered. "I'll take you home."

The phone rang before she could tell him it wasn't necessary. Stacey just wanted to be alone to think things out.

He glanced at his watch with a scowl. "Who the devil could be calling at this hour?"

"Probably your attorney," Gwen answered. "He phoned earlier and said he had to talk to you about something important. I offered to take a message, but he said he'd call back."

Sean stalked out of the room, swearing under his breath.

Stacey accepted the diversion gratefully. "I'll be running along."

"Don't you want Sean to take you home?" Gwen asked.

"No, I . . . just tell him I took a cab."

"I'm so glad we had this chance to meet," Gwen called as Stacey almost ran to the door. A self-satisfied smile lurked around the corners of her mouth.

She was curled up on the couch when Sean returned, her caftan arranged in graceful folds.

He looked swiftly around the room. "Where's Stacey?"

"She took a taxi home."

"What did you say to her?" he demanded.

Gwen's eyebrows climbed. "Not a thing. She just said she had to leave."

"And you have no idea why," he said sarcastically.

"Well, I suppose she might have felt a trifle constrained. Stacey is a dear little thing, but she *is* a bit unsophisticated."

"Thank God for small favors!"

Gwen contemplated his taut body and barely controlled anger with complacency. "Is that why you chose her? Because she's my complete opposite? Were you trying to blot me out of your consciousness?"

"I *chose* her because I'm in love with her," he replied savagely.

"How can you be sure? You were in love with me once," Gwen said softly.

Sean looked at the beautiful woman on the couch, trying to summon up past feelings. He couldn't. All he could recall, besides the destructive arguments, were obsessive nights—followed by boredom. Sean couldn't bring himself to tell her that, so he looked for another way to explain.

"We shared very satisfying sex," he said quietly. "If we'd left it at that, we could have remained friends. Our mistake was in confusing passion with love. Neither of us was committed to the other."

"You wouldn't have been so upset about my little, mm...transgressions...if you didn't love me."

He smiled bitterly. "No man likes to be publicly cuckolded."

"Most men would have found consolation with other women. The fact that you didn't proves you loved me," she challenged.

Sean's face was austere once more. "Perhaps you destroyed my interest in women."

"Only temporarily it seems," she said mockingly.

"Fortunately," he answered, just as mockingly.

"So now, after all this time, you've found your true love."

"Yes." His voice softened.

Gwen drew in her breath sharply. She'd never seen that look on Sean's face. "What makes her different from any other woman?"

"If you can't see for yourself, I can't explain."

"She's very impressionable. Are you planning to play Pygmalion and mold her into your image of a perfect woman?"

Sean chuckled unexpectedly. "You don't know Stacey very well. She's changed me more than I've changed her."

Gwen slanted a guarded look at him. "A new romance can be very exciting, especially someone totally outside your normal sphere."

"It's kind of you to give me the benefit of your experience."

"Don't be bitter, darling. I'm only trying to warn you against doing anything hasty." She put her hand on his arm. "I really care about you."

Sean's raised eyebrow indicated disbelief. "You'll still get your alimony check."

"That was unkind," Gwen whispered, giving him a hurt look.

"Okay, your warning has been duly noted. Now you can send me a wedding present—preferably from Europe. I don't want you popping up here anymore."

She looked at him searchingly. "I can't believe it's all over between us."

"Didn't the divorce papers give you a clue?"

"I always hoped we'd get back together," she murmured.

Sean was unmoved. "That wasn't what you wanted when we were *married*. What's the matter, Gwen, did your latest boyfriend throw you over?"

Her startled look was quickly masked by lowered lashes. "Can't you manage to be pleasant for the short time I'll be here?"

Sean's face hardened. "If you mean tonight, I'll try. First thing tomorrow morning you're going to a hotel."

"Let me stay this week, Sean." She traced the outline of his lapels. "Just a week for old times' sake."

"No!"

"This will be the last time we have together," she coaxed. Her voice held a throbbing note.

His eyes narrowed. "I don't know what you want, Gwen, but experience tells me you want *something*. Why don't you save us both a lot of time and tell me what it is?"

"What would you say if I told you I came back because I realized our divorce was a terrible mistake?"

"I'd still ask what your angle is."

"You didn't used to be this hard." Gwen bent her lovely head. "You've changed, Sean."

"Because I don't want to be burned twice."

"I hurt you, and I'm sorry," she said remorsefully. "But we're both older and wiser now."

"Older, anyway." His appraising glance swept over her.

Anger flashed in Gwen's eyes for an unguarded second. Then the pleading look returned. "We could make a go of it this time. It wasn't all bad. You can't deny we were good together."

"It's over, Gwen! I'm marrying Stacey. I love her. You'll just have to accept the fact."

She stared at him for a long moment. Gwen's blank face didn't reveal any of the furious thoughts coursing through her brain. Finally she made up her mind.

"If that's what you truly want, I'm happy for you." She gave him a melancholy smile. "For what it's worth, you have my very best wishes."

Sean's rigidly held body relaxed. "Thanks, Gwen," he said quietly.

"Can we have a drink to celebrate?"

He hesitated. "I want to straighten things out with Stacey."

"Just a short drink," Gwen said wistfully. "She wouldn't begrudge me that."

After Sean had reluctantly poured Scotch over ice, Gwen raised her glass in a toast. "To love and marriage."

He smiled. "I'll drink to that."

"Where are you going on your honeymoon?"

"I don't know. We haven't discussed it."

Gwen rested her head on the back of the couch and looked into space dreamily. "Remember our honeymoon? We stayed at that funny little inn high on a hill. You ordered champagne, and we drank it out of tumblers because they didn't have any wineglasses."

"What's the point in dredging up the past?" Sean asked impatiently.

Her smile held sadness. "Memories are all I have."

He set his glass down and stood up. "I'm leaving now."

Gwen sprang up from the couch and put a restraining hand on his arm. "Running away isn't the answer. There's still the same magic between us. You feel it, too, but you just won't admit it."

"I should have known better than to think you'd give up," Sean said disgustedly. "Is your pride hurt? Is that it? As long as I didn't remarry, you could tell yourself I was carrying the world's biggest torch?"

"I didn't get married again, either. Doesn't that tell you something?"

"Nothing I don't already know. Your alimony payments would stop."

"Oh, Sean, how can you be so dense?" She put her arms around his neck. "I want to come back home where I belong!"

His hands fastened on her waist, urging her body away from his. "It's interesting that at no time have you said you love me."

She lifted her face until their lips were just inches apart. "Stay with me tonight and I'll show you," she whispered.

Sean's eyes blazed with contempt. "You're really incredible! Do you honestly think I'd do a thing like that to Stacey?"

"You aren't married yet." Gwen tried to move closer.

He reached up and yanked her arms free. "That's about what I'd expect from you."

"All I'm asking for is one night," she said urgently. "After that I'll get out of your life if you say so."

He grabbed her wrists as she reached for him once more. "I want you out of my life *now*! After tonight I don't want to see you here again."

Before she could answer, he strode angrily to the door.

Gwen stood where he'd left her, frowning thoughtfully.

Stacey had turned on all the lights when she returned home, unconsciously trying to dispel the darkness that had eclipsed her life. The discovery that Sean was still in love with Gwen was a crushing blow, even though she'd suspected as much earlier in their relationship.

How could he be so loving, even propose marriage, when he'd never stopped wanting Gwen? Stacey's pain deepened as little things began to come back to her.

Sean's initial reaction to the idea of marriage had been lukewarm, to put it charitably. When she'd backed off he'd been quite content to leave things as they were—until he discovered Gwen was returning. That was what triggered his urgency. Was he using marriage as a safeguard, because he knew he couldn't resist Gwen? She'd returned before for a whirlwind reunion and then left him.

Stacey wrapped her arms around her trembling body, as though to ward off a mortal blow. Her dreams had gone up in smoke, yet it was nobody's fault. Sean couldn't fall out of love because he wanted to. He'd used her, but perhaps not even consciously. He was fond of her, in spite of his obsession with Gwen. He would even have been a good husband.

For a fleeting instant Stacey considered going through with the marriage. Maybe in time Sean would come to love her. She gave up the notion with great despair. Whenever he was even a little withdrawn, she'd wonder if he was thinking of Gwen.

Stacey's shoulders drooped as she turned out the lights and went into the bedroom to get undressed. If she needed any proof of Gwen's power, Sean's actions had supplied it. He'd chosen to stay with her. Stacey closed her mind to what they were doing at that moment.

She was caught off guard when the doorbell rang a short time later. Her first impulse was to ignore it. Stacey went to the door reluctantly, knowing Sean wouldn't go away. She really didn't want to talk to him. What could he say that she didn't already know?

The deep lines in his face revealed the trauma he'd been through. "Why did you run away, Stacey?" he demanded.

"What was there to stay for?" she asked.

"You're angry about Gwen, but I had no idea she'd be there."

"I know you didn't, but the fact is she *was*. And she always will be."

"No! We had it out after you left. I told her to leave and not come back."

Stacey sighed. "It isn't that simple, Sean. Even when she's an ocean away she's a tangible presence in your life."

"Perhaps she was until I met you, but not the way you're implying. I didn't realize how I'd allowed her to poison my thinking," he said slowly. "It wasn't until I met you that I became whole again."

"That's what you want to believe."

"It's the truth!"

"I was there tonight, Sean. I saw how deeply Gwen affected you."

"I was surprised to see her," he said defensively. "And when she started reminiscing about the past, I could tell how it upset you."

"Me? Or you?" Stacey asked skeptically. "Those remembrances of that New Year's in Spain weren't exactly painful memories."

Sean raked his fingers through his hair in frustration. "Do you want me to say my marriage was unrelieved hell? It wasn't. I want to be honest with you. Gwen is what's called a fun date. That's what she should have been. Unfortunately, we got married."

"But you're divorced now! Why does the mere fact of seeing her send you into a tailspin?"

"Because I knew you'd get the wrong impression when we came home and found her acting as though she belonged in my apartment."

"She does stay with you when she comes to town," Stacey said in a small voice.

"I know she gave you that impression, but it was only once, three months ago. I was just as surprised then. She descended on me without warning, and there was nothing I could do about it, short of putting her out physically. I was merely annoyed then, but this time I realized it could be a catastrophe."

Stacey wanted with all her heart to believe him, but there was too much evidence on the other side. Her voice was muted as she put her fear into words. "She wants you back."

"Believe me, she doesn't! I don't know what's going on in her head, but I won't let it come between us. We're going ahead with our plans."

"Just supposing she was serious," Stacey said hesitantly. "You two have a lot of emotional ties. I know you're . . . well . . . fond of me—"

"Is *that* what you call it!"

"Please, let me finish, Sean. I'm trying to say it would be misplaced chivalry to consider yourself bound by a promise you made when you didn't know there was a chance for a reconciliation with Gwen.

Sean's sigh came from his toes. "Darling Stacey, I've really failed you."

Her heart plunged. "It's all right. I understand."

"That's the whole trouble—you don't. I love you so much that the thought of losing you terrifies me. I can't seem to convince you that Gwen means nothing to me. What more can I say? What can I do?"

He looked as miserable as Stacey felt. "I want to believe you, Sean. Maybe after she's gone."

"That will be tomorrow," he said grimly.

"She agreed to leave?"

"I didn't give her any choice."

Did he hope out of sight would be out of mind? Sean was obviously fighting Gwen's attraction, but how could things be different just because she was staying at a hotel instead of his apartment?

Stacey sighed. "I suppose it doesn't make any difference."

"You know better than that. You'd be imagining all kinds of things!"

"She's a stunning woman," Stacey murmured. "I can see how a man could find her irresistible."

"Have you ever looked in a mirror?" he demanded.

"I realize some men consider me attractive," she said slowly. "But I don't have her, her... Oh, how can I put it? She's so *sexy*! You've said as much yourself."

"Beautiful Stacey!" He put his arms around her. "Don't you know you're so much more desirable? There isn't a time when I don't ache to make love to you. I want you near me always. You must know that by now."

Stacey raised her head to look at him searchingly. The ice around her heart cracked as she found pure love in his eyes.

Her arms tightened around his chest. "Oh, Sean, I thought I'd lost you!"

"Never in a million years."

His mouth sought hers eagerly. For a blessed few minutes Stacey was lost in the throbbing world of sensation Sean always created. She clung to him tightly as he swung her into his arms and carried her to a big chair, where he sat down, holding her on his lap.

"Now, how about setting a date for our wedding?" he asked.

She smoothed his cheek lovingly. "I haven't talked to my mother yet."

"What are you waiting for?"

"She's out of town."

"When is she coming home?"

"I don't know. I don't even know where they are. Dad hates to be tied down to a schedule."

Sean made a low sound of annoyance. "At this rate our wedding and the turn of the century will occur at about the same time."

Stacey laughed. "Well, at least you won't have trouble remembering our wedding anniversary."

"I want to get married *now*!" His face cleared suddenly. "Why couldn't we get married secretly? No one else would have to know. You could still have your big celebration later."

A little chill touched Stacey's spine as her suspicion was revived. "I couldn't deceive my parents like that."

Sean sighed. "You're right, honey. I just got carried away."

"There isn't any real hurry," she said tentatively.

"I suppose not. I simply want our marriage to be an accomplished fact before anything else happens."

She slipped off his lap before he could stop her. "Gwen really shook you up," she remarked casually.

His jaw firmed. "She's good at that."

Stacey hesitated. "Did she say how long she'll be in town?"

"No, and I'm not interested." He held out his arms. "Come back here where you belong. I want to whisper outrageous things in your ear before I undress you slowly."

For once Stacey wasn't responsive. How could she let Sean make love to her when unresolved doubts still tormented her? He could reduce her to mindless ecstasy with his lips, his hands, his body. But she wanted his heart, too. Did Gwen have that, in spite of his protestations?

Stacey avoided looking at him directly. "I'm rather tired. It's been quite an evening. Would you mind terribly if I didn't ask you to stay?"

Sean became very still. "I thought we'd straightened everything out."

"We did," she said hastily. "I'm just . . . tired."

"I see." He stood up and walked over, but he didn't touch her. "I love you, Stacey, but evidently that isn't enough. I'm sorry."

His stern face frightened her. "You're wrong! I love you, too. That's why I need to be sure your ties with Gwen are broken."

He looked at her without emotion. "That's something you'll have to work out for yourself."

Stacey stared at the closed door after he left, torn by indecision. She wanted to run after him, tell him that nothing mattered but being together. Yet something stopped her.

Doubt battled with regret all the time she was getting ready for bed. If she hadn't sent him away, Sean would be beside her now, holding her in his arms, making her feel cherished. Was she a fool to send him back to Gwen, practically gift wrapped?

Stacey stirred restlessly as she pictured how the other woman would greet him. Sean wouldn't tell her about their problems, but she'd guess by his manner. Gwen would be balm to his hurt feelings. And when she offered more than consolation, would he accept?

Stacey buried her head in the pillow, trying to stifle her tortuous thoughts.

Chapter Nine

Stacey tormented herself needlessly, picturing Sean in Gwen's arms. He didn't go back to his apartment that night. After leaving Stacey he drove around aimlessly for hours, trying to figure out what had gone wrong. How could she believe he was still in love with Gwen?

Sean realized he'd made the initial mistake in not proposing marriage earlier, but his explanation had been truthful. He hadn't given Stacey all the gory details of his marriage because it wasn't something a gentleman did. Yet surely the small glimpse she'd gotten should have been enough.

When his jaw ached from clenching his teeth and his eyes burned from staring at the road, he drove to the nearest motel.

In spite of his fatigue, dawn was breaking before he fell asleep. He continued to ask himself unanswerable questions until his tired mind rebelled. As a result, he didn't awaken until noon.

He ordered breakfast from room service and went to take a shower. By the time he was dressed, his food arrived.

The lack of a razor was an annoyance, but at least his timing was right. Gwen would be gone by the time he returned home.

Sean was unprepared to find her there when he entered the apartment some time later.

"Is that you, darling?" Gwen called from the guest room.

"What are you doing here?" he asked, startled into rudeness.

Gwen came into the living room, still wearing her nightgown and trailing clouds of perfume. "What kind of greeting is that?" she pouted.

"I asked you a question." His voice was ominous.

"Don't be tiresome, Sean. Stacey isn't here. You don't have to put on a big act."

"I told you last night you couldn't stay."

"Why on earth not? One of us ought to sleep here," she remarked pointedly.

"This happens to be *my* apartment!"

"Which you aren't using. Why should you object if I do?"

"I don't have to explain my sleeping arrangements to you," he said tautly.

Gwen gave a tinkling little laugh. "I'm not asking you to, pet. I know how virile you are. I didn't expect you to come home last night."

A vein pulsed in his temple. "I wasn't with Stacey last night."

"How deliciously gallant." She smiled indulgently. "You're protecting her reputation."

Sean gave up on the subject. He stared at her moodily. "What are you doing in Los Angeles, Gwen?"

"I came for a visit."

"Why now?"

Her smile wavered slightly. "Why not?"

"I know you," he said slowly. "You never do anything without an ulterior motive."

"That's unkind," she said reproachfully.

"But true. If you said you came for a party or to check out a new couturier or hairdresser—any of the trivial things you consider important—I'd have believed you. But for no reason at all? Come on, Gwen!"

"You're the reason, Sean, whether you choose to believe it or not." She cupped his cheek in her palm and looked up at him with limpid blue eyes. "I've never stopped caring, and I don't think you have, either."

He jerked her hand down. "We went through all that last night. I don't intend to do it again."

She laughed softly. "Look at you. You're tied up in knots. Don't try to pretend you're indifferent to me."

"I wouldn't be indifferent to a man-eating tiger in my living room, either, but that doesn't mean I'd want it to stick around. Did you phone for a hotel room?"

"You're not really putting me out, are you?"

"In your nightgown, if necessary!"

"But that's so foolish, Sean. You have plenty of room."

"Perhaps you enjoy these little scenes, but I don't," he said grimly.

Gwen's shoulders slumped. "Okay, you win."

"When you're ready I'll drive you wherever you want to go," he said more kindly.

Her eyes widened. "I meant I won't bother you anymore. You can come and go as if I weren't here."

"That's impossible, and you know it!"

"If I upset you that much, you can to go to Stacey's for a few days," she said, watching his reaction intently.

"Why should I be put out of my own apartment?"

"You two haven't argued, have you?"

"What could we possibly have to argue about?" Sean asked sardonically. "My fiancée was delighted to find that my ex-wife had moved in for an indefinite stay."

"I explained about not knowing you were engaged. Surely she can't be jealous of me."

"If she wasn't, it's not your fault. You gave the impression that Scarlett and Rhett were a couple of awkward teenagers next to us!"

"We did have our moments." Her smile was seductive.

"Indeed we did. Like the time I forgot my wallet and came back for it unexpectedly. That was a night to remember."

Gwen bit her lip nervously. "I admitted I made mistakes."

The incident he spoke of had been sordid. It was also the final blow to their marriage. The degrading episode continued to rankle long after the divorce. But Sean suddenly realized it no longer bothered him.

He laughed naturally for the first time. "One of your mistakes was not locking the bedroom door."

Gwen caught the new note in his voice. She masked her concern behind lowered lashes. "You'll never know how much I regret that night."

He grinned. "It's the little things that trip you up every time. But I'm sure you learned by experience. Boyfriends tend to get just as upset about those things as husbands."

"Please, Sean," she murmured, having no other defense.

"Who are you going with these days? Still that Italian playboy—what's his name?"

"Marcello Panzone," she answered unwillingly.

"That's the one. He's noted for appreciating beautiful women, but I hear he has quite a temper. Better watch your step."

Gwen's long nails bit into her palms. "I don't see Marcello anymore."

Sean looked at her more closely. "Is that why you came back to California? Did you run through all the men on the continent?"

"Don't be ridiculous," she snapped.

"No, that couldn't be it. There are all those smaller countries you haven't mined yet."

"If you insist on being insulting, I'm going to my room."

Sean's amusement faded. "To pack, I trust."

"I'm going back to bed. You've given me a headache."

He followed her down the hall. "Listen, Gwen, you've had your fun. Now it's time to be serious. You simply cannot stay here."

"I woke up feeling rotten, and you certainly haven't helped matters." She tossed aside her filmy peignoir and got into bed. "I think I'm coming down with something."

Sean stood by the bed, glaring down at her. "There's not a thing in this world wrong with you!"

"Why, thank you, darling. That's the sweetest thing you've said since I got here."

"You know what I mean," he muttered.

"I believe I'd better call a doctor. Do you still use that nice Dr. Richardson?"

Sean scowled at her for an indecisive moment before stalking out the door.

In his own room he took a suitcase off the top shelf of the closet. Since Gwen clearly wasn't going to leave, *he'd* have to. Stacey would never believe Gwen refused to go. Sean scarcely believed it himself! His frustration boiled over as he threw shirts and socks into the suitcase.

The two women in his life were both being unreasonable, and he couldn't talk sense into either of them. Should he try to talk to Stacey again? Maybe she'd had a change of heart overnight. Sean yearned for the sound of her voice. Whether together or apart, they always started the day by reaffirming their love.

He missed the warm feeling that brought. Should he phone? The memory of her cool dismissal the night before changed his mind. He'd feel even worse exchanging polite conversation with her. Stacey might also ask if Gwen were still there, and what could he say?

When he was all packed, Sean faced the dilemma of where to go. He had no idea how long Gwen intended to stay, and a lengthy sojourn in a hotel room held no charm. Suddenly an alternative appeared. He'd planned to go to New York in a week. Why not now?

The prospect of getting away from his problems for a short time was irresistible. He picked up the phone and made a series of calls.

Gwen saw him pass by her open door, suitcase in hand. She sat up in bed. "Where are you going?"

"To New York," he answered without stopping.

She jumped up and ran down the hall after him. "You're being ridiculous, Sean! That's no solution."

"Maybe not, but I need a few days to myself. If anyone calls, say I went to New York on business. I'll be back in a week." Sean didn't mention Stacey by name, not wanting to confirm Gwen's suspicion that they'd argued.

Gwen started to protest, then changed her mind. Sean was proving unexpectedly difficult. Perhaps it would be better to let him cool off for a bit.

His engagement had come as an unpleasant surprise but not an insurmountable one. Gwen couldn't accept the fact that Sean had no feelings left for her. She still felt a certain fondness for him. She'd even had a moment's regret at fouling up his romance. It couldn't be helped, though.

If only she and Marcello hadn't had that terrible fight. They'd both said awful things to each other, but hers were especially cutting. She'd tried to apologize afterward, but his male ego had been wounded. Would it make a difference if she could talk to him now that he'd had a chance to reconsider? Or would he still reject her?

Gwen stared at the telephone. What if he'd had a change of heart and was trying to get in touch with her? Marcello wouldn't know where to reach her unless she phoned. Gwen lifted the receiver and dialed the operator.

Static crackled over the wire as a servant announced, *"Residenza de Signor Panzone."*

"Is Signor Panzone there?" Gwen asked.

"I am sorry, no."

"Is that you, Roberto? It's Gwen Garrison."

"Ah, Signorina Garrison. Come sta?"

"I'm fine. When will Mr. Panzone be back?"

"That I do not know. He went on the yacht of the Count de Villois. I think they go to many places."

"I see."

Gwen bit her lip. She knew about the French count and his fabulous cruises. They always abounded with beautiful women. Marcello was consoling himself royally. He probably hadn't given her a second thought.

It was a lost cause, but Gwen gave the servant her phone number. "He can reach me here if he likes."

Stacey's spirits were as low as those of the other two that morning. She didn't even feel like getting out of bed. The knowledge that she might have sent Sean straight to Gwen's arms was painful. Yet how could she have done otherwise? If he was that undecided, it was better to find out now rather than later.

The shrilling telephone sent a bolt of energy through her. Sean would scarcely call if he'd just left Gwen's bed! The sparkle died out of Stacey's eyes as Claudia's voice greeted her.

"I don't care if I did wake you. I have wonderful news!"

"What's so great?" Stacey asked dully.

"Everything! The whole world's beautiful!"

"Maybe to you."

"Don't be grumpy. Life is too exciting to waste sleeping."

"I haven't had my coffee yet, Claudia. Either tell me why you called, or call back later."

"You were right and I was wrong."

"That's one in a row," Stacey muttered.

"I took your advice and called Mike." Claudia's voice was filled with love and laughter. "He was terribly stiff at first. When I told him I was sorry I'd jumped to conclusions, he said I damn well should be."

"A strong offense is a good defense," Stacey observed moodily.

"You've certainly changed your tune," Claudia remarked, but she was obviously too happy to dwell on the fact. "Anyway, I asked him if he'd like to come over and have a talk. He didn't exactly jump at the opportunity, but he did agree." She laughed. "When he first arrived we were like two foreign diplomats, terribly polite to each other but neither saying what was really on our minds. I didn't know how to begin, and Mike wasn't about to make it easy for me. Would you believe we even talked about the weather?"

Stacey smiled unwillingly. "That couldn't have taken long. It's always the same in Southern California. I presume you eventually got around to the important stuff. How did he explain the brunette?"

"You were right again, Stacey! She was working on the case with him. Pauline is associated with Mike's law firm."

"I told you it was probably something like that," Stacey said, although she had private reservations. Her own experience with Sean made her wonder if anything was the way it appeared.

"I know, and I should have listened to you," Claudia answered remorsefully. "I put us both through all that agony for nothing."

"Mike explained why they were working at his apartment rather than the office?" Stacey asked deliberately.

"Yes, and it's so simple. Pauline lives here in the valley near Mike. She had to go home after work to fix dinner for her family, which meant she would have had to go all the way downtown again afterward. They were merely saving time by working at Mike's apartment."

"That makes sense." Stacey was wondering why he hadn't gone to the woman's house if work was all they had in mind, but she had no intention of asking.

Claudia answered her unspoken question. "Pauline has two small children, so they wouldn't have gotten anything done at her place. Her husband took care of the kids while she went to Mike's."

Stacey was ashamed of her doubts. She'd never been a suspicious person before. What had Sean done to her?

"I felt small enough to hide in a kitten's ear," Claudia was saying. "And that's what I felt like doing. But Mike said he was glad it happened. He said he wasn't sure I cared that much for him. Can you believe it?"

"I guess men can be insecure, too," Stacey said slowly. It was a new concept to her.

"But not men like Mike who have women throwing themselves at him!"

"That isn't necessarily what they want."

"I guess not." Claudia laughed softly. "I haven't told you the best part yet. He asked me to marry him."

"What did you say?"

"Are you kidding? I accepted before he got all the words out!"

"You haven't known him very long," Stacey said tentatively.

"I knew that first night when he stayed and helped me with the dishes," Claudia answered confidently. "You'll understand when you fall in love yourself. Some kind of built-in radar tells you this is the one."

Stacey couldn't help but agree. She thought back to the first time she'd opened her eyes and seen Sean's darkly handsome face. The chemistry had been there even before she discovered the qualities that made her love him. That was also before she knew about Gwen.

"You're lucky Mike felt the same way," Stacey said wistfully.

"I would have known if he didn't."

"That wasn't how you felt when you found Pauline in his apartment."

"I wasn't thinking straight or I would have believed him in the first place. It's all a matter of trust, as Mike pointed out. If you really love someone, you take him on faith."

Claudia prattled on about Mike, how wonderful he was, their coming wedding and a lot more. Stacey wasn't really listening. Claudia had touched a tender spot with her talk about knowing when someone loved you and giving him the benefit of any doubt.

Was she as guilty as Claudia of making her own problems? The rapturous times she and Sean had spent together were too memorable for a casual affair. The memory of his ravaged face when he left the night before rose up to haunt Stacey. She never should have sent him away! Was the damage irreparable?

Stacey broke in on Claudia's ecstatic monologue. "I'm so happy for you, and I want to hear all about your plans, but I have an important phone call to make. I'll get back to you later."

Her heart was pounding as she hung up and dialed Sean's number. She could only hope he'd be as understanding as Mike had been.

"Hello." Gwen's voice was breathless with anticipation as she answered the phone.

Stacey felt as though someone had poured a bucket of ice water over her. Sean had assured her Gwen was leaving, but she was still there.

"Hello," Gwen repeated. "Who is it?"

Stacey reminded herself how fatal it was to jump to conclusions. Any number of things could explain Gwen's continued presence—she'd overslept, she was still packing.

"Hi, it's Stacey." She struggled to manage a normal tone of voice.

"Oh...hi, how are you?" Gwen sounded disappointed.

"Fine. I didn't expect—I mean, is Sean there?"

After a slight pause Gwen said, "No, he slept late, and then the poor dear had to rush out of here. He had some pressing business to attend to, I believe."

"I see. Well, would you leave him a note to call me?"

"I'll do better than that. I'll give him the message in person," Gwen promised. "He might not be home for some time, though."

Stacey willed herself not to overreact. "I got the impression you were leaving."

Gwen's laughter sounded like ice tinkling in a crystal glass. "You didn't seriously think he would put me out?"

"He did offer to take you to a hotel," Stacey replied evenly.

"Sean knows I abhor hotels. The poor darling was simply in a terrible spot. It's ridiculous of course, but he was afraid you'd be upset if I stayed with him. You aren't, are you?"

"Should I be?"

"I suppose that depends on how possessive you are."

"We're engaged," Stacey said pointedly.

"I was married to him," Gwen answered calmly.

"But you aren't anymore!"

"The ties that bind you to someone you've shared your life with are never really broken."

"Are you saying you still love him?"

"What really matters is how Sean feels," Gwen replied softly.

"I know how he feels." The slight quaver in Stacey's voice betrayed her insecurity.

"Then you have nothing to worry about, do you? I told Sean that. We had a lovely talk when he came home."

"How long are you staying?" Stacey asked abruptly.

"That depends on a lot of things. I promise to give you equal time with him, though," Gwen joked.

Stacey had reached the bottom by the time their conversation ended. She tried to tell herself not to fall into Gwen's trap. The woman as much as stated that she wanted Sean back. If she succeeded in making trouble between Sean and Stacey, she might accomplish her goal.

Stacey reminded herself of Sean's distaste for his former wife. She summoned up his tender words and actions. But balancing that was the disturbing picture of Gwen and Sean sharing the apartment, having cozy late-night talks. And inevitably...more?

Stacey deeply needed Sean's reassurance. If only she could talk to him. Everything would be all right when he called, she promised herself.

Gwen knew she had caused what could be a serious rift between Stacey and Sean. That had been her intention. It didn't elate her the way it should have, however. Stacey was a nice enough person, and they were obviously mad about each other. It was too bad, but unavoidable. Gwen stared pensively at the ceiling. She had no other option at the moment.

With a sigh, she reached for the phone and dialed Francine Wilson's number.

When Gwen arrived at the restaurant they'd selected for lunch, Francine was already at the table. A half-consumed martini was evidence that she'd been there for some time.

Gwen slid into the booth with an air of breathlessness. "I'm sorry I'm late."

"You always are, darling," Francine answered indulgently. "I didn't expect you to change."

"I honestly try to be on time, but something always comes up."

"As long as you can get away with it, why worry?"

"It drives some people up the wall. I wish everyone were as understanding as you."

"I'm your best friend, remember?"

Gwen smiled at the other woman. "It's so good to see you again, Francine."

"And such a surprise. It's only been a short time since you were here last."

"Three months." Gwen's eyes were shadowed.

Francine stared at her speculatively. "You couldn't wait to return to Europe then."

"You know me. I like to keep on the move." Gwen paused to give her order to the waiter.

"Where are you staying?" Francine asked as the man left.

"Didn't I mention it? At Sean's, naturally."

Francine's eyebrows climbed. "He's been having an affair with a little ingenue type. She's not going to be very happy about that."

"Stacey? She's rather sweet."

"You've met her?"

"Last night when he brought her home." Gwen laughed ruefully. "Poor Sean, I really should have given him advance warning."

Francine's eyes gleamed avidly. "I wish I could have seen his face—and hers!"

"It was all quite civilized. Sean introduced us, and we made small talk."

"And afterward?"

"We went to bed, what else?"

"An orgy? I didn't think Sean went for that sort of thing—not to mention his prissy little girlfriend."

"Don't be crude, darling. Of course we didn't have an orgy. After a suitable time, Stacey went home. As a matter of fact, she left alone."

Francine smiled knowingly. "I should have known. That little twit isn't in the same league as you."

Gwen looked at the other woman appraisingly. "You seem to dislike her a lot."

Francine shrugged. "Actually I have no feelings about her one way or the other. I just think she and Sean deserve each other."

"When did your attitude toward Sean change so drastically? At one time I got the impression that you wouldn't have minded consoling him in my absence."

"That's ridiculous!" Francine's denial was both prompt and vehement, but her eyes swiveled away.

Gwen laughed indulgently. "Don't feel badly, darling. Sean is deliciously old-fashioned. He believes in fidelity."

Francine changed the subject hastily. "Are you still seeing that fascinating Italian?"

"All Italians are fascinating," Gwen answered lightly.

"Don't be coy. You know who I mean. The gorgeous one who's on the international polo team."

Gwen glanced around. "Where *is* that waiter with our lunch? The service around here has certainly deteriorated."

Francine's gaze sharpened. "Are you trying to change the subject?"

"Why would I do that?"

"Don't try to kid an old friend. You and Marcello Panzone have been a hot item for months. Everything he does is news. That's the only way I've kept track of you, through the gossip columns."

"Then why ask me? Go read the newspaper."

"Is that any way to treat a pal? I want the inside stuff."

"The columnists have already printed everything there is to know about us."

"They haven't gotten wind of your trip home. Is it all over between you two?"

Gwen frowned in annoyance. "You're making a big deal out of nothing. I do come back to see my friends every now and then."

"You were just here three months ago."

"That was business; this is pleasure." Gwen's unconsciously grim face didn't indicate as much.

"You're staying with Sean again, so he must be the attraction," Francine mused.

"Oh, for heaven's sake, Francine! I might as well have had lunch with a reporter."

"Well, if you insist on clamming up, don't blame me for drawing my own conclusions."

Gwen sighed. "All right, I'll level with you. I did come back to try for a reconciliation with Sean."

"How about Marcello? What happened to your big romance?"

The waiter had brought their lunch, and Gwen gave full attention to her shrimp salad. "He was fun for a while, but it was never anything serious."

Francine looked shrewdly at her friend's bent head. "You mean *he* wasn't, or *you* weren't?"

"Neither of us was," Gwen answered curtly.

"Too bad. You seemed made for each other. But it will be nice to have you back, anyway."

"I don't know if I'll stay."

"But you just said—"

"I didn't realize Sean was involved with someone."

"Surely you're not worried about Stacey? When he knows you're available he'll drop her so hard, she'll bounce."

Gwen looked pleased. "You really think so?"

"I wish I could be so sure of everything in life."

Francine's confidence would have been shaken had she known Sean's state of mind. His flight to New York was literally that—an escape. He was fed up with life in general and women in particular.

As he stared out the plane window into the clear blue sky, Sean asked himself if anything was worth what he was going through. Gwen was merely a minor annoyance, but Stacey was putting him through hell.

His failure to convince her that Gwen meant nothing to him was both puzzling and ominous. Sean knew all about distrust. He didn't want another marriage based on it, even though this was the reverse of his former situation.

His eyes burned as he searched the limitless sky for answers. This could be just the tip of the iceberg. If he and Stacey got married, would she continue to suspect him of one thing or another? If so, their marriage was doomed from the start. Could she really love him and still feel this way?

Sean's teeth clenched as another thought occurred to him. Did he really love *her*? Or was the major attraction between them physical, as Stacey had often indicated? His first impulse was to reject the idea violently, yet he forced himself to consider the possibility.

Last night had been a painful experience. When Stacey rejected him after he'd thought they'd reached an understanding, he'd felt like a puppet on a string. He'd been both hurt and angry then, but now he felt only a kind of relief at leaving all his problems behind. That wouldn't make them go away, yet he couldn't deny he was looking forward to the respite.

For the next three days Sean immersed himself in business meetings that spilled over into social events, since the two were intertwined. He mingled with producers and famous stars at lavish apartments and renowned restaurants. The theater was his ostensible reason for being in New York, so he attended plays, then wound up the evening at late-night discos.

This was the life he was accustomed to before meeting Stacey. Sean slipped back into it easily, but he felt more like a spectator than a participant. He was not only bored, there was an emptiness inside him.

Much as he tried, Sean couldn't blank Stacey out of his mind. He kept picturing how delighted she'd be at the choice theater seats, the posh restaurants and the celebrities who peopled them. Her enthusiasm was infectious. If she were here he wouldn't feel this detachment. Sean set his jaw grimly, forcing himself to remember less desirable facets of her nature.

At a cocktail party one night his heart almost stopped beating when he glanced idly across the room and saw a woman with long auburn hair. Her back was turned so he couldn't see her face, but she also had Stacey's slender body. Common sense told him she wasn't Stacey, yet he was drawn to her like a magnet.

The woman turned and smiled at him. She was very lovely. "Hello, I'm Terry Lansing." As Sean started to introduce himself, she stopped him. "I already know who you are."

He raised an eyebrow. "How would you know that?"

"Because I pointed you out and asked who the handsomest man in the room was."

"That's very flattering, coming from the most beautiful lady here."

Sean had recognized the gambit and responded automatically. He was puzzled, though. Her compliment hadn't been delivered with the usual lowered lashes and throaty voice.

"You didn't have to say that," she replied. "I was being truthful."

"So was I."

"Then beauty must truly be in the eye of the beholder," she answered in a mocking tone. "There are some gorgeous starlets here tonight."

"Is that what you are?"

She shook her head. "I'm not even in show business, except marginally. I'm Cal Rothenstein's secretary." He was a Broadway producer.

"I'm surprised we haven't met before." Terry's lack of artifice reminded Sean of Stacey. She was the first woman he'd met whom he'd like to know better. "We have a lot of things in common. Would you like to go someplace quieter so we can have a drink and talk?"

"I'd like to talk, but I'd rather have a chocolate soda." She laughed at the surprised look on his face. "Don't panic. I'll have a drink instead."

"I was merely thinking it was something my...a friend of mine might have said. You'd better have been serious, because I'm going to find us a soda fountain."

He located one in the coffee shop of one of the big hotels. They sat in a red leather booth under bright lights and got acquainted over tall ice-cream sodas.

Sean found out that Terry had many of Stacey's qualities. She was without pretense, witty, good company and undeniably lovely. He waited for a familiar spark to ignite, knowing in his heart it wasn't going to.

An hour passed pleasantly before Terry said, "You're really a good sport to bring me here when you'd much rather be at a nightclub."

"You're wrong. I can't think of anyplace I'd rather be than having ice cream with a charming redhead."

"Why do I get the feeling you have some other redhead in mind?"

"Whatever gave you that impression?" Sean fenced.

She smiled a little sadly. "A woman can sense these things."

"Because I haven't made advances, as they say in Victorian novels?" He gave her a mock leer. "Wait until I get you home."

"It won't be any different. You're in love with someone, aren't you?"

Sean started to deny it, then reconsidered. His laughter died as he said quietly, "Very much so."

"I'm not surprised. The good ones are always taken." Terry sighed. "She's a lucky girl."

"No, I'm the lucky one. I just lost sight of it for a short time. Thank you for setting me straight."

As soon as Sean took Terry home and returned to his hotel room, he dialed Stacey's number. Because of the three-hour difference in time, it was only ten o'clock in Los Angeles, but he would have called no matter what time it was. He had a burning need to hear her voice.

When no one answered, Sean was bereft. Where could she be at this hour? Common sense told him it wasn't very late. She could be any number of places, but that didn't ease his disappointment. He forced himself not to keep calling. She might be out late, and he would only succeed in frustrating himself.

The one thing that didn't torture Sean was the fear that Stacey was out with another man. He knew there would never be anyone else for either of them.

He went to bed with a smile on his face. Tomorrow he would wind up his business and book a flight home, after one other errand. A stop at Tiffany's to buy engagement and wedding rings.

Stacey heard the phone ringing as she turned off the shower. She grabbed a towel and rushed into the bedroom, but the ringing stopped as she reached for the receiver.

She was flooded with intense disappointment, which was completely irrational. There was no reason to believe it had been Sean. He hadn't called for three days. Not since Gwen had arrived. What more proof did she need that they were through?

Sean had every right to be angry, but she had phoned the next day. Even if Gwen had purposely forgotten to give him her message, Sean would have called if he'd really wanted to.

Stacey fought back her tears and climbed into bed.

Chapter Ten

Sean didn't finish his business in New York until late, so he took the midnight flight home. It was either that or waste another day until he could see Stacey, which he didn't intend to do.

He arrived in Los Angeles early in the morning and took a taxi to his apartment, hoping Gwen would be gone. If she wasn't, they were going to have a final showdown. She'd made enough trouble.

Lobo greeted Sean rapturously, almost knocking him down with joy.

"Easy, fella, you don't know your own strength." Sean braced himself against the dog's lunges. "You'd make a great tackle for some lucky football team."

Lobo put his paws on Sean's shoulders and licked his face.

"Did Mitch feed you and take you out every day? It wasn't like being with Stacey though, was it? Well, don't worry, you'll have her back soon."

The dog barked his approval loudly.

"What on earth is going on?" Gwen came into the living room, scowling. Her face cleared when she saw Sean. "You're back!"

"And you're still here, I see."

Gwen glanced at him warily, gauging his mood. Encouraged by his calm tone of voice, she said, "I missed you, darling. It's been lonely here without you."

"You didn't have to stay," he replied with deceptive mildness.

"I knew you'd be back sooner or later." She trailed after Sean as he led Lobo to the kitchen. "Your general manager has been calling frantically."

"What did he want?" Sean took a box of dog biscuits from the cupboard and fed one to Lobo.

"Something about an awards show." Gwen ran her fingers through her short curls and adjusted her nightgown strap to a more seductive angle.

Her efforts were wasted on Sean. He didn't even notice. "Did you tell him I was out of town?"

Sean was frowning. He should have called the theater office and told them himself, or at least checked in from New York. But he'd wanted to distance himself from everything and everybody in Los Angeles.

"The man really didn't give me a chance," Gwen answered. "When I told him you weren't here, he said to have you call him as soon as possible. That was our whole conversation."

Sean ground his teeth in annoyance. "It didn't occur to you that it might be important?"

She widened her eyes in hurt innocence. "I'm sorry, darling. If you'd told me what hotel you were going to, I would have called you."

He was about to point out that his manager could have tracked him down, but what was the use? "I'll take a quick shower and get down there."

"But it's practically the middle of the night. Why don't you grab a few hours sleep first, and then we can have breakfast together. I'll have that nice housekeeper of yours fix all your favorites."

He raised a sardonic eyebrow. "For a minute there I thought you were going to offer to cook for me yourself."

"I will if you want me to, but that isn't where my greatest talent lies," she murmured.

"That comes from practicing one skill more than the other." He walked past her, unbuttoning his shirt.

She followed hopefully. "I'll take the phone off the hook so you won't be disturbed."

"Forget it, Gwen. I'm going to the theater."

"I've been sitting here for three days just waiting for you to come home," she sulked. "Doesn't that mean anything to you?"

"It says you're persistent." He halted his progress toward the bedroom and turned to face her. "You never did take no for an answer, but this time you'll have to. We're all washed up, Gwen."

"No! I won't accept that."

She stared at his hard face, searching for some chink in his armor. None was visible. Suddenly Gwen played her trump card. She stripped off her nightgown and stood before him completely nude.

"Look at me, and then tell me you don't want me," she taunted.

He looked her up and down deliberately, then turned away. "Better put on a robe before you catch cold," he said over his shoulder as he went into his bedroom and closed the door.

Sean turned the shower to a needle spray. The stinging pellets of water felt good, cleansing him of the nastiness of his latest encounter with Gwen. Sean's spirits rose as he realized how completely unaffected he'd been by her undeniably lush body.

He put Gwen out of his mind and turned his thoughts to Stacey. God, how he wanted to hear her voice! It was too early to call, though. She'd been out late the night before. He'd go to the theater and settle whatever problem had arisen so he could spend an uninterrupted day with her.

Maybe he wouldn't even phone first. With any luck he'd get through in a hurry and arrive at Stacey's before she was out of bed. Sean's muscles tightened as he imagined how he'd wake her.

His plans were well-intentioned but doomed to failure. More than the usual pandemonium reigned at the theater. The atmosphere had an underlying air of panic.

"Thank God you're here!" John Rhine, the general manager, exclaimed when he saw Sean. "I've been trying to get in touch with you for days."

"What the devil is going on?" Sean asked. "The theater is supposed to be dark."

"That's what I wanted to tell you. The Players' Guild is having its annual awards presentation here tonight."

"That's not possible! It's being held at the Grammercy."

"It was supposed to be there, but the Grammercy burned down two nights ago. All the other theaters with enough seating capacity were booked, so they asked if they could have it here. When I couldn't get in touch with you, I gave the okay myself, but I had no idea what it entailed. They want extra lights and special stairs going up to the stage. Our carpenters say that isn't in their contract, and we can't bring in outside workers or the union will be on our tail.'' The man was practically wringing his hands.

"Calm down, John. We'll work everything out."

"I haven't told you the rest of it yet. These people are impossible to deal with!"

"Come into the office, and we'll take it step by step." Sean smiled to reassure his manager. "We'll tackle the impossible first and leave the hard stuff till later."

The morning passed without Sean's noticing. He was a calm eye in the middle of the hurricane, mediating between warring factions, finding solutions and putting his foot down when necessary.

He never sat down. Someone brought him a sandwich at one point, which he ate while walking around. The snags and foul-ups were like dandelions. Two appeared for every one that was rooted out. Because of the last-minute change in plans, everyone was trying to cram a week's work into twelve hours.

Finally by about five o'clock, everything started to come together. Frayed tempers were mended, and people began to apologize for snapping at one another.

Sean massaged his tired neck muscles. "You see, John? You were worried for nothing."

"You're a miracle worker!" John said fervently. "This thing would have been a fiasco without you."

"You'd have managed."

"No way! I realize now I never should have given them the theater without making sure you'd be on deck, but I kept expecting to hear from you. You've never taken off before without letting me know. Was it an emergency?"

Sean was abruptly reminded of his tangled affairs. "You might say that."

"I'm sorry. Is there anything I can do?"

"No, it's all taken care of." Sean looked at his watch and swore. Where had the day gone? "I have an important phone call to make."

He drummed his fingers on the desk top, listening to the phone ring. Stacey just had to be home! When she answered, he couldn't speak for a moment.

Stacey was similarly affected at hearing Sean's voice after she'd given up hope of hearing from him again. Her legs started to tremble so badly that she had to sit down.

"You sound wonderful," he said softly.

"You sound the same as always," she answered through stiff lips.

"Is that good or bad?" he teased.

Anger replaced Stacey's numbness. How dare he expect to take up where they'd left off without phoning for four days? "What do you want?" she demanded.

He chuckled deeply. "If a telephone supervisor happened to be listening in, I could get arrested for answering that question."

"I don't think that's very funny," she replied coldly.

Sean's euphoria dimmed a little at her frigid tone. "Are you still upset, angel? I thought you'd be glad to hear from me after three days."

"Four," she said curtly. "Not that it matters."

"I tried to call, but you were out."

"Don't hand me that stale line," she said indignantly. "I have an answering machine, remember?"

"It wasn't on last night."

Stacey recalled the ringing phone as she got out of the shower. It *had* been Sean! But where had he been before that? She didn't intend to let him set her up for another fall.

"I was out," she lied. "Having a wonderful time—with Walter Caldwell."

"Who?"

"Walter Caldwell, my old boyfriend."

"Joe College?" Sean laughed. "Come on, honey. You wouldn't go out with him to stop a prison riot."

"You're pretty sure of yourself, aren't you?" she muttered, annoyed at being seen through. Why had she picked Walter the wimp?

"No, I'm sure of *you*, sweetheart—of us." Sean's voice held a throbbing note.

"There is no us," Stacey said flatly. "That's all over."

"You know that's not true. I realize you're angry that I didn't phone, but I had to have time alone to work things out. This hasn't been easy for me, either."

Only one word meant anything to Stacey. "Alone? Gwen isn't staying with you anymore?"

"She's still at the apartment, but—"

"Don't bother to explain. I know you must have a lot of catching up to do."

"What are you talking about? I wasn't with Gwen."

"Oh, Sean, please!"

He was beginning to feel the same frustration he'd thought was over. "If you'd cared enough to phone, you'd have found that out."

"I *did* phone—the next morning. I had a lovely conversation with your wife."

"*Ex*-wife. Didn't she tell you I'd gone to New York?"

Stacey was startled out of her anger for the moment. "No, she . . . she indicated that you'd be home that evening."

Sean swore vehemently. "And you believed her?"

"I had no reason not to."

"You had *every* reason. I wanted to stay with you the night Gwen showed up. You were the one who sent me away."

"Right back to her," Stacey said bitterly.

"If you truly believe that, then I guess it really is over between us. I never worried for an instant that you'd turn to another man, but you didn't have the same trust in me."

"It isn't the same thing," Stacey protested. "How would you feel if some man I'd been intimate with in the past had moved in with me?"

"I would have thrown him out bodily, which is what I wanted to do to Gwen. But a man doesn't have that option. Civilization has its drawbacks," Sean remarked dryly.

"Okay, but you admit you would have been disturbed."

"I know what you've been through, sweetheart, and I wish I could have spared you. But you can't let it destroy our relationship."

"She's still there," Stacey pointed out.

"Maybe not. We had it out this morning when I returned from New York. I can't imagine she'd stay after what happened."

"What did happen?" Stacey asked in a small voice.

"It doesn't matter. What's important is that I want to see you. If I don't touch you soon, my nervous system is going to suffer irreparable damage. Do you feel the same way?" he asked in a husky voice.

"You know I do. That's the whole trouble," she answered soberly.

Relief welled up in Sean. "The whole world should have such trouble!"

Stacey sighed. "No, I wouldn't wish this uncertainty on anyone."

"Come down to the theater, and I'll get rid of all your doubts. I'd come to you, angel, but I'm stuck here with an awards presentation."

"I thought the theater was dark."

"It's a long story. I'll explain when I see you. Will you come?"

Stacey had very real doubts. Nothing had actually changed. Gwen was still living with Sean, and he was still making excuses for that fact. But he was also reiterating his love, something that fell like balm on her wounded heart. After four barren days Stacey was starved for the sight of him.

"I'll be there," she whispered.

Sean had told her the show wouldn't be over until ten o'clock at the earliest, so she had plenty of time to get to the theater. In spite of her eagerness to see him, she spent a long time getting ready.

Since Hollywood went all out for its galas, Stacey had an opportunity to appear at her most glamorous. She wanted to look so smashing that Sean would wonder what he'd ever seen in another woman.

She had a moment's indecision, remembering that he claimed to prefer the natural look on her. Then she thought of Gwen. What a man *said* he liked and what he really did were often two different things.

Her most outstanding outfit was one she'd bought for a New Year's Eve party. The narrow lavender satin pants and matching chiffon top covered with paillettes and bugle beads were so formal that she'd never had occasion to wear them again. Tonight she was about to get her money's worth.

Stacey's eyes were like twin sparkling emeralds, and her cheeks were pink with excitement as she hurried toward the theater. A lot of heads turned to follow her, but she scarcely noticed. Only Sean's approval mattered.

This time she had no trouble finding him. The stage manager had been alerted to watch for her.

"Mr. Garrison has been waiting for you," the man said. "I'll take you to him."

"That's all right. I see him."

Sean was standing in the middle of a group of people, as always. His shirt was open at the collar, and his hair was ruffled, but he radiated confidence.

Stacey stood by the door, drinking in the sight of him. She was oblivious to the people around her. Francine had to speak to her twice before she got her attention.

"I said I almost didn't recognize you," she repeated. "That's a stunning outfit."

"What?" Stacey stared at her blankly. "Oh...thank you."

"I guess you're not Sean's date tonight."

"Why do you say that?"

Francine glanced over at him. "He's too busy to party."

"I can wait," Stacey answered calmly.

"You must have been doing a lot of that since Gwen moved in."

"Is that what she told you?" Stacey was determined not to let the woman ruffle her.

"She didn't have to. I know how they feel about each other."

"Isn't it strange that they got a divorce then?"

Francine shrugged. "It's just a piece of paper. Sometimes people are more faithful when they're not legally bound."

"That's an interesting theory, although slightly bizarre."

"You'd understand if you were part of Sean's world," Francine said condescendingly.

Stacey's temper started to get the better of her. "I *am* part of his world. I'm going to marry him."

"Perhaps when Gwen is through with him. And I should warn you that she isn't yet. Which one of you is living with him?" Francine taunted.

"Who is he with tonight?" Stacey countered.

She looked over at Sean for confirmation, reminding herself that Francine was not only spiteful but prejudiced.

Sean was glancing across the bustling area, not really seeing any single individual. His gaze swept indifferently over Stacey, then snapped back as he recognized her.

Intense emotion replaced his businesslike manner. He walked away from the group surrounding him, oblivious to their querulous demands. The light in his eyes was like a beacon, guiding Stacey to him.

She started toward him, not even noticing the obstacles in her path. As far as she was concerned there weren't any. Nothing could keep her from Sean.

Francine was a concerned witness. She knew how Stacey felt, but the expression on Sean's face was a revelation. Francine didn't wait to see any more. She hurried off in search of a telephone.

Gwen was watching television and feeling sorry for herself. The phone call didn't make her any happier.

"You'd better get down here right away," Francine concluded after briefing her friend.

"I know he's seeing Stacey. What's the big deal?"

"You haven't seen her tonight. Our little ingenue has turned into a full-fledged femme fatale."

"So what? Sean has always been surrounded by beautiful women. They were never any threat to me."

"Stacey told me they're getting married."

"That doesn't make it so," Gwen said without conviction.

"If you'd seen his face when he looked at her, you wouldn't be sitting there doing nothing."

"Maybe I'd be better off letting Sean get her out of his system," Gwen said slowly.

"Okay, if you want to wait until he gets married and divorced."

"Don't be ridiculous! He isn't about to get married again." Gwen's voice rose shrilly. "Stacey is just another one of his girls."

"Not from what *I* saw. I think he's completely dazzled by that innocent act. She's going to pick him off like a ripe avocado."

"Over my dead body!" Gwen's eyes were narrow slits.

"That's the old spirit!"

"Thanks for alerting me, Francine. I owe you one."

"Glad to do it. I owe *Sean* one, and this should make us even," Francine answered with satisfaction.

Stacey and Sean were a small island in the middle of the activity backstage. They gazed into each other's eyes with a hunger born of separation and yearning.

He lifted her hair gently, letting the shining strands spill through his fingers. That was the one concession Stacey had made in her quest for sophistication. She'd left her hair loose and natural the way he liked it.

"You look fantastic," he said softly.

"So do you," she whispered.

"Did you miss me as much as I missed you?"

"When you didn't call I wanted to die," she said simply.

He took both of her hands and held them tightly. "What would I have done without you?"

As they gazed wordlessly into each other's eyes, someone jostled Stacey. Sean reached for her protectively, then held her close for a moment.

"Let's go to my office," he murmured in her ear.

"Do you have to stay until the show is over?" she asked as he guided her around a stack of chairs.

"Yes, unfortunately." Sean was holding on to her hand, as though he had to remain in contact. "This thing came up so suddenly. It's been crazy around here. I have to stick around to make sure everything goes off okay."

"I understand."

His hand tightened around hers. "This wasn't the way I expected to spend today."

Stacey laughed, filled with incredulous happiness. "This wasn't the way I expected to spend *tonight*."

"Wait until you find out what else I have planned," he said softly.

The stage manager joined them with a clipboard in his hand. "Can you take a look at this list of presentations?" he asked.

"No," Sean answered curtly without slowing his pace.

"But you know these people. You can tell if they're being called on in the right order. All hell will break loose if someone feels upstaged."

"Find an official of the Players' Guild. It's time they did some of the work on this thing. I'm going to my office, and I don't want to be disturbed," Sean stated firmly.

When the man had gone Stacey said, "You're busy, Sean. I can wait."

"But I can't."

He led her up a flight of stairs and into a small cluttered room. The furnishing consisted of a large desk, a leather couch and some filing cabinets and tables. Posters were stacked in corners, and every flat surface was covered with programs, photographs and clippings.

Stacey didn't really register any of this immediately, because Sean took her in his arms the minute the door was closed. He held her so tightly that she could feel his heart beating against her breast.

"I've been waiting to do this for days," he groaned, burying his face in her hair. "I never want to be away from you this long again."

"At least tell me the next time," she pleaded. "Don't just leave me like that."

"There won't be a next time, sweetheart."

His mouth covered hers, bringing reassurance by its urgency. He parted her lips and plunged deeply, conveying all of his longing. Her own yearning was as great. She pressed against him, almost bruised by his hard frame yet seeking closer contact. They were fused together by their burning need for each other.

When she traced the straining muscles in his back, uttering incoherent little cries of pleasure, a long shudder ran through Sean. His hand caressed her waist before moving to cup her breast. Suddenly he drew back with an almost comic look on his face.

"What the devil do you have on? It feels like a suit of armor!"

Stacey gazed at him uncomprehendingly for an instant, then started to laugh helplessly. "Is that the thanks I get for trying to look glamorous for you?"

"You always look wonderful." He flicked one of the nickel-sized paillettes that covered her bodice. "I could do without these, however."

"You really don't like my outfit?" she asked wistfully.

"I like you in anything." His eyes took on brilliance. "I like you even better in nothing."

He pulled her into his arms again. While the tip of his tongue explored the delicate contours of her inner ear, his hand moved under the beaded top and stroked her bare back.

"Mmm, that's better," he murmured.

Stacey felt fire race through her veins as his hand moved to her midriff and then higher. She quivered when his fingertips feathered across her breast, teasing the sensitive tip until it curled into a sculptured rosette.

"Your body is so exquisite," he said hoarsely. "I want to kiss you everywhere."

"Oh, Sean, please don't!" she begged. Her legs were threatening to give way.

"You're right. I'm just frustrating both of us." He swung her into his arms and sat down in the swivel chair behind the desk, holding her on his lap. "We have the whole night ahead of us."

She rested her head on his shoulder and slipped her hand inside the opening of his shirt. "I can hardly wait."

"Don't push your luck, angel. The only thing that prevents me from taking you this very minute is that chain mail outfit you have on."

Stacey smiled. "You just don't appreciate haute couture."

"Not if it keeps me from touching you." His hand slid sensuously along her thigh.

"Sean," she said warningly.

He sighed. "I can't seem to help myself."

"Maybe I'd better sit on the couch."

His arms tightened. "No, I'll behave. Let me have this much at least. This is what I dreamed of all the time I was away."

"Did you have a good trip?"

He shrugged. "I got my business done."

"New York is a fascinating city. Don't tell me you had your nose to the grindstone every minute."

"No, I went to some parties and a couple of discos."

"That's more than I did," Stacey pouted. "I *should* have gone out with Walter."

Sean chuckled. "You can do better than him."

"You sound as though you wouldn't have cared," she said uncertainly.

"I wouldn't, because I trust you." He smoothed her hair fondly. "When two people really love each other as we do, there isn't any room for doubt."

Stacey's eyelashes fell as she remembered her past suspicions. "About Gwen..." she began.

Sean put his finger on her lips. "We're never going to talk about her again."

"I think we should," Stacey said slowly. "I want to tell you how I felt."

"I saw how you felt."

"But not why."

"Maybe you're right. I never could understand it. You must know how I feel about you."

"That isn't necessarily love," she explained painfully.

"Sweet, innocent Stacey. If sex was all I wanted, I could find it every hour of the day—in varieties you couldn't even imagine."

"I know that, but you still don't understand. I worried that perhaps you were using me to break Gwen's hold on you."

He looked at her in honest bewilderment. "What hold could she possibly have over me?"

"I was afraid you were still in love with her, in spite of all your efforts to fight it," Stacey whispered. "And I thought you hoped marrying me would put an end to your indecision. She couldn't keep drifting in and out of your life if you were married."

"If I was so obsessed with Gwen, what would prevent me from continuing our relationship whenever she showed up?"

"I knew you wouldn't do a thing like that once you'd made a commitment."

"Well, thanks for small compliments! I'm glad to hear you don't think I'm a complete fink!" Sean was blazingly angry.

"You have to admit you were ambivalent about getting married until Gwen arrived," Stacey said defensively.

"That's not strictly true. I made the original error, which I explained and regret. But I distinctly remember urging you to set an immediate date for our wedding."

"After you heard Gwen was coming home."

The stern look Stacey dreaded was back on Sean's face. "I suppose the bare facts could be interpreted your way—if you leave out all the personalities involved."

Sean was right. They never should have discussed Gwen. "I was only trying to explain why I acted the way I did," she pleaded. "I don't feel that way anymore. I'll marry you tomorrow if you like."

A muscle twitched in his taut jaw. "You still seem to have some reservations, or you wouldn't have brought it up. Maybe you'd better think about it a little longer."

"I love you, Sean." Stacey had tears in her eyes. "Please don't let her come between us."

His hard expression softened when he saw her distress. He gathered her close. "My darling love, do you think I'd ever let you go?"

As Sean's mouth sought hers, Stacey clasped her arms tightly around his neck.

They were both too preoccupied to hear the door open. Gwen stood on the threshold for a long moment, assessing the threat facing her. She drew a deep breath and closed the door with a sound calculated to be heard.

They were both startled, but Sean was also annoyed. "Don't you have anything better to do than follow me around?"

Stacey got to her feet, evading Sean's efforts to stop her.

"You used to have better manners," Gwen remarked pointedly.

"That was before you were underfoot every moment," he answered grimly. "What are you doing here?"

"I was worried about you, darling. You left early this morning, and I didn't hear from you again. That's not like you."

"Since when do we report to each other?" he demanded.

"That's true. We've always given each other space." Gwen turned to Stacey. "I'm terribly sorry. I didn't mean to break in on you, but I had no idea. Sean doesn't usually conduct his little . . . dalliances . . . in the office."

"Whatever you're trying to pull, Gwen, it won't work." Sean looked at her with something akin to loathing. "Stacey knows how I feel about you."

"That's very astute of her, since I don't know myself. When we're alone you're...unbelievable." Gwen's expression conveyed unspoken delights. "And then when Stacey's around, you pretend our only contact is a handshake. That really isn't worthy of you, Sean. You're keeping us both dangling."

"You and I cut our losses a long time ago," he said with narrowed eyes. "Don't try to pretend there's anything left."

"Do you really think two people who once loved each other can ever stop caring?"

Sean flicked a glance at Stacey. "First you have to care. We never did."

"I loved *you*," Gwen said softly.

"You don't know what love is! I didn't know myself until I met Stacey. Why are you doing this to me?" he demanded with deep frustration. "You made a new life for yourself. Why are you trying to sabotage mine?"

"I'm only trying to make you be honest with all three of us." Gwen looked at Stacey. "Are you willing to marry a man who still has ties to another woman?"

"Sean doesn't." Stacey returned her gaze steadily. "You had your chance, and you failed him. I don't know if you're trying to get him back out of vanity or mere selfishness, but it's too late. We love each other, and we're going to get married."

"It doesn't bother you that he'll come back to me as often as I want him?"

Before Sean could burst into an angry denial, Stacey said, "That's wishful thinking."

Gwen smiled. "He really has you brainwashed. You probably believe he was in New York these past three days. That's what he told you, isn't it?"

"I *was* in New York!" Sean said explosively.

Gwen gazed at him ruefully. "I know I agreed to go along with you, darling, but it really is dirty pool."

Stacey's heart seemed to stop beating. Would Gwen tell such a monstrous lie? She looked at Sean in a kind of daze.

"I can prove I was in New York," he fumed. "Any number of people can vouch for the fact!"

"His friends are very loyal," Gwen murmured.

"You don't believe her, do you?" he demanded of Stacey.

"No...of course not."

But Stacey's voice didn't carry conviction. Could Gwen possibly be telling the truth? Had she and Sean spent the time together? It didn't bear thinking about.

Sean was aware of her uncertainty. He gripped her shoulders tightly. "Look at me! What reason would I have to lie? If I wanted Gwen, why would I have called and begged you to meet me tonight?"

Gwen sighed. "I do sympathize with you, Sean. I've always wanted it all, too. That was the root of our problems. We couldn't resist having little flings, even though they never meant anything."

"I won't bother to deny your ridiculous allegations," he said. "Just answer me one question. Why are Stacey and I planning to get married?"

"I'll bet it wasn't your idea." From the tiny sound that escaped Stacey, Gwen knew her random shot had hit the mark.

Sean knew it, too. He was coldly furious. "This has gone far enough. I'm used to your dramatics, but I won't have you upsetting Stacey any further."

"Somebody has to save her from making a dreadful mistake."

"You haven't done anything but make a nasty scene," he snapped. "We're getting married as soon as I can get a license."

Gwen was watching Stacey. "Are you willing to go along with that after what I've told you?"

Stacey refused to let herself be swayed. She was sorry for her momentary weakness. Gwen had already demonstrated that she would do anything to come between them.

"Sean was speaking for both of us," she said evenly.

Gwen drew a deep breath as she realized there was only one course left open to her. "I hoped it wouldn't come to this, but you leave me no choice. I'm going to have Sean's baby."

After an electrifying second, he erupted. "This is a new low, even for you!"

Stacey felt her whole world crashing down. "Did you know about this?" she whispered, looking at Sean with stricken eyes.

"Of course not, because it couldn't possibly be true!"

"We've been living together," Gwen murmured.

"No, we haven't! I was in New York, remember? But even if we had been, do you honestly expect anyone to believe you could know you were pregnant after only three days?"

"It happened three months ago when I was here."

"Nothing happened then, either! You slept in the guest room. I didn't come near you."

"It's not necessary to keep up the pretense for Stacey's sake. You hadn't met her then. She can't blame you for something that took place before you even knew her."

His eyes blazed with anger. "If you think you're getting away with this, you're crazy."

"We had our differences, Sean, but I didn't think you'd deny your own child." Gwen regarded him with large, sad eyes.

"My God, what are you trying to do to me? How can you stand there and lie like this?"

He turned helplessly to Stacey, but she was staring at him as though he'd sprouted horns and a tail. This was one story Gwen couldn't have made up. Her pregnancy would show very soon. If you knew what to look for, the signs were already there. No wonder she was so desperate to get Sean back!

His jaw clenched as he saw the accusation on Stacey's face. "You've made up your mind, haven't you?" he asked harshly.

"What do you want me to say, Sean? That the baby isn't yours, even though it was conceived while she was staying with you? She comes and goes as though you're still married. What do you expect me to think?"

"I expect you to have a little faith in me."

"And ignore everything Gwen said?"

"It's her word against mine, yet you choose to believe her. Why?"

"I don't *want* to, but what other explanation is there?"

"*If* Gwen is indeed pregnant, which I'm not willing to accept blindly, did you ever consider that another man might be involved?"

Stacey and Sean had been ignoring Gwen as though she weren't in the room. She spoke up hastily now.

"Any court in the land would declare you the father, under the circumstances."

Sean's eyes never left Stacey's. "That's hardly true, but I'm not concerned with legalities. Is that the way *you* feel?" he asked Stacey.

Her heart was breaking, but she couldn't back down. "Your life-style is so different from mine. You and Gwen have a relationship that's incomprehensible to me."

"That answers my question," he said without emotion.

His glacial calm added to Stacey's misery. "I'm not judging you, Sean," she said in a small voice.

"Yes, you are. And you found me guilty without a trial." When she started to protest he cut her off. "Never mind, it's no longer important. Would you leave Gwen and me alone? We have some things to discuss."

Gwen was visibly nervous as Sean's enigmatic glance swung to her. She seemed about to speak, then thought better of it. The game was played out.

Chapter Eleven

The silence after Stacey left was like the calm that precedes a hurricane. Sean's detachment frightened Gwen more than his ranting and raging had. The fixed, almost clinical way he inspected her was nerve stretching.

Gwen stood it as long as she could before bursting out, "What are you going to do?"

"I haven't decided yet. Your performance was so downright mind-boggling that I'm still in shock."

"I know you're angry, Sean, but Stacey wasn't right for you. She said herself that your values are different. You wouldn't have been happy together." Gwen realized she was babbling, but she couldn't seem to stop.

"I'm not interested in discussing Stacey right now. You and I have more pressing matters to talk about. Are you really pregnant, Gwen?"

"Yes," she murmured.

"Do you know who the father is?"

Her eyes slid away from his. "I was staying with you. Everybody knows that."

"But we both know I never touched you," he said softly. "Are you going to tell me the real story, or make me get it the hard way?"

Gwen twisted her fingers together distractedly. "We could be happy together, Sean. We've learned from experience. We could make it this time."

"I'm waiting," he said inexorably.

"Won't you at least think about it?" she begged.

"You're incredible!" His composure showed signs of cracking for the first time. "After ruining my life, you have the effrontery to suggest that if I accept another man's child as my own, we'll live happily ever after."

"We could have more children," she said eagerly. "Your children."

"I can't quite see you turning into a baby factory. It's too out-of-character."

"I've changed, Sean! You'll see."

"We're getting off the subject. Who is the father, Gwen?"

She realized the futility of trying to convince him. "A man named Marcello Panzone," she answered in a low voice.

He nodded. "That's better. Now tell me the rest of the story."

"What do you want to know?"

"Why you named me as the father instead of him." Sean looked at her shrewdly. "Did he run out on you?"

"Of course not!"

He merely waited.

"Marcello doesn't know about the baby," she finally said tonelessly.

"Don't you think it might be a good idea to tell him?"

"I don't know if it would do any good."

"He must be a real prince," Sean remarked sarcastically.

"You don't understand. Before I could tell him, we had a dreadful argument. I said some things I shouldn't have. He won't even talk to me now."

"Then send him a cablegram! He'll probably hop the first plane over."

"I wish I could believe that," Gwen replied wistfully. "But you don't know Marcello. Even if he forgave me, domesticity isn't his bag. He likes to jet around the world at a moment's notice. The idea of a baby would freak him out."

Sean's eyes were narrowed slits. "You never intended to tell him, did you? When you found out you were pregnant, you hotfooted it back here to present me with your problem. That was the reason for the big seduction act with 'Auld Lang Syne' playing in the background. I was supposed to make love to you, and in due time you'd bring forth a 'premature' infant. Wasn't that the plan?"

"I didn't know what else to do," she faltered.

"And after that, what?" Sean's face was white with fury. "Was I to receive the pleasure of raising the child while you went back and reconciled with your Latin lover?"

"No! I wouldn't abandon my baby."

"How touching. You don't mind substituting fathers on him, though."

"It's better than no father at all," she whispered.

"Thanks for the splendid compliment," he answered sardonically.

"I didn't mean it that way, Sean. Can't you see my side of it?" she pleaded.

"Sure. I know how your mind works," he said bitterly. "Panzone wouldn't take care of you, and you were afraid I might go to court to stop your alimony payments if I found out you were pregnant by another man."

"What would I live on?" she asked helplessly.

A vein throbbed in his temple. "It didn't bother you that you destroyed two lives along the way, all because you didn't want to upset your playboy boyfriend."

"You're wrong, Sean. I was going to tell him—I *wanted* to tell him. I was just waiting for the right time."

"Always playing the angles," he said disgustedly. "Only this time you outsmarted yourself. Panzone walked out on you, and I won't take you back."

Gwen panicked. "You wouldn't throw me out! What would I do? Where can I go?"

"I ought to let you figure that out for yourself."

She looked at him with dawning hope. "I can stay? You'll say the baby is yours?"

"Not on your life!" he answered grimly. "I'll take care of you and pay your medical bills, but I won't marry you, and I won't claim the baby. If you try to spread any rumors to the contrary, you'll be on your own. Is that clear?"

She bent her head. "Yes."

"Okay, as long as we understand each other."

There was a long silence. Then Gwen spoke. "Sean...I'm sorry."

He stared at her. "Yes, I suppose you are—not that it matters now."

"I'll tell Stacey the truth."

"Forget it," he said curtly.

"But everything will be all right between you two after I tell her the real story."

"It was over between us the night we came home and found you in my apartment."

"My behavior was inexcusable, but she'll understand once she realizes why I acted as I did."

"Nothing changes the fact that she didn't believe me."

"You're being too hard on her, Sean. Any woman would be upset under the circumstances."

"I might be able to forgive her for thinking I'd take up with you again while I was engaged to her. I *did* forgive her for that. But if Stacey can believe I'd deny my own child, she must have serious doubts about my character. What kind of marriage would we have?"

"She really loves you," Gwen said gently. "It's written all over her when she looks at you."

A spasm of pain passed over Sean's face. It was gone in a moment, leaving his expression austere once more. "Isn't it a trifle late to turn into little Miss Matchmaker?"

"I'd like to make up for the damage I've caused. I know I'm selfish and self-centered. I could see how you felt about each other, but that didn't stop me from trying to save my own skin."

"Forgive me for being slightly suspicious of your sudden repentance. If I changed my mind about marrying you, you'd take me up on it in a minute."

"That's true," she admitted. "But I know you're not going to. Stacey is the love of your life. Don't let stubborn pride foul up your chance for happiness."

"You haven't managed your own life well enough to give advice," he commented bitingly.

"If you want to be pigheaded, there's nothing I can do about it. But I'm telling you, you're making a mistake."

"It isn't the first one," he answered somberly.

* * *

Stacey's world fell apart the night of Gwen's disastrous revelation.

At first she nursed her anger and betrayal. Nothing Sean could do would make up for his behavior. She didn't want him to call with excuses and pleas for forgiveness. He was very good at those, she thought bitterly, but gullibility had its limits!

As the days passed and Sean made no attempt to contact her, Stacey was reminded of his trip to New York. Could he be out of town again? Had he left purposely to give her time to cool off? If so, it wasn't going to work. This was more than a little misunderstanding. She wasn't about to fall into his arms again the way she had before.

But as time stretched on, it became apparent that Sean didn't expect her to. She kept track of him through the newspaper. Stacey learned from the entertainment page that a new play had opened at the Majestic. At least he'd been truthful about that! An item in "Show and Tell," a gossip column, told her that Sean and Gwen had taken up where they'd left off.

"Show and Tell" gushingly related:

All of Hollywood is delighted to see that fun couple, Sean and Gwen Garrison, back together again. He's the beaucoups rich theater mogul. Gorgeous Gwen has been absent from the local scene much too long. Congratulations on coming to your senses, you two.

The item only confirmed what Stacey suspected.

Her heart no longer leaped when the phone rang. Sean Garrison was a closed episode in her life. She was lucky to have found out what kind of man he was before she married him.

However, Stacey didn't look like a woman who should count her blessings. She looked like one of the walking wounded.

The atmosphere was no more cheerful at Sean's. Gloom was an almost tangible presence in the apartment, although he was scrupulously polite to Gwen—when they met. Sean was gone for long stretches at a time.

Gwen suspected that he sometimes slept on the couch in his office. When she couldn't endure his stoic suffering any longer, she pleaded with him to let her call Stacey.

That was the only time he came to life. His refusal was both vehement and ominous. If Gwen contacted Stacey in any way, she would have to find other living accommodations.

Gwen moped around, feeling sorry for herself. She was bored and lonely. Sean wouldn't accompany her to any of the social events they were invited to, and for the first time she didn't enjoy going alone. She didn't actually enjoy anything—not shopping, or lunch with friends—none of the things that used to interest her.

She also cried a lot. At first Gwen attributed everything to her pregnancy—until she couldn't deny the truth any longer. Nothing was the same without Marcello. She was in love with him. That was the reason she'd never even considered not having his baby. Gwen's tears fell faster as she faced a life without Marcello. Now she knew how Stacey and Sean felt.

Marcello's transatlantic phone call came as a blissful surprise. Gwen was singing when Sean happened to return home. It was so unusual that he went to her room.

She stopped packing to give him a brilliant smile. "The most wonderful thing has happened! Marcello called. We made up!"

"Did you give him all the facts?" Sean asked cautiously.

"He's thrilled about the baby! He said this separation made him realize how much he loved me. He phoned as soon as he returned home and found out where to reach me. We're getting married! Oh, Sean, I've been such an idiot. If only I'd told him about the baby right away. I've been going through hell for nothing!"

The lines in Sean's face deepened. "You've had a lot of company."

Stacey found out about Gwen's departure through the gossip column. Her heart started to pound as usual when Sean's name leaped out at her.

Sean Garrison's reconciliation with his lovely Gwen didn't last long. She's off to Europe to marry dashing Marcello Panzone, the international playboy. Rumor has it that the happy couple are also shopping for a baby carriage to go with the wedding ring. Those Italian men are so impetuous!

The implication hit Stacey like a lightning bolt. Sean had been telling the truth! The baby wasn't his! Gwen's allegations had been lies from start to finish.

Stacey was filled with remorse for ever doubting Sean. How hurt he must have been. A smothering weight was lifted from her shoulders as tremendous joy washed over her. She ran to the phone, eager to make amends.

Sean was at the theater. Stacey gave her name and quivered with anticipation, waiting to hear his blessed voice.

She received a rude shock when the stage manager returned after an interminable time and informed her that Sean was busy.

"Did you tell him who was calling?" she demanded.

"Yes, Miss Marlowe, but he's tied up at the moment."

"I see. Well, did he send any message?"

"Afraid not."

Stacey hung up reluctantly. Sean had every right to be angry, but he might at least have listened to what she had to say. A little chill ran up her spine. He must not have missed her the way she missed him.

After a moment's indecision, Stacey set her chin firmly. She would not allow his hurt feelings to finish what Gwen had started. Sean was entitled to an apology, and that's exactly what he was going to get!

She grabbed her car keys and drove to the theater, nervously rehearsing her speech. She'd seen Sean in one of his autocratic moods, and it wasn't something she looked forward to. Stacey sighed. He'd probably make her pay dearly before forgiving her, but she deserved it.

Sean was conferring with the general manager when she entered the backstage area. He looked very masculine in a close-fitting black pullover and tight jeans. Both accentuated the lithe body she remembered so well.

Stacey's heart was beating rapidly as she walked slowly across the stage. She was not encouraged by her reception.

Sean stiffened for a moment, as though he'd seen a ghost. Then all expression drained out of his face, leaving it a stony mask.

"This is a surprise," he remarked, leaving the impression that it was one he could have foregone.

"I tried to call, but you were busy," she said tentatively.

"Yes, I got the message." He didn't bother to deny it.

She glanced at the general manager, then back at Sean. "Can we talk for a few minutes?"

The other man took the hint. "I'll be in your office," he told Sean.

That was where Stacey had hoped to make her apology, not in the middle of a lot of people. The things they had to say to each other were personal. Sean might even shout a lot. But after a suitable period of venting his anger, he was bound to relent and take her in his arms. That was what she was counting on. But none of those things was likely on a crowded stage.

He was looking at her disinterestedly. "What did you want to talk about?"

She moistened her lips nervously. "I haven't seen you in a long time. How have you been?"

He raised one eyebrow. "Is that what you want to talk about?"

"No. I...I read in the paper that Gwen went back to Europe to get married."

"That's correct."

"You didn't...I thought you might call me."

"Why?" he asked bluntly.

This was even worse than Stacey had expected. His clipped answers were like bullets piercing her thin skin. "I don't blame you for being angry, Sean. I came to apologize."

"It's not necessary. Your actions were justified."

"How can you say that? You aren't the father of Gwen's child. None of the things she said were true!"

"But you believed them." Anger kindled in his eyes, warming the ice. "If you thought I was capable of any of the things she accused me of, you had every reason to walk out."

"I was wrong, and I regret it deeply."

His momentary flash of emotion was gone. "We all make mistakes. Don't worry about it."

"Can't you forgive me?" she pleaded.

He shrugged. "Sure, if it will make you feel any better."

"That's not forgiveness. That's revenge!"

His jaw clenched. "What do you want me to do, give you an award for crowning me rat fink of the year? You believed every rotten thing Gwen told you about me. The love you and I shared meant nothing to you. The nights in my arms were just satisfying sex."

"No! You're wrong!"

"Am I? Then how could you throw it all away?"

"It broke my heart," Stacey whispered. "But I thought, deep down, you really wanted her. I didn't think I could compete."

A tender look crossed his face for just a second. It was gone immediately. "You really should do something about that inferiority complex."

"Please give me another chance, Sean. I'll make it up to you. I'll never doubt you again, I swear it!"

He stared at her as though making up his mind. Stacey's hopes rose as his rigid expression softened, but they were dashed when she realized he was saying goodbye.

"It wouldn't work, Stacey. I wanted to live with you for the rest of our lives, but what kind of life would it be now? I'd always remember you didn't trust me when it counted."

Tears shimmered in her green eyes. "Everybody deserves a second chance."

"At what? Hurting each other? That's all we've done lately."

"Why can't you remember the way it was before?" she asked passionately. "Not just our lovemaking, but the wonderful times we had together, the companionship and the laughter. *You're* the one who's throwing it all away!"

"Don't make it any harder," he said tautly.

"You talk about trust, but how about love?" she challenged. "If you really loved me, you couldn't just walk away."

"That's another misconception of yours." His face was very white. "The thought of it is killing me, but a clean death is better than dying by inches. Goodbye, Stacey."

She watched, heartsick, as he strode into the wings and disappeared.

Stacey sat outside in her car, too numb to drive home. How could this be happening? She'd expected Sean to be angry but not unreachable. He'd admitted he loved her, yet he couldn't forgive her. She had hurt more than his pride, Stacey realized.

The feeling of desolation that weighed her down was actually painful. How could she get through the rest of her life knowing she'd failed the man she loved? Nobody should have to live under such a sentence. Sean would have to give her another chance to prove herself. How could he forgive her, though, when he obviously didn't intend to see her again?

If only they could have had their talk in private. He had weakened a couple of times. Would the outcome have been any different if she'd been free to throw her arms around him? Could Sean have resisted the awesome force that always drew them together? Stacey didn't think so.

The problem was how to get him alone. Her mind worked furiously, searching for a solution. Finally she smiled. There was one sure way to bring Sean to her house.

* * *

Mitch greeted Stacey like a long-lost friend when she drove up in front of Sean's apartment building a short time later.

"Good to see you," he said jovially. "I was beginning to think you'd forgotten all about us."

"You'd be surprised at how often I think about this place," she answered. "How's my friend Lobo?"

"He misses you something fierce. Mr. Garrison's wife has been staying here, and—"

"*Former* wife," Stacey corrected firmly.

"Yeah, I guess so. She sure acted like she owned the place, though." Mitch belatedly realized how that sounded. "She's a very nice lady, but I don't think she was too crazy about Lobo."

"Have you been exercising him?"

"As much as I can. Not like you do, though. Are you going to take over your old job?" he asked hopefully.

"That's why I'm here."

"Great! I'll get him for you as soon as I bring Mrs. McAllister's car around."

"You're busy. Just give me the key, and I'll get him myself."

Lobo went wild with joy when he saw her. He leaped around like an overgrown puppy and licked her face, alternately barking and whining.

"Well, at least somebody in the family is glad to see me." Stacey put her arms around the dog and hugged him. "You missed me, didn't you, sweetheart? Your master did, too, only he's too stubborn to do anything about it. But we're not going to let him get away with that, are we?"

Lobo barked as though agreeing with every word she said.

Stacey took him into the kitchen for dog biscuits. Then, on an impulse, she walked down the hall to the master bedroom. The housekeeper had left it spotless—too neat in fact. Stacey wanted to see Sean's robe tossed over a chair, the imprint of his head on a pillow.

"Maybe I'll change the color scheme in here when I move in," she told Lobo. Laughter caught in her throat. "That's what's called whistling in the dark to keep your spirits up." She touched a silver brush gently before turning away. "Come on, Lobo, we have to get into our battle gear."

Stacey had no idea what time Sean would return home, but she knew it would be late. She had plenty of time to get ready—too much time, in fact.

She drew a bubble bath and stayed in it for a long time, trying to relax her taut muscles. The water was soothing, but it didn't really ease her tension. Too much depended on the next few hours—her whole life, actually.

After applying makeup with meticulous care, Stacey put on a nightgown and matching peignoir that she'd been saving for a trip or a stay at some fancy hotel. The fragile peach-colored chiffon ensemble had been a birthday gift from her mother. Eileen had half-jokingly said it was the start of Stacey's trousseau. If all went well tonight, she'd be right.

Stacey looked in the mirror, seeking reassurance. Her eyes were a feverish green as she adjusted a lacy shoulder strap. Was the effect too blatant?

The sheer chiffon nightgown veiled rather than concealed her body, allowing tantalizing glimpses of her breasts, which were strategically covered by rosettes of lace. The rest of her body was seductively visible through the pleated folds of transparent fabric that swirled gracefully to the floor.

No woman would ever expect to sleep alone in an outfit like this. Sean would know instantly what she had in mind. Stacey wavered. What if he rejected her? She set her jaw, refusing to let the possibility deter her. Too much was at stake to worry about a thing like pride.

She was lying on the couch, trying to read, when the telephone rang. She took a deep breath to steady herself before answering.

"Do you have my dog?" Sean demanded without further greeting.

"Yes, he's here," she answered in a slightly uneven voice.

"I knew it! What do you think you're pulling?" he asked furiously. "You can't just waltz into a man's home and steal his property."

Stacey giggled out of sheer nervousness. "Lobo isn't property; he's family."

"Even more reason! And I'm glad you find this amusing."

"I don't, Sean, honestly. I didn't think you'd mind."

"Yes you did, or you'd have asked me first."

"What would you have said?"

"I'd have said no, but that's not the point. You can't go around taking what you want whenever the mood strikes you."

"I missed him," she said softly.

"You think that's an excuse? I could tell you a few things about—" He broke off abruptly. Sean struggled for composure and lost the battle. "I want that dog back here in twenty minutes or I'm calling the police!"

"I was just getting ready for bed," she protested. "It would take me that long to get dressed again. Can't I keep him overnight?"

"No! Don't think you can drag this out for days. If you won't bring him back, I'll come and get him myself." He hung up before she could argue the point, not realizing that wasn't her intention.

Sean apparently broke all speed laws getting to Stacey's house. Her nerves tightened almost unbearably when she heard his car outside, an incredibly short time after their phone conversation. From the sound of his brakes screeching as he slammed to a stop, Sean hadn't cooled off on the way over.

When she opened the door Stacey had trouble breathing. Sean's face was austere, with deep lines bracketing his compressed mouth. There wasn't a hint of softness in either his hard expression or his taut body, but he still looked wonderful to her.

They stared at each other wordlessly for a moment. Then his eyes flicked over her revealing outfit. His only reaction was a deepened frown and a further tightening of his already rigid jaw.

Stacey's cheeks flushed. Sean had seen through her plan. Even more humiliating, he wasn't the slightest bit interested.

She pulled her peignoir together in a futile attempt to make it less revealing. "I . . . I was just going to bed."

"So I see." His stony expression didn't change.

"I intended to bring Lobo back in the morning," she murmured.

"You shouldn't have taken him in the first place. I had a long, trying day, and this didn't help matters."

"I'm sorry." She bit her lip nervously. "Would you like a drink, or a cup of coffee?"

"No thanks. I still have some book work to do."

Stacey's hopes shriveled and died. Her dream of a romantic reunion had been hopelessly naive. Sean was like a man made out of ice. His emotions were frozen under that cold exterior. There was no way to reach him. Further efforts would only prolong the misery.

She turned away to hide her desolation. "I'll get Lobo's leash."

The dog's tail started to wag furiously when he saw the leash. Stacey held it out to Sean, but he didn't take it.

"Maybe I'll have some coffee after all," he said, almost reluctantly. "If it isn't too much trouble."

"No, I . . . of course not."

She studied his face covertly, looking for some reason for his change of heart. He didn't appear to have weakened. Why didn't he just take Lobo and go?

Sean followed her to the kitchen. He leaned against the doorjamb and watched her jerky movements as she poured water into the coffee maker.

"Is that what you usually sleep in?" he asked abruptly.

Her cheeks flamed as she realized Sean would have no way of knowing. They'd always slept nude in each other's arms.

"Sometimes I wear pajamas," she murmured, scarcely audibly.

He seemed to have regretted the question. "How's your novel coming?" he asked, moving to safer ground.

"Slowly. I seem to have trouble finding time to write."

"I know what you mean. Time is a precious commodity."

That seemed to cover the subject. She cast around for another one while she was putting out cookies to keep from looking at him. "How's your new play doing?"

"Quite well. I'll send you a couple of tickets if you like. You can bring a date."

She didn't see the intent way he was watching her. Stacey was crushed by the indifferent offer, but she was determined not to show it. "That's very generous. Maybe we could have a drink afterward with you and *your* date."

"I don't go out much anymore," he answered.

"That doesn't sound like the man I once knew," she remarked with a forced laugh.

"That was the whole trouble. You never really knew me," he answered quietly.

She turned to look at him then. He was so near and yet so far. The few feet that separated them might as well have been a chasm.

"Perhaps you're right," she said. "The man I *thought* I knew was more forgiving."

"Don't try to shift the blame!" Sean finally came to life. "*You* were the one who leaped to judgment."

"Gwen was too clever for me," she said hopelessly. "I couldn't conceive of that kind of deviousness."

"Now you know what I lived with," he said grimly.

"But can't you understand how foreign it would be to me?" she pleaded. "How could I help but believe her?"

"After all we'd been to each other, you should have believed *me*."

"You're right." Stacey fought back her tears. "I don't know why I didn't see through her. I realize it's too late to make amends, but I want you to know I'm sorry. It's no wonder you've lost all faith in women. I just hope someday you'll find one who's worthy of you."

"I thought I had," he said softly.

"Don't let my weakness destroy your faith," she said earnestly. "All women aren't like Gwen and me. You were just unfortunate to meet up with two of the worst examples of our sex.''

"I would never lump you together with Gwen."

"We have a lot in common," Stacey replied sadly. "I tricked you into coming here tonight."

Something flickered in his eyes. "I wouldn't have come if I hadn't wanted to."

"You came for Lobo," she said dully.

"Did I?"

She looked at him uncertainly. "You wouldn't be here otherwise."

"Perhaps not tonight . . . but sooner or later." He walked slowly toward her. "I've tried using pride to keep me warm, but it couldn't compare to you."

Stacey was afraid she was only hearing what she wanted to hear. "You were so angry when you came in," she faltered.

Sean's smile transformed his face. "I couldn't be sure you hadn't taken Lobo for the reason you gave—that you missed him, not me. I was afraid to risk another rejection by jumping to the wrong conclusion."

"But after you saw me!" How could he possibly have misunderstood? She spread out the folds of her gown. "You don't honestly think I go to bed dressed like this?"

His laughter held an undercurrent of excitement. "Never in *my* experience."

"You saw through me right away. You just wanted to make me suffer!" she exclaimed indignantly.

His eyes glittered as they traveled over her from head to toe. "No, darling. I just wanted to keep on seeing through you."

"I feel like an idiot in this getup," she mumbled.

"Then maybe you'd better take it off." He closed the distance between them.

All uncertainty fled when she saw the love and longing on his face. Stacey went into Sean's arms with a little cry of joy.

He held her fiercely, parting her lips for an onslaught that was almost out of control. His hands roamed restlessly over her body in an erotic exploration that made her tremble.

"I've been so miserable without you," he murmured brokenly. "I need you, sweetheart."

"Show me how much," she whispered, tightening her arms around his neck.

"I plan on showing you over and over again, my love."

He lifted her in his arms and carried her into the bedroom. After setting her gently on her feet he removed her peignoir. Instead of pulling the gown over her head, he slid the straps down her shoulders and let it slither to the floor.

Sean's eyes were lit by inner flames as he stroked her breasts and continued down her body with arousing caresses. "I've dreamed of this every lonely night since you left. I can't believe I'm not still dreaming."

Stacey's mouth curved in a smile. "Then I'll just have to convince you."

She unfastened his shirt, then his slacks. When he was standing taut and naked in front of her, she slowly stroked his body the way he'd stroked hers, lingering where he was most vulnerable.

Sean uttered a hoarse cry and clasped her so tightly in his arms that his pulsing desire burned away their last shred of restraint. He placed her on the bed and knelt over her for one breathtaking instant.

"This is how much I need you, my dearest one."

His possession was urgent yet tender, filling her with remembered rapture. Stacey arched her body to meet his surges. She was bathed in pleasure so intense that it was almost unbearable. The mounting spirals of sensation culminated in a throbbing explosion that brought release and fulfillment. They descended from the heights slowly, clinging together out of love.

Much later Sean cuddled her closer without opening his eyes. "We're getting married tomorrow, with or without your parents in attendance. I don't want to hear any excuses."

Stacey smoothed his hair lovingly. "I wouldn't dream of disagreeing with you, master."

"Don't give me any of that phony 'master' stuff. I expect to lead a dog's life after we're married."

"What kind of thing is that to say?" she asked indignantly.

He chuckled. "I'm hoping you'll love me as much as you do Lobo."

"I already do," she murmured, moving against him seductively. "But in a much more exciting way."

*   *   *   *   *

FOUR UNIQUE SERIES
FOR EVERY WOMAN YOU ARE ..

Silhouette Romance

Love, at its most tender, provocative,
emotional ... in stories that will make you laugh and
cry while bringing you the magic of falling in love.

6 titles
per month

Silhouette Special Edition

Sophisticated, substantial and packed with
emotion, these powerful novels of life and love will
capture your imagination and steal your heart.

6 titles
per month

Silhouette Desire

Open the door to romance and passion. Humorous,
emotional, compelling—yet always a believable
and sensuous story—Silhouette Desire never
fails to deliver on the promise of love.

6 titles
per month

Silhouette Intimate Moments

Enter a world of excitement, of romance
heightened by suspense, adventure and the
passions every woman dreams of. Let us
sweep you away.

4 titles
per month